Federico F.

a novel

Gianfranco Angelucci

translated by
Giuseppe Natale

Bordighera Press

Library of Congress Control Number: 2008924273

All the characters and events portrayed in this story, although based on a faithful chronicle, are entirely fictitious. Any resemblance to real persons, living or dead, is coincidental and not intended by the author.

Cover: "Self-caricature," by F. Fellini,

Printed in the United States.

Published by
BORDIGHERA PRESS
John D. Calandra Italian American Institute
25 West 43rd Street, 17th Floor
New York, NY 10036

VIA FOLIOS 50
ISBN 1-884419-95-X

to my father

I like much more to remember than to live!

What's the difference, anyway?

Ivo Salvini in *The Voice Of The Moon*

Table of Contents

Chapter I

Premonition

I was walking along Corso d'Italia. *I was supposed to take a message to Federico Fellini's office. When I arrived at my studio, however, I noticed that the shutters were half-closed, the way I leave them when I am not there. So I turned to ring the buzzer, but instead of the usual row of buttons next to the front door. . . .*

I see this dream now, drawn on one of the last pages of the big, leather bound book in which Fellini for years would secretly record those frequent, eagerly anticipated night visitations. They were detailed, colorful, fanciful little stories, sketches that reproduced the full intensity and enigma of those mysterious and fascinating visions. Usually, Fellini furnished them with his comments. He would scribble them in his minute, barely perceptible handwriting on the imaginary white margins of the page, alongside the drawings. Or he would enclose his words in a little cloud, a *balloon,* like in the comics, especially when he related the dialogues between the people in his dreams. He even allowed for a few of these drawings to be published, thus violating their secrecy, but he did so on the sly, just to please a friend. He even annotated their possible interpretations, which were as inspired and astonishing as the drawings themselves.

For the dream of Corso d'Italia, he portrayed himself as seen from behind, facing the closed front door, with an envelope in his hand:

. . . I was supposed to take a message to Federico Fellini's office. When I arrived at my studio, however, I noticed that the shutters were half-closed, the way I leave them when I am not there. So I turned to ring the buzzer, but instead of the usual row of buttons next to the front door, I found a rectangular slab of gray marble, like a tombstone, with a mail slot. . . .

Oscar Rinaldi, who for years had been his aide, his shadow, was haunted by this dream.

The last time Rinaldi and I met was almost a year ago, at the *Caffè Canova* in Piazza del Popolo. I saw him sitting outside at a small table, so I decided to stop by, and then I waited with him for Federico to arrive.

That was the morning when Fellini received the news of his fifth Oscar, his lifetime achievement award: it was January 20, his birthday. He materialized from Via del Babuino, walking gingerly, with his long arms dangling down, and his burgundy scarf wrapped around his neck. His eyes were darting, his hands were busy in that peculiar gesture of his, alternatively crossing the index and middle finger, like a wary cat snapping his tail while studying the environment. The sudden applause bursting from the taxi parking lot, next to the *Chiesa degli Artisti,* told us that he had arrived. Fellini waved in salute, and a taxi driver yelled:

"Ehi, Federì, we're great!"

He was associating himself and an entire group of people with the Maestro's fortune and fame. But who was "we"? We Italians? We Romans? We *Fellinians*?

Then Federico joined us at the table. Almost immediately a television reporter arrived asking for his comment on the recent news of his latest Oscar.

"It's an invitation to stop bumming around and start working again," Fellini said.

Since filming *The Voice of the Moon* a couple of years before, he had been idle. During that time, just a few months before, the dream visited him:

I was walking along Corso d'Italia. *I was supposed to take a message to Federico Fellini's office. When I arrived at my studio, however, I noticed that the shutters were half-closed, the way I leave them when I am not there. So I turned to ring the buzzer, but instead of the usual row of buttons next to the front door, I found a rectangular slab of gray marble, like a tombstone, with a mail slot. Written on it:* THE LOST OF THE LOST. *I realized that it was the name of the letter's recipient, and that I was supposed to deliver the letter to myself. At that point my curiosity got the best of me: I had to know what was in the envelope, what was so urgent about it. I couldn't resist taking a look before dropping it in the slot. As my fingers fumbled with the envelope, a sheet of paper slipped out and opened. I found out that there was nothing written on it: it was totally blank.*

The intense surprise of that discovery woke me up.

Fellini had passed away. His heart stopped beating at noon on Sunday, October 31.

He was the most beloved, fortunate, celebrated, and prized of all film directors, the *auteur* who redefined the role of filmmaker. He was the champion of wild individualism and absolute creative freedom. Through his uncompromising attitude he set all film directors free, and restored for them the dignity of art and self-expression. He was the reluctant inspirer of proselytes and callings. He was the creator of *8 1/2*, the magician, the wizard, the guru. He took his leave.

As the events precipitated, he passed away within a few weeks: GOODBYE FELLINI, GOODBYE MAESTRO, read the grieving titles of the newspapers.

A Jesuit priest, a personal friend of Fellini and exegete of his work, was in a distant city at a film-studies conference at the time of his passing. Still unaware of what had occurred, he fainted right in the middle of the conference at the precise moment of Fellini's death. They carried him to his hotel room and laid him on the bed, still swooning. Highly sensitive people reacted like that, as if a vacuum of energy suddenly opened before them, and an eddy, a black hole, swallowed them up.

On the second of November–All Souls' Day–his lying-in-state was set up at Studio 5 in Cinecittà, and the wake was opened to the public.

I was going there now myself.

Like others who decided to become directors, I also owed my inspiration to him and to the deep emotions that his films indelibly engraved in me; first through the screen, then by being on his movie sets, in the sorcerous light of his halo.

The first time I set foot in Cinecittà to meet Fellini, he was shooting *Roma*. Someone escorted me from the offices on the first floor, directly inside the big womb of Studio 5. Once past the little padded door, which was tightly watched over by suspicious guards, the most incredible vision unfolded before my eyes. It was the episode of Via Albalonga: streetcars clanging along the rails and brushing by the tables of an open-air *trattoria,* amid a swarm of extras, trucks, cars, bicycles; building façades enlivened by tenants leaning out of windows or sitting on balconies *al fresco;* lowly women with bulging boobs; wild screaming kids; unlimited varieties of attractive flappers; gigantic plates of pasta *alla pajata;* sidewalks alit with shop-windows, shining stores, and neon signs; large clouds of incense hovering over the set, enveloping my senses to the point of bewilderment. I felt like I was becoming part of a new church, a church whose existence I only had dreamed of until then; and now I was finally able to measure its magnificence, its unsettling, geometric confusion. It was an exciting secular church, where rituals of re-creation were officiated under the command of a High Priest, and no one else could play that role better than Fellini.

I knew that Oscar Rinaldi had been at Fellini's side through his entire illness, until his very last hours. In fact, he had been at his side for decades, mostly as a friend, but also as an aide and scriptwriter. He helped Fellini to draft a few screenplays, and he was always the first person with whom he would discuss a new idea for a movie, a subject, a film treatment. In time, Oscar became the *ghost* of Fellini, his *ghostwriter,* a sort of writing alter ego, a logographer, as he gleefully used to describe himself:

"I write what they ask me to write, in whatever form they prefer."

When talking about Oscar, Fellini said with amused admiration that he should have been the director of a newspaper, given his ability to handle any topic in limited time, while displaying the ease of an essayist and the tone of a narrator.

"He really has a rare gift," he told me in confidence. "I don't understand why he doesn't want to be a professional journalist."

The two of them played hide and seek through their writings, to the extent that it became quite a challenge to distinguish them apart. Federico was constantly overwhelmed with all kinds of requests: interviews, speeches, prefaces, and statements. If there had not been someone to help him, he would have spent all day just replying to the thousands of solicitations that came to him from all over the world. He got along well with Oscar. He treated him like a son, or maybe like a younger brother, a pupil, even though he never wanted to consider himself the master of anyone. Nonetheless, in a veiled way Oscar could evoke the figure of an apprentice wizard.

The film director had sincere affection for him; their relationship was based on congeniality and respect, but above all on close familiarity. Knowing that Oscar could be trusted, Fellini confided in him, as he had done through time with a number of other young people who had come and gone. However, he and Oscar shared an intangible complicity, a peculiar affinity that was quite easy to discern. Leaving aside the great gap in age, differences between them were minimal. At any rate, if one of them could be considered an eternal adolescent, it was Federico. Oscar was not a kid anymore, either. In the end, even their human, personal experiences came to resemble each other. They say that when two people spend a lot of time together they grow more and more similar, or at least that is the general impression.

When I reach the studios on Via Tuscolana the gates are open, and the public is flowing in like an endless river. Alfredo, the last of the old security guards still in service, is at the entrance.

"I've never seen so many people.... Not even when Totò died. ..." he whispers, amazed.

Oscar Rinaldi, thoughtful as always, had called earlier to let me know that there was a pass ready for me to pick up at the entrance to Cinecittà, so that I could get in with my car.

Avoiding the main avenues, I drive to the rear of Studio 5. After parking, I slip through a little side door to find a kind of blue-colored limbo sunk in semi-darkness. A sky furrowed with soft clouds is the studio's backdrop. High from above, the luminous cones from the searchlights cross over the coffin, forming a sparkling double circle, the focus of the slow-moving stream of people.

I push along the right wall of the immense theater to the area where a small group of Fellini's closest friends have gathered. Marvisio, his assistant director, is scanning for familiar faces amongst the sea of heads. He intends to separate the immediate family and friends from the seething mass, so they can have a private moment to pay tribute and share their condolences. The security guard is worried because the crowd is moving too slowly, bottlenecking. It is like a human snake, whose tail already protrudes beyond the gates, stretching onto Via Tuscolana, where it holds up the traffic and blocks the subway exit.

A signature book located near the exit is the cause of the congestion, and it slows down the crowd's exodus. It becomes necessary to move the table outside the theater to allow those who want to sign, and bear witness of their presence, to do so without hindering the others. Fortunately, it soon stops raining and the situation quickly improves: the crowd of devotees resumes its slow but constant flow. It is a calm stream, a controlled flood. Its silent glide keeps time with the music by Nino Rota, Fellini's appointed composer. They are theme songs selected by Nicola Piovani, and recorded on an endless loop tape.

One has the feeling of witnessing a rarefied, prodigious event. Time passes by, suspended in awe, like the imposing crowd that came to pay its silent tribute to the *Maestro.*

One by one, his closest friends arrive. Some of us burst into inconsolable sobbing. Our fragile veneer of decorum shatters especially when we are face to face: we then become defenseless, and entrust ourselves to this mutual feeling of compassion and sorrow. A young poet holds a white poodle tightly to her chest and exhales between tears, her voice gravelly like Pythia's. Her face is arcane, a tellurian image of ancient pain engulfed in vapors, a lost echo of the underworld risen from the womb of Mother Earth herself.

With her lush Titian mane, her wide, dull, pale face, a sensual Dutch writer emerges from the throng. She comes up and hugs me, holding me tight for a few moments against her soft showgirl body. The last time I saw her, with Federico, she was wearing red spiked high-heels and was suffering from a consuming Electra complex. Now she is wearing a black cape raincoat, her heels are still spiked, but her Electra complex is gone, having found its way to the pages of a book.

"I signed the contract right before leaving Amsterdam," she whispers in my ear, her voice still resonating with that inscrutable, portentous event. She is not there by accident.

A TV journalist, nicknamed the "Bard" for his lyrical style, has already dispatched a small troupe, with the impeccable timing typical of all reporters. Motivated by the still inchoate idea to produce a special report on the great Maestro and friend, he wants to gather some uniquely suggestive material.

The female reporters, who in the foggy nights of October meticulously and tirelessly documented all phases of Fellini's agony from Rome's Policlinic, are also present *en masse.* They now watch the crowd from the press area, a tier box cordoned off by passementerie. Every now and then they disobey orders, jump over the dividing cordon, and run to embrace some newly arrived mourner, whispering words of sympathy and regret.

Oscar gracefully kisses a few of them, breathing the cajolery he learnt from the Maestro into their attentive ears. Rumor has it that a conceited journalist wrote an article in his hard-line newspaper where he rudely desecrated that spontaneous and affectionate gathering of the Roman people. No one has been able to get a copy of the paper in question. It would take a feat to reach the newsstand near the entry gates; one would have to go against the hosts of visitors flowing in the avenues of Cinecittà, marching on the wet asphalt, amid the black pines. They are the same pine trees that Fellini once described in *Interview,* when he mentioned flying over their highest leaves and branches in a revealing dream.

Surrounded by that grieving army, Oscar has to stop every few feet, held back by his acquaintances for a greeting here, an embrace there. Sometimes it's not easy to recognize familiar faces outside of their usual environment; like this couple here who runs one of Federico's favorite restaurants, and now wears a sincere and well-meaning smile. They are simple, friendly people, with suffering on their faces.

Taking the initiative, a daring set manager is able to reach the newsstand and get a copy of the paper with the incriminating article. When he comes back into the theater he is already disgusted after skimming a few lines:

. . . The death–and the life–of Fellini are events much less moving than

the newspapers would lead us to believe.

Fellini was an intellectual director liked by intellectuals, and the box-office failure of many of his films is clear proof of this. Intellectuals, who enjoy showing off to be exactly that, also produce newspapers. For instance, the front-page editorial in La Stampa, *written by an excellent female journalist, begins with nothing less than this statement: "It will be difficult and ugly to live on without Fellini. . . ." Is that so, Madam? Would you say the same thing to your descendants or to the factory workers at the gates of FIAT Mirafiori? Already Fellini had virtually exhausted his repertoire, and lately he was wearily repeating himself.*

I read the article in the diffused light trickling down from the floods set on the ceiling trusses. The river of mourners has swollen beyond measure, and it continues to flow silently. Entire families have flocked in. Fathers who left work early are there carrying their children on their shoulders, or pushing strollers. Once in front of the coffin, they cross themselves, pay their mental tribute to Fellini, and move on. It is rare to see anyone betraying the faintest frivolous curiosity for the few seats that the scenographer has placed to the right of the casket, where celebrities–actors, directors, and female TV stars–pause, absorbed in prayer. Sonia D'Ambrosi is there with her "rascal face" that intrigued Fellini so much, looking as sumptuous and restless as a tiger. Marcello Mastroianni is also there, wearing black glasses, rigidly standing at attention in front of the coffin. He is visibly shaken, distracted, and he barely reacts when someone tries to rouse him from his inertia. Anita Ekberg, true to her latest role in Fellini's film, glides down next to the coffin like a mythological figure, with her Hydra face capable of bewitching and paralyzing when she opens wide her icy eyes.

"You said beautiful things on television," a flattering voice whispers into her blond hair cascading over her shoulders.

"Oh, really?" she replies raising her eyebrows, casting a surprised glance that fades beyond the sky backdrop, as if those words were directed at someone else, someone whom she cannot remember or does not know. Nevertheless, as a sign of appreciation she draws her interlocutor close to her large bosom.

The extra-large senator arrives, duly accompanied by the

presidents of the Italian National Television and Cinema Corporation. This is the best moment to discuss creating a fund in Rome aimed at preserving Fellini's cultural legacy. Monique Larouche, a Dante and Fellini scholar, with her typically French self-confidence steps forward, in the shadow of the senator. He's so heavily built that he resembles the bulky Giolitti in Galantara's drawings. She spiritedly lays out her excellent arguments, rolling her R's. The senator, pleased to be the object of her benevolent attention, stoops down toward the attractive and pugnacious scholar. Smiling like a prelate, he says:

"It will not be easy to take a Fellini fund away from his native Rimini," is his resolved preamble. "I know very well how stubborn the people of Romagna can be. Apart from this, my dear lady, in Italy *there are no funds for a fund.*"

His witticism, worthy of a variety comedian, baffles those present. No one knows whether to be amused or irritated. His remark sounds like a cursive caption from the *Corriere dei Piccoli,* or a quip by vaudevillians like Sergio Tofano or Macario.

The president of the Italian Television Corporation nods respectfully, betraying a slight flicker in his watery eyes behind his glasses.

The mood radically changes when Antonioni arrives accompanied by his young wife. Now that he is older, undermined by illness, his face carved in stone, he almost looks like one of those cardinals that Fellini immortalized in his films. He silently sits on one of the few chairs lined up along the bier, his still eyes shedding tears. He is a fascinating appearance: under the halo of his snow-white hair, he is much more attractive now than he was in his youth. Thanks to the affection they gather from the love they bestow on others, artists do become more beautiful as they get older. He wipes his eyelashes thoughtlessly, with a mechanical, ancillary gesture.

Solemnly wrapped in his Hermès white silk raincoat, the Bard has been hanging around with the chorus of Fellini's close friends for quite some time. As soon as he runs into Oscar, he draws him close and whispers words of affection:

"I'm moved, you know?" he sighs wantonly, paternally drawing Oscar's head closer to his shoulder. "In moments like these I'm not able to talk. My voice quivers. I need to have a eulogy for

Federico. Would you help me?"

He looks fondly at Antonioni and at his gleaming tears streaking down his hollow cheeks.

"I'm acting like him now. It must be old age!"

Oscar clumsily tries to reassure him. "It's a consequence of the stroke he suffered," he whispers. "Dr. Jacobsen told me that."

The Bard turns suddenly pale, and goes as white as his raincoat: that incurable hypochondriac already considers himself at risk.

"Really? Do you think that I too could suffer a stroke?"

"What are you saying?" Oscar asks with an uneasy smile. "It's not a warning sign; it's a consequence of an injury that has already taken place, an after effect. I've said something stupid that I shouldn't have!"

They hug again and start walking up and down the theater, arm in arm. They talk about Federico, his premature death, and the clear faults of those responsible for the treatment he received.

"Write me an article," urges the Bard. "I will add my own commentary. It will be syndicated worldwide."

Step by step, he nears the exit. His armed escort in a bulletproof car has been alerted, and waits for him outside in the humid night.

"Shall we dine at the *Fico Nuovo*?" he proposes.

Oscar says he cannot leave: they still need him at the theater. He politely declines the invitation, feeling slightly sorry. Meanwhile, a godsend young actress providentially joins them, her eyes shining alluringly. At first the Bard takes up a defensive position, pretending not to recognize her, but then he makes a sudden lunge, like a perfect seducer:

"Oh, Barbarella dear, it is *you*! After we saw you with Federico, we kept asking him when he was going to introduce us to you."

He caresses her goodbye like a monsignor, his hand lingering for a moment: he will be waiting for her call. However, before taking shelter in his car, he can't refrain from adding a comment to his small circle of listeners:

"Actually, what we asked him was quite something else!" he sneers, his head still half-turned.

The car door closes. The Bard's hand waves in blessing behind the window. Oscar Rinaldi heads back to the theater, accompanied by a towering blond girl, taller than he is. I recognize Else Jacobsen, the Norwegian neurologist made famous by a photo-reportage in a widely circulated magazine, which portrayed her and Fellini during a work session. She is dressed in decidedly Nordic attire, wearing a thick wool coat and a sober anthracite-gray suit. Moved by a secret sweet kindness or torment, she smiles at whomever approaches her. She, too, has just read the absurd article in the newspaper. The inappropriate publication is passing from hand to hand, arousing everyone's indignation.

"We must not react to this provocation," says Rinaldi, "better let it fall on deaf ears. We shouldn't even dignify it with a comment."

A few minutes earlier, the Bard had expressed a different opinion; in fact he had come to the conclusion that an appropriate reply was absolutely necessary, and a slap-up one, for that matter. He loves to imitate Dumas' musketeer:

"I'm going to provide that scoundrel with what he deserves!"

Claudio Ciocca, a friend of Fellini's who owns a restaurant in the Castelli area and also acted in some of his films, had been going around all afternoon carrying a bag full of sandwiches, thoughtfully imagining that somebody might need to eat. From time to time, he goes back to join Mirella, his gentle-mannered and fearful-looking wife. They really insist on having us to dinner. Claudio invites also Dr. Jacobsen: Fellini had told him about her with his typical excitement and enthusiasm. He scrutinizes her with the eyes of a connoisseur:

"Yes, she's attractive all right," he comments once we are alone, "but she's just your typical Scandinavian woman. I was fancying who knows what!"

Having seen Mastroianni and other celebrities pray alone in front of the coffin, a utility actress whose stage name is Leyla Shed imploringly asks to be allowed to do the same. She would love to find herself in the limelight for once, to be the object of television cameras and flashlights, even through a fallacy. The press director for Cinecittà grants her wish.

A young reporter from Belgian TV begs for an interview with Rinaldi, who in the meantime has entered the theater at the side of the attractive neurologist. Since Else speaks French fluently, she is drafted to act as interpreter. The small group walks to the tier of seats reserved for the photographers, on the opposite side of the theater that is partially illuminated by the floodlights.

Else reveals the ease of a veteran interpreter, as she unravels into French Oscar's unstoppable stream of words, his maelstrom of emotions:

"What is left of Fellini? His immense creative energy simply passed from him into the vast public who absorbed it through his movies. The proof is right here, the thousands of people lining up behind us. This never ending chain of grief, regret, love, and gratitude is the tangible evidence, the most tangible manifestation of such a miracle."

It is past nine thirty, and Claudio Ciocca is patiently waiting for us at the entrance to the theatre. We leave Cinecittà, bound for the Castelli. While the passengers in the back seat are chatting, Rinaldi, who is sitting in the front next to me, moves closer to whisper something about Else:

"What a lovely creature! Fellini made her materialize when he was taken to that little out-of-the-way hospital, near Ferrara. All of a sudden there she appeared, with perfect synchrony, like a radiant Minerva in a Homer's tale, sent to assist the wounded hero.... Federico became infatuated with her. He realized that he could perform his alchemy on her through me, his faithful apprentice."

As we return from the restaurant at eleven o'clock, we notice that the crowd shows no sign of abating: it is a swollen, dense river. It had been decided to keep the gates open–all night long, if necessary–until that incredible influx of people would finally dry up.

We have to wait for the subway to close, the security guards say. Only then the tide will ebb.

Reporters fan out to turn in their articles to meet the printing deadline, except one, the TG1 reporter, who had just arrived. A famous comic-strip writer, who is now leaning motionless against a light tower, wearing a duffel coat, trying to hold back his tears, accompanied him.

In the now empty press box sits Petulia, the young woman lawyer who Federico once met at a newsstand on Via Po. He saw her arrive astride her powerful motorbike, clad in black leather. She introduced herself, proclaiming to be an unshakable fan of his. After that, they started to see each other often. They would call each other and look for each other. Federico admired her exuberant energy, her constant running around from a board meeting to a court trial, her nervous hopping from one country to another, her virile command disguised under her seductive gracefulness. He was amused and flattered by the young woman's attentions. She called him from every corner of the world many times, and he was always courteous and solicitous with her. "Call me when you get back so we can spend some time together," he would say adroitly, invitingly.

Petulia wanted to put together a group of backers willing to produce his next movie. She had immediately become the daughter, lover, and disciple of that analyst and magician, that prophet and artist, who was capable of penetrating your inner self and revealing it to you.

At one o' clock, the flux of visitors finally stops. The gates are closed with no particular rush. Inside the huge theater now there remain a small number of people, just a handful of us, as if obeying some tacit, imaginary orders.

All this time Elena, a beautiful and provoking blond lady, has been kneeling on the blue-gray wool felt that covers the dais, leaning on the coffin. Whenever someone thoughtfully tries to pull her away with the excuse of a sip of water or a short break, she amiably and obligingly agrees; but soon she regains her position, invisibly gliding back to her previous spot, still burning with the same pain and passion as before. Wrapped in her raincoat as if it were a mantle, her slender and soft body is clamped in a vice-like grip, and her hair is braided into a curl on her delicate nape. Her back is shaking with sobs.

"Everything started with her," Rinaldi whispers.

"Everything what?"

"Have you ever met her?"

"I don't think so."

"Before last summer in Rimini, I didn't know her either. You knew Federico, how he was, always secrets on top of more secrets, and to each one his own."

Chapter II

Enchanted Enclosure

"Federico resided within the nourishing sphere of femininity till his last flash of life, with all his might. You knew him: women were his creative magma, his placenta, his food. They were his unexplored universe and at the same time the sacred perimeter in which he felt sheltered. When, after the onslaught of his disease, he had no other means left, he unconsciously turned to me and used me as an instrument to carry out his indispensable magic spells."

As Oscar knows, this surprising confidence will find me an unbiased listener.

"Also with Dr. Jacobsen?" I deliberately tease him, so intrigued am I by the striking neurologist.

"Especially with her!"

"And all the women concerned . . . do they know?"

"I believe so."

I expect him to go on with his story, but we are not able to remain alone long enough in that place. Maybe because of its large scale, that makeshift funeral chamber conjures epic images: the death of an emperor on the battlefield, the somber bivouac among the tents, the banners fluttering in the fires' reflection, the restlessness preceding the final parting, the nervous insomnia at dawn, the ears perked at the imminent trumpet blares, the shuffling of the horses' hoofs. The die-hards linger on, taking turns on the few seats available or standing in groups of two or three, small clusters of people that continuously recombine into new aggregates. The air teems with a soft chattering about the myriad reasons of his death. A magician cannot depart like that!

The *carabinieri* with their three-cornered hat also have left, along with the municipal policemen who formed the guard of honor around the coffin. To make up for it, the two brothers from the *Osteria del Curato* arrive, totally unexpected guests, deferentially carrying in large trays of food as a pious act of consolation for the mourners. Dressed identically, with green quilted jackets, they bow in front of everyone as if parading on a walkway, like a duo from a variety show.

They go upstairs to the dressing rooms to prepare their fragrant food, and then come down to pray. Sitting upright, they spend a long time absorbed in prayer, their lips whispering. With the same young-friar gracefulness they take their leave, thankful for being granted the honor to pay their respects with their provisions.

Grateful for those delights, the night guards accept their offering without much ado. With their empty stomachs, and their uniforms drenched from the rain that is once again pouring down, they quickly help themselves to thermoses of hot tea, coffee, and milk.

A violent storm breaks out. Thunder and lightning are so violent that even the thick soundproofed walls start shaking. Two frightened dogs appear at the entrance. One of them is Peter, a dappled mongrel who already knows most of the people present, and charmingly wags his tail. He trustingly comes in and wanders about the coffin, sniffing the funeral cushion flowers and affectionately rubbing his nose against the velvet pall. The other one is a shy little German-shepherd dog. She irresolutely paws the threshold, ready to scamper at the first sign of danger. She is tempted to look inside for shelter from the lightning flaring around her like turquoise tongues of flame, and yet she is unable to overcome the prohibition acquired from years of discipline spent with the patrolmen.

Amid the deafening roars, Oscar picks up the thread of his story.

"Do you remember the time we met at *Caffè Canova,* in Piazza del Popolo, before Federico left for the States to receive his honorary Oscar? Already ill, he talked with subdued sarcasm about the lack of energy that marks the end of an artist's career."

I remembered it clearly. I was also struck by his confession and its helpless, prophetic tone. Fellini dwelled on the fact that his work no longer appealed to him.

"It's as if I were inhabited by someone who has left me. I don't want to sound too rhetorical or pedantic, but I have the impression that the man who used to be within me, the one who used to make decisions, devise plans, meet people, and sign contracts, has slipped away without warning. He's gone. And I don't feel like doing anything anymore. I wouldn't even know where to begin."

His TV reporter friend had prompted him to comment on his birthday.

"What can I say?" Federico replied playfully, dodging the question as usual. "I'm 73 years old for the first time. I don't know how it feels yet."

His swerves, his shifts. . . . Fellini the man, like Fellini the director, was the true prototype of the clown-artist, the tightrope walker admired for his virtuosity, thrilling nimbleness, weightlessness; he was the circus performer who never betrays, not even for a second, the physical writhing, the animal strain that makes his act possible.

Federico was endowed with that same grace, that invisible muscular tension that makes it all look like magic. His films exude that seemingly effortless beauty derived from a winged somersault, an aerial caper, a whirlwind.

His clownery, his intellectual acrobatics. . . . Those were the things that separated Fellini from his fellow directors and made him so unique! He possessed the same elusive diaphanous quality that Nino Rota was able to translate into his music, into his enthralling, mercurial compositions.

All successful artists are able to turn energy into creative expression under our very eyes; in Fellini's case this exciting phenomenon is perhaps the most visible.

After his last film–that short flight to the moon and the subsequent descent back to earth, to the water wells echoing with whispers and calls–the old magic acrobat had begun to fear that his muscles would betray him, that they had become too stiff and wooden with age.

He meant it literally, not just metaphorically. His insecurity turned somatic. Lately, he could hardly walk; the blood circulation in one of his legs became alarming; cataracts were clouding his sight, especially in his right eye.

"To a film director the eyes are everything," he said, shaking his head, feeling symbolically wounded in the function that best defined him.

Every time we met, I could not help watching him closely, trying not to make myself noticed. In the mornings, when the sun was still low and the light would strike slantwise, I seemed to be able to detect the veil blurring his crystalline lens. I now wonder if he felt it to be an annoyance or simply the natural, progressive, and inevitable dimming of things he did not care to see anymore.

"He did not want to attend the Oscar ceremony, as you probably know," Rinaldi resumes. "He did everything possible not to go. I spent two whole days with him–the 17th and the 18th of March–trying to come up with a plausible excuse, a fabricated impediment to feed to the Academy Award Organization that would not sound offensive. He seemed amused rather than embarrassed by our enterprise. We wanted to prepare a statement declining the invitation, to be both faxed to the Academy and recorded for a video that the RAI news correspondent would personally take to Hollywood, in time for the ceremony.

Federico decided against going.

"I really don't have the energy," he kept saying.

In view of Federico's obstinate opposition, even his wife Giulietta and his most faithful press agent stopped pressuring him. The reasons for not going–the hardships of the trip, the fatigue, and the stress–finally prevailed.

Fellini went from doctor to doctor for his cervical arthritis that caused him dizziness, and above all for the circulatory disorder in his leg where complications had set in. The specialists believed a bypass was now unavoidable and arranged to have him in Zurich on April 2 for a consultation. In order to go to Hollywood, Federico had to face the exertion of a second trip with little or no time to spare in between. It was a waste of energy that he felt was beyond his strength.

On the other hand, so as not to provoke disquieting rumors that would result in unscrupulous scoops or, even worse, a jinxing, we did not want to mention his illness in our faxes to the president of the Hollywood Academy. Therefore, after the second or third exchange of messages in real time across the ocean, we settled for a formulaic statement that would explain everything and say nothing. We carefully weighed each word, considered all possible implications, and relied on an elusive, almost cryptic style, like this:

I am compelled to inform you in confidence that I cannot help but follow the advice of those who, at this time, would caution me from making a trip....

But then, almost responding to an innate compulsion, Federico could not refrain from one of his unexpected, surrealistic turns, one worthy of his old contributions to the satirical magazine *Marc' Aurelio.*

I am compelled to inform you in confidence that I cannot help but follow the advice of those who, at this time, would caution me from making a trip....

... *by sleigh,* he treacherously added. And then, in an attempt to convince himself, he said:

"With the problems of international communication and translation, perhaps someone could have made a mistake or have misunderstood. For now, the sleigh introduces a tangible, objective element, an obstacle so absurd that it seems all the more real. Try and read it again...."

I read it again, but when I got to the sleigh fib we burst out into a *fou rire* that grew in a senseless crescendo. Fellini found the response we had conceived so amusing that he felt the urge to share it immediately over the phone with his faithful press secretary: he joyously anticipated the disconcerted reaction of that scrupulous professional. This time it was Federico himself who, with comic gravity, tried to read the message, but after the first few words his voice began to crack with an infectious laughter.

His secretary also started laughing heartily, but then he became increasingly worried:

"The president of the Academy takes everything seriously," he was anxious to point out, "he would not understand."

So we had to forgo the sleigh.

While Oscar tells his story, I keep glancing at the attractive blond lady, her face a thin wax mask, who during all that time did not move away from the coffin. Rinaldi notices it:

"I will get to her in a moment. Believe me, it's not that I like approaching things in a roundabout way, but in order for you to understand the meandering mental process of this story, you must follow each and every step from the very beginning."

Bereft of the crowd of visitors, the theater seems even vaster than before, a pagan netherworld inhabited by a few dejected, wandering souls.

"We walked to the restaurant on Via Brunetti, the one near his place on Via Margutta," Rinaldi continues. "There, Federico started talking about his health and the sophisticated clinical tests that had led to his diagnosis. It was as if he wanted to convince me, and convince himself in the process, that a trip to America was objectively not feasible. Back in his office, he further elaborated:

"I sense my energy failing, abandoning me," he said to justify himself. "When I think back to films like *Satyricon* and *Casanova,* and how complex they were, with all their plot connections, the thousands of threads to be tied together like umbilical cords. . . . Well, today, I would find it impossible even to imagine an undertaking of such magnitude. To juggle constructions like that you must rely on an almost inexhaustible vital force, you must let high-tension voltage run through your body and yet survive unscathed. And perhaps *that* is the real fun, a sort of irresponsible euphoria that makes you reckless but nimble, that makes you find quick solutions to every hitch, solutions that almost unfailingly have been there all the time waiting to be found, like the carnival scene in *Casanova,* or the last scene of *8 1/2.*

Without energy nothing can happen. If the most striking, most desirable, most tempting woman I ever saw now came through that door, I wouldn't be the one to decide what to do next, because our encounter would depend on someone else; someone who is in no position to judge, and also has no expectations, no claims; someone who would be happy just to devote himself to the event regardless of its outcome. Simenon, after he gave up writing at seventy years of age and confined himself to dictating his memories on a tape recorder–his *jouet,* his little toy, as he called it–confessed to me: 'I don't have the energy to write novels any more.' Only now do I understand what he meant. The drive that allowed him to engage in the creative process had failed him. It's the same for me. It's as if we were talking about someone who used to live within me and who now is gone. I no longer have the same confident expectation that made me take my place behind the movie camera and rest my eye against the frame-finder. I no longer have the curiosity of knowing what might happen next. I can't even say that I'm depressed, I'm just indifferent. And I don't even feel like talking about it, or trying to escape it with an elusive side-step, or a somersault, as I've have always done."

Belying his own predictions, Federico left for Hollywood, even though he was unsure until the very last moment, so much so that he had already recorded the statement of regret for the RAI correspondent and the Academy.

"I feel mortified, even chagrined, not to be able to participate in person," he was saying in his flute-like voice. "For someone of my generation, someone like me from Rimini, cinema and America are the very same thing–two worlds that mirror each other, creating a parallel, essential third universe."

In the tone of his voice and his choice of words one could detect an authentic melancholy that his defection had caused him. His aversion to all kinds of award ceremonies notwithstanding, he regretted not taking part in the celebration. He felt that he was behaving "like a clown, an acrobat who had dreamed all his life to be in a circus, and when he's finally asked to join, he won't go."

The message ended with his heartfelt thanks to the American audiences who always had a liking for him, and his affectionate thoughts for the two actors who had kindly agreed to stand in for him on the Academy stage:

"Amid so much sadness, it's a comfort to know that I will be represented by Marcello Mastroianni; so many times he has been called my fictional alter ego, and this time he wants to be it for real. I thank him, along with beautiful Sophia Loren, for accepting this award on my behalf. It represents the trust, loyalty, and affection of the American audiences, my colleagues, and the members of the

Academy, all of whom I hope to repay by making a few more films."

Friday of the same week–it was late in the morning–Fellini called and left a brief message on my answering machine to inform me of his sudden decision to go:

"Hi, Oscar. I collapsed miserably, and not because of the dizziness from my cervical arthritis. . . . I collapsed in the face of this unending surge of condemnation, insistence, pleading, of pain in the ass. So, I might leave tomorrow or Sunday, I don't know yet. I'll call you later on in the day. Take care."

While he was gone, I stayed in Italy to oversee the reprinting of his films for a Fellini film festival scheduled for the fall in New York, a grand homage that featured a thorough retrospective spanning his entire career.

Time was getting short, and new problems kept popping up at every turn. The original negatives of some of his first films had crystallized and needed meticulous restorative work, which had to be done by hand, frame by frame. The negatives of more recent films like *Amarcord* were so worn out that they could not withstand any more printing or regeneration, and could only be saved through a delicate process that was extremely expensive and time-consuming. The project involved the most skilled technicians in Cinecittà and all of Rome. Unforeseen, complicated obstacles had to be overcome through the goodwill and cooperation of everyone.

When Fellini came back from the States, on April 5, we met in the late afternoon at Piazza del Popolo, intending to continue the evening at a restaurant.

Punctual as the usual, Fellini was already waiting for me at *Caffé Canova.* Seated at an outdoor table, he was smiling politely and amiably, returning the greetings from the many people promenading and chattering at dusk, that suspended hour swelling with expectations.

Giulietta had gone out to dinner, and Federico was enjoying an evening of loafing. Sporting his raincoat with the collar raised, he kept glancing all around with his usual, inexhaustible sense of wonder, while sipping a beer and nibbling on a few *salatini.* Later on that night, while we were driving leisurely across Ponte Margherita in order to get to the restaurant on Via Germanico, I took advantage of the opportunity to update him on the restoration of his films.

Cinecittá International had organized a film series at Palazzo delle Esposizioni on Via Nazionale. That evening they were showing *La Dolce Vita,* using a new, sharp, and bright print of which I was very proud:

"If you feel like it, we can stop by later," I dared saying.

"I wouldn't dream of it!"

"We could go in when the movie has already started, no one will see *you*. . . ."

"But *I* don't want to see myself," he replied with an uneasy smile, resorting to one of his habitual verbal pirouettes. It was his most typical attitude–always trying to flee, draw away, escape the snares of his past. Nonetheless, he indulgently listened to me while I described the meticulous task of preservation being carried out at the film works, despite the carelessness, indolence, and lack of financial resources that unfailingly plagued our nation.

A storm had rolled through Rome, cooling off the air. Federico, however, would not relinquish his little outdoor table under the striped canvas awning. While waiting for the waiter, he sneaked into the kitchen–as was his habit–and returned with a dish brimming with hand-sliced *prosciutto.* We ate it with freshly baked, fragrant bread, and sipped Chianti that we ourselves poured from the straw-covered bottle. Simple, yet sophisticated, that is the way the meals were with Federico: always different, unconventional, free of restrictions and set menus, always characterized by improvisation, variety, and extreme refinement. Talking about the restoration of his films led me, I don't know how, to dwell upon *La Strada,* that imaginary and timeless tale, mysteriously imbued with a malaise that remains unchanged after so many years. For the first time in our long relationship, Federico revealed a glimpse of that work yet unknown to me.

The making of that movie had been for him a painful, near-psychic experience that drove him dangerously close to mental illness.

"One day, a week before the end of the shooting, I was having lunch with the troupe at *Bastianelli,* a restaurant on the wharf in Fiumicino. All of a sudden, I felt something in me crack, just like the snap of a coiled spring. In those days I was filming the first scenes, the ones at the beach that according to our shooting schedule should have been last. After the lunch break, I went back to the movie camera, and I felt like a castaway clinging to flotsam, striving to stay alive; it was as if a part of me had to hold on to the other part that got separated. I finished the day's shooting feeling totally out of sorts. My sense of malaise was so strong that even Giulietta noticed it. That night I couldn't sleep. In fact, I didn't sleep a wink for a whole week: sleepless at night and busy shooting during the day. Giulietta knew the girlfriend of a Jungian analyst, Professor Servadio, and through her she managed to get me an appointment. I went to see him one afternoon after shooting. That was the first time I had ever set foot in a psychoanalyst's office. He saw his patients in a skimpy, little room, half filled with a small couch: it was so small that it felt claustrophobic, suffocating. I was totally uncomfortable. There was nothing there that could be of any help. That first visit, I remember, I almost didn't say a word: I wasn't in the right frame of mind. I didn't want to be. While I was in the doctor's office, a big storm broke out. When I got out, I had to take cover from the torrential rain under a tree. A young lady was already there, also waiting for a cab to show up.

"Now, what do you think? Will some kind soul help us out?" she said to me. Her inflection and accent were typically Riminese. I asked her where she was from and she said *San Marino.* Lea was her name. We waited together for a cab. Even though she was wearing a loose-fitting dress–a sacque, as they called it in those days–when she whirled around I caught a glimpse of her glorious buttocks. A cab arrived, and we both climbed into the back seat. We agreed to drop her off at her boarding-house first, and then I would continue on my way. When we reached her destination, however, I got out of the cab to walk her to the door, and I asked the driver to wait for me. In the twilight of the entryway she stopped hesitantly, perhaps to thank me. Acting on impulse I embraced her, and she let me...."

The legendary Lea! So many times did her name crop up in

his tales, like a flare, a dazzling Bengal light, and now, unexpectedly, Federico was describing to me their first encounter, the birth of their burning passion.

That night, we drove aimlessly around the silent city–Piazza Venezia, the Colosseo, Via Cristoforo Colombo–and we headed back through the Passeggiata Archeologica, Via dei Fori Imperiali, Via del Corso, Trinità dei Monti, Via del Babuino, and finally Via Margutta, to his office. I dropped him off at his front door at eleven o'clock. During our dreamy and heedless wandering, the splendid Lea from San Marino sat with us, a leonine figure of outrageous sensuality and insatiable lust. She was the woman who more than any other had swept him away. The insatiable female who, in *The Voice of the Moon,* turned before everyone's eyes into an unstoppable, puffing locomotive, a frightening steam engine that derailed the mind of her frail, improvident young husband. The bellicose lover, who, during a stop along a highway in Umbria, got overexcited and started pelting Federico's brand new Flaminia Sport with cobblestones, nearly destroying it. The legendary Lea from San Marino, who died in a mental hospital.

Chapter III

Magic Chain

"Federico left for Switzerland at the end of May," continues Rinaldi, "while I stayed in Rome to oversee the reprinting of his films, as scheduled. I had the incomparable opportunity not only to enjoy the uncanny Roman summer, but also to watch all of Fellini's films, one after another, on a wide screen, under optimum technical conditions. When would I ever be able to do that again?

I arranged to have the film screenings at lunchtime, around one or two o'clock: just when the heat was most oppressive, I had to drag myself to the studios through a seeming lava flow.

In Rome, summer breaks out with primeval, African fierceness. The metal bodies of the cars snarled in traffic rise to a red heat, and the streets steam in the sun. I had to reach Via Tiburtina, near the belt highway, in that arid and dusty urban periphery defaced by building speculation. The square, air-conditioned construction that housed the studios finally welcomed me, cool like an oasis, muffled like a luxury clinic for chronic patients.

The kind and accommodating technicians did not question my unusual schedule. I entered the carpeted viewing room and took my place in a plush, velvety seat near the console, at a slight angle from the row, while the laconic film printer settled behind me in order to verify the outcome together.

While the labs could vary, the distant drone of the projector and the impeccable air-conditioning were the same everywhere. The inimitable images of *Satyricon, Amarcord, Roma, Casanova, The City of Women, And the Ship Sails On, Ginger and Fred, Interview,* flowed on the dazzlingly clear, flawless screen.

As I read the credit titles for *The Voice of the Moon*–in a gaudy white lettering against a blue background–I was struck by the following phrase:

Angelucci

Story and Screenplay
By Federico Fellini

I did not remember having seen that peculiar caption before in any of Federico's films. It almost looked like a trademark with which he wanted to seal his career, the simple signature of a craftsman who took pride in his work. Then the film started with the whispers rising from the water wells, calling by name the improvident and excited Salvini: it was an insidious, irresistible murmur, in which one could easily recognize Federico's barely disguised voice.

The print did not present the slightest imperfection; the colors were extremely luminous, intense, and faithful: it was a feast for the eyes.

The film ran smoothly; the images were ethereal, light, transparent, and elusive like those of a dream from which you'd never want to awaken. Even the few, minor blemishes that I had originally noticed and thought to be extraneous authorial whims had now disappeared, simply dissolved in the limpid tale. Every face, feature, and pose of the actors seemed marvelously unique, irreplaceable, and unchangeable. The story materialized out of its own "unnaturalness," like poetry. I sat there spellbound. I absorbed that flow of words and images imbued with both lyrical and physiological urgency, like a thin fog, a vapor that rises from below, from within, and magically swirls you in. That film, as elusive as the voices from the wells, as sorcerous as the unfathomable calls bewitched me.

Sitting in front of a cinema screen we all are like the protagonist Salvini. I, too, let myself become enraptured with pure heart and infinite patience, oblivious to obstacles and intrusions. What a delight it was to be able to plunge into Federico's visionary magma, sheltered from all possible interferences, with no spectators restlessly moving their legs or making their seats creak, with not even a sigh to disrupt my concentration. I can assure you, it was a near transcendent experience!

There are moments when we need a different contact with the mystery of artistic communication, a contact that is more adamant, intimate, nocturnal. When this happens, the message of art reveals itself as pure truth.

If only we could be a little more silent, states the film toward the end. It is an invitation for us all to heed and reflect; to bow our heads and collect our thoughts; to lend our ears to the revelations that might come from a whisper, a puff hidden behind the daze of words, beyond the uproar of empty voices; to detect what might be conveyed through a metaphoric image or a neglected echo.

It is no accident that Fellini decided to devote his final film to the moon, the satellite that mirrors earth with her double face: by day, Diana, the aloof virgin, the elusive and swift huntress; by night, Hecate, Proserpine, the goddess of the netherworld, the lover of Pluto and all that is buried within us and is secretly gleaming. The film embodies her feminine fragility and charm, her innermost nature, her double profile, and it proves to be as fascinating as the mysterious silver star herself.

For those who are able to hear the moon's voice–to discern it among the many other voices that reverberate around her, and to recognize her ectoplasmic features in the faces of the two clownish characters–every small detail in the film, even the most trivial one, will take on unexpected meaning.

In any accomplished work of art, what really moves us, or stirs us is not the subject itself, but the accuracy of the representation, the perfect dovetailing of the artist's soul and the final product, the dazzling revelation surfacing from the mirror's depths. As we watch Fellini's films, at first our eyes are sated, lit with pure astonishment, swept by the overall composition. Such subtleties often pass unnoticed, yet they leave their mark in our hearts. Despite its apparent cheerfulness, the *Voice of the Moon* is so disconsolate. It is not unlike Federico's other stories, in which the events merrily unwind with noisy, even comic gaiety, and contrast with the invariably doleful and tormented tone of the film. The same apparent incompatibility intertwines Nino Rota's music, his impalpable ornamentations, his irresolute motifs that are pervaded by remorse and hope.

Fellini usually gives this contrast a pleasant and harmonious representation. In *The Voice of the Moon,* however, he turns it into a harsh and corrosive cacophony that jars us deep down, right from the start. He achieves this effect through the set design of that town so fictitious and yet so real: the jumble of architectural styles; the streets inundated with cars; the square disfigured by a neoplastic fiberglass church; the ground unceasingly ripped open by the Micheluzzi brothers, who wickedly capture the moon and insanely explant her from the sky!

After the party at the disco, Salvini-Benigni runs into his sister and his brother-in-law. In the fearful and worried face of that young woman, in the gentle and compassionate look of that young man, one can see the typical expression of all sisters- and brothers-in-laws of the world, easily recognizable even by those like me who do not have any in their family. The modest, neat apartment where they live, and the maternal gesture of Salvini's sister when she rests her cheek on her insane brother's forehead and kisses it, conjure the oldest and truest sense of home: the main shelter from the ravages of life. Compassion makes us defenseless and magically allures us into the dark, inscrutable zone where artists take their deep roots and absorb their creative sap. There they set free some of our repressed thoughts, and unlock revelations that we would not otherwise be able to recognize or hear without the silence they entreat.

In a similar state of uneasiness, I had watched *The City of Women* and *Ginger and Fred,* two foreboding films marked by mystifying restlessness and enigmatic parables. *And the Ship Sails On,* mysteriously lit by the flashes of hatred of the bellicose, desperate Serbs, is a film whose impending enigma became clear to us only ten years later. Federico fictionalized by spying on reality, absorbing its inner vibrations like the diviner who discovers a vein of water. How did he know so far in advance? How did those two ideas–the Balkan stage shaken by thunders of war and the doleful collapse of harmony–coalesce in his mind? What message was he able to perceive in the silence that he entreated? What was he able to fathom, to grasp among the imperceptible plots of sensible reality, where only poetry can provide bearing, like a spectroscope, a sonar, a magnet of cosmic dust?

In *Interview,* Federico openly invited the viewer to join his game by playing with nostalgia and irony, arming the redskins with television antennas instead of spears, setting them off to a ragged and glorious charge against the besieged, agonizing cinema. No point in scanning the horizon hoping for the usual, *here come our men*! The prairie no longer existed, for the horizon was now made of tall buildings that formed a long, wide barrier inexorably encircling the studios.

The Voice of the Moon was the conclusion of this journey, the final song of a seer-poet who went beyond the confines of prosody. Universally acclaimed as a show business man, because of his talent and vocation Fellini was instead a darkly conscious rhapsodist, an indispensable prophet in a society that has lost its bearings and its contact with the deep.

Believe me, Fellini was a saint in a jacket and tie, and his films were his miracles.

On Friday, June 25, around five in the afternoon, Fellini finally called from Switzerland and left a message on my answering machine:

"Hi Oscar, this is Federico. I just wanted to say hello. I haven't been able to call you sooner because they only let me use the phone for a few minutes; they even stand by the door to make sure that I don't overstep the time limit.... The surgery was a little more complicated than expected. I will have to stay here two or three more weeks, I believe. But things are starting to get better, even though very, very slowly. It has been quite an adventure... also quite nourishing for the mind, I must say.... The hospital is exceptional. The simple fact that there is a place like this, where 1,500 people work and 300 or 400 patients enter and leave every day is a miracle! A miracle that really gives you hope, trust... with none of that chattering, rhetoric, and humbug we have in our country, none of that shame.... Okay, Oscar. I will get in touch with you at another time, maybe tomorrow, or the day after. Anyway, I just wanted to say hi. I'm thinking of you. Bye, Oscar...."

The next morning, I finally managed to hear him in person. His voice no longer sounded broken, panting, and tired as it did on the answering machine; instead it was clear, streaked with humor, and full of playfulness. He was telling me about the young black girl standing at his door, who was in charge of removing the phone after he made a few short calls so that he wouldn't get too tired. In the short time he had available, he excitedly told me more about that model hospital:

"If I had had surgery in Italy, I wouldn't be here talking to you," he maintained.

He felt very much protected, reassured by a specific statistic showing that there were four-and-a-half staff members to every patient. He was impressed not only by the professionalism of the nurses of every race and color, but also by their unremitting presence and solicitude:

"As an organization it's even more reassuring than the American one: it's efficient without being too robotic or impersonal."

Probably seen from afar, Italy must have indeed appeared to him like a messy barracks: a country erroneously pleased at its own kindliness, its mystique of individualism, its alleged *dolce vita* in which the respect for the others is so feeble that it leads to an asocial assertion of independence.

"This is true democracy," Federico argued from Switzerland. "Here you really feel like a citizen. A hospital like this restores your confidence in the community."

His irrepressible love for reversals, however, prevailed once again:

"The surgeon truly looks like a Wermacht officer," he added, "one of those with a *von* in front of their last name, one who immediately operates on you with his eyes."

He then told me that not just one, but *three* consecutive surgeries had been necessary. He went under anesthesia three times, and was confined to the operating room from seven in the morning until nine in the evening. He was unable to come out of his artificial sleep, and kept raving even after the effects of the narcotics had worn off.

Every once in a while he interrupted his conversation to say, *One moment . . . just one moment . . .*, evidently addressing the young black nurse who was standing nearby, signaling him to hang up. He cajoled her with his thin, charming voice, only to inform me:

"Her ass is so big that you could rest your typewriter, phone, books, and elbows on it; you could even stretch out on it like on a couch. If only you could see the nurses here: how beautiful, well mannered, and kind they are. There's nothing whorish about them, nothing of the brothel stereotype, only a femininity and grace that revitalizes and soothes you." And he hung up, leaving me with these triumphant images of healing womanliness. During his phone call, I told him that I was going to send him a letter I had already written, keeping him abreast of the reprinting of his films. I decided to write it on a whim, right after the screening of *Toby Dammit,* a movie so modern that it looked like it had just been shot. Its language is clear and spasmodic at the same time; its narrative style is neurotic, pressing, and visionary. It's a style that young film directors and ad-writers alike would avidly use as a source of inspiration during the next few decades. One more unpaid debt that we owe our Merlin.

The later we go into the night, the deeper Rinaldi's words seem to isolate the empty hall of Studio 5, placing it under an invisible glass cover. We all are prisoners inside a glass bubble held in the palm of the Genius of the Lamp under his sly, gentle gaze.

An old actress and psychic who comes all the way from Apulia turns on a tape-recorder hidden inside her purse, filling the immense, silent nave with medieval songs from the time of Emperor Frederick II. She had collected the songs personally in a state of trance, traveling throughout southern Italy from castle to castle, retracing the steps of the Emperor's strolling-minstrel. Sorrow is rampant, but the sorceress wants none of it. Sulky faces will not be tolerated, because affliction holds back the soul of he who is about to withdraw from this world, and prevents it from flying free to rejoin the common spirit and dispersing into the universe as it longs to do.

Her exhortation produces the desired effect. The typical euphoria of a movie set takes hold of those present. The crowds swirling around all day long, the mobile spotlight towers, and the fake sky restore the studio to an unmistakable charm that envelops us all. We are within the safe shelter of a "privileged enclosure," a mandala, a sanctuary where events morph into magic, and magic in turn unites all disciples into a strong, indissoluble bond. The atmosphere inside that makeshift funeral chamber is light and serene. In addition, an almost palpable sensuality hovers around the studio; the preponderance of female figures creates an ideal harem around the coffin. Some of them are very attractive, even provocative, regardless of their age or intent. Alba Moreno, the script girl for the Maestro during the last thirty years, exudes the same feline eroticism that Fellini captured in the thousands of drawings he dedicated to her: a she-cat with a gluttonous smile and the tail raised over her provocative buttocks.

The young Rinaldi watches her too, and perhaps intuits my thoughts as he remarks:

"She is the one who ushered me into Federico's world. She was the threshold guardian, the herald announcing the disciples' arrival: a twist of fate that I should have recognized right then."

"What do you mean?"

At the time I was working on my dissertation on Fellini, discovering that the art of cinema allows for total expression. Not only could a man freely fantasize about those unreachable demigoddesses who smiled at him from the screen, but also he was entitled to conjure them, filch them, snatch them from that world of dreams and make them materialize. Anita Ekberg's lips! Her tiger eyes! Her breasts! Her legs! So, there is Paradise!

Art. Psychoanalysis. Magic. Was there anything that Fellini the great alchemist had not been able to project onto the white screen? Not to forget his love, admiration, and boundless curiosity about the women's universe, which he described without false shame or hypocritical moralism.

I happened to be born just a few miles from Rimini, Federico's hometown. Only a short bike ride separated me from that joyously pagan, dynamic world of his. Who knows? Perhaps that fortuitous coincidence would allow me to cross over and enter into the other dimension. And so, once I had finished researching everything ever written about his films, with a letter of introduction from a mutual friend I went to Rome to meet him in person.

Worried that I might be late, I walked into the legendary Plaza Hotel at noon sharp. The Plaza is a stately building, located halfway up Via del Corso, across from the Church of the SS. Ambrogio and Carlo. The gleaming revolving door, made of Art Nouveau frosted glass, spun me right into the middle of the hall that was bursting with life. What I witnessed was a kind of movie in itself, with the characters milling around the set, slowly gathering at an intended focal point. Among them was the most famous director on earth.

"I have an appointment with Fellini," I uttered to one of the tailcoated employees who were standing pompously behind the reception desk. Was he the right person to ask? Did I choose well? Without bothering to reply, he lifted a receiver, black and shiny like his tails, and warily whispered a few vague words:

"They are coming," he informed me, imperceptibly raising his eyes at the glass door dividing the atrium from the vast hall laden with rugs and shiny fittings, hinting at the place of the impending apparition.

In front of me rose a wide, curving marble staircase, embellished with a flaming red runner. At the end the handrail spiral stood a giant lion, leaning toward the lobby with a majestic step, his mane bristling, and his jaws half open to discourage the brash visitor. His sheer presence and size constituted a threat; he was there to guard a passageway that was obviously prohibited, or perhaps open to only an elect few. Nonetheless, both staircase and animal looked quite familiar: I had seen them perfectly reproduced in *8 1/2*.

Then suddenly I saw an alluring smile, two inviting vermilion lips on a sinuous mouth that shaped captivating words:

"You look so young! You are just a boy! You are here to see the Maestro, aren't you? I'm Alba Moreno, Fellini's script girl."

As she offered me her hand, her scarlet silk blouse, studiedly left partly unbuttoned, quivered over her unruly breasts that refused to be restrained by that pliant cloth screen. Her smile did not fade away, nay, it lit up her whole face, spangled her dark brazen eyes that nonetheless looked as listless as those of a Shulamite. While she talked, she moistened her lips with the tip of her darting tongue that sassily and promisingly peeped through her mouth.

"Come, the Maestro will see you right away. You are from Bologna, aren't you?" she said, as if being from Bologna was a laissez-passer.

"I *study* in Bologna," I corrected her pedantically, still unaware of the rules of that world in which questions are asked almost absent-mindedly, out of politeness, without really expecting an answer.

"Good for you!" she said, revealing a slight Tuscan accent. "These days it's not easy to find a young man who has the will to study; a boy at your age would rather . . . well . . . enjoy himself!"

She preceded me by half a step, while her languid body softly molded the air around. Her smile visibly turned into an absolving snicker: if I indeed enjoyed myself instead of studying, she would not blame me.

As you can see, Alba is shaped like an amphora. She reminds me of the old pre-war drawings by Barbara, Boccasile, and Walter Molino–those women with thin ankles and rounded bottoms, not tall but very well proportioned: the real Italian women, that is. In his numberless caricatures, Federico always portrayed her the same way: the she-cat face, the feline curves, and the idling gait of an enchantress.

Through her, I was introduced to Fellini's world. For the first time I found myself standing before one of his creatures in the flesh, not just a silver ghost on the screen that I had to tirelessly enrich through my imagination."

"What happened between you and Alba?"

"Nothing! Alba was just some kind of harbinger, a herald, an Olympus messenger. I realized it only later. In fact, to be honest, I realize it only now that I'm discussing it with you. The significance of that first meeting unveils itself if I put it in relation to the events of last summer, when, after being discharged from the Swiss hospital, Federico unreasonably decided to return to Rimini. It was a fatal decision, perhaps, in light of the ensuing dramatic turn of events. It was a decision that also favored the precipitation of hallucinogenic salts, and Federico the alchemist was the only one able to control their hidden influx and to master the visions that they induced.

Chapter IV

A Renaissance Angel

On August 3, while at the Grand Hotel in Rimini, Fellini suffered a stroke and was immediately taken to the Ospedale Infermi.

Following the directions I was given at the information desk, I ventured inside the meanders of that vast hospital complex: *wing C, go to the rear, fourth floor.*

The electrified reaction of a squad of reporters at the opening of the elevator's doors indicated that I had reached the right ward. Ignoring who I was, but suffering from news bulimia, the reporters sprang toward me asking questions, rummaging for possible indiscretions. A photographer, who once had sent me his portfolio at Cinecittà so that I could submit it to Fellini, recognized me and glanced at a screen that blocked the access to a corridor:

"That way," he advised sympathetically.

At that very moment, Giulietta Masina appeared from behind the screen. With her blank eyes and wiped out, taut face she looked like ectoplasm.

We hugged and kissed each other on the cheeks, as usual.

"I don't know if you can see him," she whispered, "he's not doing well."

She went back around the dividing screen and led me into the ward. At the end of the corridor were two doors. Loretta, Fellini's personal assistant, emerged from one of them.

"Come, Oscar, follow me."

Giulietta returned to the elevators, and I followed Loretta into a double room that had been provisionally turned into a secretary's office and waiting room. Behind the closed door of the opposite room was Federico.

"He's had many visitors," said Loretta, trying to summarize the situation for me. "He got all worked up and got tired. Even his blood pressure went back up. Now, before letting any more visitors in, we must get clearance from Dr. Saraceni."

Mario Saraceni was Fellini's attending physician. Being the one who issued the medical bulletins for the press and read them in front of the TV cameras, he suddenly found himself in the spotlight.

August 6, 1993, 10:00 a.m.

Federico Fellini's clinical picture has shown a modest initial improvement. The patient has never lost consciousness. Initially his responsiveness came only under stimulus but now it is spontaneous. His motor loss remains unchanged. There is no sign of infectious, metabolic or cardiorespiratory complications. His third CAT scan has confirmed the absence of brain hemorrhage. The prognosis, however, remains uncertain.

Loretta quickly described for me the events that marked those first days at the hospital: the speculations, the anxieties, the visits, the vain parade of the most unlikely people, the irrepressible hyperboles of the journalists. As we questioned each other about the possible outcome of that sad development, Saraceni entered the room displaying his theatrical, *boulevardier* manner. Compared to when he was in Rome, his innate histrionics had become even more pronounced. Given his double role of spokesman for the hospital and attending physician of the venerable patient, he pitched his voice on a formal and sumptuous level, trying to sound reassuring, yet at the same time he relied on a bombastic and tremulous tone. The popularity intoxicated him, the responsibility thrilled him. He had a momentous problem on his hands: he had to decide whether or not he should alter Fellini's prognosis. Even though the patient had gotten over his ischemia, Saraceni was fully aware that it was no cause for unwarranted optimism. The stroke had taken place despite an anticoagulant therapy that already kept his blood at the lowest density level, below which it was impossible to go. At any rate, there was no other viable treatment. At the Ospedale Infermi, Fellini was given the same therapy that he had been prescribed at the Zurich Cantonal Hospital, still that did not prevent his cerebral ischemia, or his left side paralysis.

The CAT scans showed that the situation was not deteriorating, so, all in all, prospects seemed good. Saraceni, however, felt under the world's microscope, as transpired from his dazed expression when, in the press conferences, he faced that vast, imaginary audience: a situation that afflicted and galvanized him at the same time.

"Would you like to see him?" he finally asked me.

He returned to the opposite room and called me in right away. Federico's voice welcomed me as I crossed the threshold:

"Come in, Oscar, have a seat." He muttered that invitation while lying in bed, with his mouth twisted. His eyes did not conform to his disjointed face: his right eye was half-closed, the eyelid almost shut, whereas his left eye remained wide open: by contrast, it seemed unnaturally big. It reminded me of the glass eyeball worn by Alain Cuny when he played Lichas, the Neronian pirate in *Satyricon.*

His left hand lay still on the sheet. Looking at it, I had the impression that it had shrunk, wizened, like a saint's relic in a shrine. Unable to overcome my horror, I turned my eyes to his left hand, sore from IVs, and leaned over to kiss him on his cheek.

"Do you see what has happened to me?" he whispered with a serious expression, suitable to the occasion. I nodded gravely in reply, while my eyes filled with deep sorrow. I could not foresee his sudden about-face:

"My dick has grown this big," he said, drawing in the air with his good hand the contours of a huge, imaginary penis.

Despite the rather grim situation, we couldn't keep from laughing. He would have liked Dr. Saraceni to detail that unprecedented phenomenon in his medical bulletin:

It is a strange illness, an unknown and astonishing disease: a gigantic penis sprouting lilies. . . .

Even though he had suffered a severe blow, he showed an intense desire to communicate. The onslaught of his illness had left him shattered. His voice came out distorted, yet he strove to express himself. He praised the Rimini hospital for its perfect organization, and expressed his resolute opposition to any rehabilitation therapy at a specialized clinic that his physician had suggested.

"I saw those clinics when my brother Riccardo got ill, poor soul. Those places are atrocious; they are like concentration camps:

I won't set foot in one."

In the meanwhile, the nurses had come in for his electrostimulation. He knew them all by name, and inquired about those who were not present. He was mentally keeping track of his cast: the film of that "spree" continued, with him as the incontrovertible protagonist.

Loretta's "office" was crowded like a highway at rush hour, and visitors streamed in and out. Roberto Benigni arrived accompanied by Nicoletta Braschi. With his lucid, smiling eyes he pretended that he had been invited there for a party. Saraceni ushered them at once. When they emerged from the room a few minutes later, the voltaic Roberto reassured everyone with forced cheerfulness:

"He's fine! He's fine!" he kept uttering as if driven by a spring mechanism. "He's even better than before!"

Back in the lobby, Roberto was immediately besieged by reporters. He then broke out in an outlandish show for their benefit, firing gibberish at will like a true comedian. But he had a dazed expression about him; he was burning inside, clearly overcome by a consuming fever.

Federico sent Pamina Trif, a young Rumanian nurse, to get him something to read:

"He asked for *Il Messaggero* and *L'Espresso*," she kept panting in her broken Italian with an astounded look on her face, while hurrying down the stairs.

"He wants to be informed about everything, read everything," Loretta observed. "And he remembers every detail. I think that he might even be entertaining some work project."

Around eight o'clock in the evening, all visitors had left the room, including the doctors with their retinues of assistants and nurses.

Summoned in by Federico, I sat at his left side, the paralyzed one, this time observing his motionless, numb hand. The speckled skin was darker and thinner, it lacked elasticity, and above all it felt icy cold despite the torrid heat of that August day, which did not spare the hospital's rooms. In his mind, Federico incessantly returned to his "blackout," the sudden darkness that fell on him at the Grand Hotel. He discussed the damage caused by ischemia, and mentioned the name of Wilder Penfield, an American neuroscientist who wrote a book titled *Homunculus.* In his work, Penfield theorized the existence of a third brain in man. In addition to the primordial reptilian brain and the encephalon linked to the cerebral cortex, there exists the brain of imagination, which works independently from sensory experiences and afferent information. By processing motor cognitions at the cortical level, this brain should be able to restore those activities that are cut off or compromised at the somatic level.

"Imagine a hand," Federico explained, alluding to his own, "a hand that does not exist, and this cerebral area, or additional brain, whatever it is, can actually create it, make it exist as a neurologic reaction, a nerve-terminal. It can even regenerate it as a new limb."

It was a fascinating hypothesis, and through his verbal virtuosity, Federico made it ring true. Clearly, he was trying to master that new subject, which he did from a most unusual vantage point in conformity with his inimitable talent, that is by penetrating those gray areas unlit by official science. Perhaps he could see a way out from what had befallen him, in that unknown territory where nature and human knowledge prodigiously come together. From a wizard like him, one had to expect the unexpected. I diligently wrote down the book's title: it didn't sound like anything very recent.

Contrary to what I had been told, I was quite surprised to find out that Fellini was perfectly aware that he had suffered a hemiparesis.

"Where's my fake hand?" he asked the nurse on duty who discreetly went about straightening the room.

"It's right here, Sir."

The skillful nurse drew near to him and raised his hand. Fellini started to pinch it and move it as if he was dealing with a foreign object, while sternly looking at it, with dismay, and disapproval.

I decided to help him in his probe, so I joined him in his tactile experiment.

"What do you feel?"

"I feel that you're fondling me."

"If that's so, you haven't lost your sense of feeling!"

He refused to participate in my rash display of optimism.

"But I can't move it," he pointed out scowlingly.

Unnoticed to him, the nurse looked at me shaking her head. "Do not believe him," she warned me, as soon we were alone. "You know, despite what he says he can't feel anything. In his physical tests, his left hand and arm do not react to stimuli. Only his leg reacts somewhat better, but the doctors say there is no hope."

Saraceni returned to the room, insisting in a commanding and solicitous tone that it was time for rest.

"I have to finish my discussion with Oscar, here," Fellini retorted.

"Five more minutes, that's it," he said, while his eyes silently appealed to my good judgment.

While I was trying to reconstruct the moment when his cerebral ischemia had taken place, Federico unexpectedly provided me with a fascinating account of the event, without omitting a single step.

He had gone out to lunch with his sister Maddalena and his brother-in-law Giorgio. On the way back from the restaurant, he felt exhausted and insisted on returning to the Grand Hotel by himself, despite the understandable perplexity of his relatives. When he arrived to his room, he sat on the edge of the bed to undress. He always had a hard time removing the tight elastic stocking from his left leg, the one he was operated on for an aneurysm: it was too big an undertaking for his limited strength. Due to the effort, he slipped down, lost his balance and fell, hitting his temple against the corner of the night table. As he collapsed on to the floor, he instinctively dragged the phone down with him in a desperate attempt to call for help.

"While I was down on the floor, I felt a flabby, dampish object. I couldn't understand what it was. It turned out to be my hand. In a sort of premonition, I was experiencing what I was going to suffer later: a complete loss of feeling. At that moment, however, I couldn't understand. I thought I was holding a small bunch of cold, slippery asparagus. I thought: *I wonder why Giulietta left them on the night table.* I kept moaning, calling for help, for someone to come and lift me up. A young boy who was passing by in the hall heard me. He must have been German or English. You always hear about the adult who saves the child, but in my case it was the child who saved the adult. He kicked the door open, making such a noise that he startled me, and came in. *Help! Help me!* I shouted. *Go downstairs, call the concierge!* It took him a while to understand what was going on, but then he quickly turned around and ran out looking for help. Some people came, pulled me up, and put me on a stretcher. I was immediately subjected to an endless series of tests. The same thing happened ten years ago–or was it eight years? Do you remember? At Pamela Harditz's house."

Pamela was a wonderful doctor, quick of mind and action. That time she saved his life with her miraculous sense of timing, turning him upside down from the edge of their clandestine bed. At the first symptoms, she immediately realized the nature of his attack and reacted properly; in fact there were no aftereffects.

Sometime past ten, I went back to the Grand Hotel to inquire about the English or German boy who had entered Fellini's room. Nobody, however, was able to give me any information. They could not figure out what I was talking about. I described to the staff the sailor-suit that Federico had meticulously sketched out, including the red child's cap and all the other details: the black patent leather shoes; the heavy woolen stockings–one pulled up and one rolled down–on his skinny little legs. That boy, however, had never been a guest at the hotel: very likely he had never existed.

Yet Fellini was sure he did owe him his life. The boy stood out vividly in his memory, as if he were standing before his eyes. He even remembered the large ice-cream cone he held in his right hand and never stopped licking while staring at him, trying to grasp the meaning of his words.

When Fellini had arrived at that last threshold, whom did he meet? Was it himself at a young age? The eternal child who always nourished his art? An angel?

While we were in that metapsychic mode, I steered the conversation to the initiative of a common girl friend of ours, a psychic who Federico held in high regard. In his name, she had entreated the prayers of a powerful Parisian Lama, who would engage in a whole night of litany, exclusively aimed at his recovery. In my eagerness to reassure him, I also invoked the immense positive energy that flowed from his loving audience–actually, from the entire population–who felt anxious over his fate and gathered around him in an ideal, protective embrace, as reported by all the media. Federico nodded with conviction:

"Marcello also has promised to come and see me," he whispered.

Despite the numerous declarations of affection that came to him from around the world, his thoughts flew to Mastroianni, his alter ego. He was waiting for him.

But he was already getting tired and couldn't keep his eyes open, surely also due to the sleeping pills that he was given at dusk in order to alleviate the distress of the night.

I whispered goodbye.

"Come back tomorrow morning," he softly said in his drowsiness.

When I left the hospital it had been dark for quite some time, and the searing heat had abated. On the sea front, the traffic moved at an exasperating snail's pace, amid an intoxicating, overexcited atmosphere: Rimini was burning with summer fever.

By the time I arrived at the Grand Hotel, Saraceni and Loretta had already finished dinner. I sat down at their table, and the doctor showed me a typed document in which he cautiously stated that his patient was out of immediate danger. He was going to release it the next day, during the usual morning press conference.

MEDICAL BULLETIN, AUGUST 10, 1993, 10:00 A.M.

Federico Fellini remains in stable condition. Seven days after he suffered a rt. parietal ictus, we have the following situation:

a) An unchanged neurological deficiency in the left cerebral hemisphere. The patient is still fully conscious and cooperates in his physiotherapy. His fourth brain CAT scan has confirmed that there is no hemorrhage complication or widening of the ischemic lesion.

b) Up to this time there have been no metabolic, infectious or cardiopulmonary complications.

Therefore we retract the prognosis quoad vitam previously issued as a direct result of the early cerebral complications caused by the ictus on August 3rd last. Nonetheless, in view of the patient's history of serious vascular problems, he will be kept under strict observation and closely monitored against the possible insurgence of systemic complications.

The next day, the atmosphere at the hospital was a little more relaxed. Giulietta and Loretta were sitting on a little balcony off the corridor, hoping for some fresh air. When Giulietta saw me coming, she called me near looking for a little solace, a word of support. Having suffered body and soul, she felt terribly worn-out and was afraid that she couldn't make it anymore. The extreme tension made her look even frailer than usual, like a bundle of nerves and pain. It was quite clear that she would not last much longer. She was smoking. Behind her sunglasses, her eyes were unnaturally wide open. Her shoulders were stooped under the weight of an extreme fatigue, an irresistible temptation to give in. She was dangerously flirting with oblivion:

"I just feel like sleeping," she whispered.

Fearing she might collapse, her doctors prescribed massive doses of carnitine and Enervit. Those were simple palliatives, however, barely sufficient to infuse some vigor into her body and keep her on her feet. The real problem was much more serious, and there was no use hiding it.

"What an awful time!" she kept whispering. Her thought went back to Zurich, to the enervating trip that nonetheless helped save her husband's life:

"Here, he wouldn't have made it."

His femoral artery had thinned down to a veil, an onionskin. Because of the newly formed aneurysm it was close to breaking up: a hemorrhage would have been fatal. In the Swiss hospital, Federico was tended to with the technology and organization of a space center, she asserted admiringly. When the worst seemed to be over, came that dreadful blow! She could hardly hold back her tears.

No longer mindful of her appearance, Giulietta looked as crumpled as her suit. Only her head was unfailingly tidy, not a hair was out of place. Her well-groomed bleached mane, to which she gave constant, manic care, was her only harmless foible.

Federico had been taken to another wing of the hospital, and at that very moment he was undergoing the umpteenth ultrasound.

"Why is it taking them so long?" she softly implored, as if reciting a tender prayer. Each clinical test was a new load of anxiety and tension that weighed unbearably on her soul.

Noonday was drawing near, and with it, the bustle that characterized lunchtime. Like an actor from an animated cartoon, Elio Tosi, the prince of Rimini's restaurateurs, emerged from the corridor's far end, holding high on his palm a tray brimful of steaming sunset clams, covered with foil. With his dramatic entrance, his faultless blue pants and snow-white tennis shirt, he definitely typified a Felliniesque character:

"I went all the way to Cesenatico to get them: I smuggled them!" he boasted. "You know, the coast down here is a no fishing zone, and you can't find them anymore. But the Maestro likes them so much! He expressly asked me to get them for him!"

"Can he eat them?" Giulietta wondered disquietedly. "We'll have to check with the doctors. . . ."

A gigantic, flamboyant *corbeille* of scarlet roses, lilies, Barberton daisies, irises, and anthuriums made its entry into the room, and found its place among the many floral gifts that had arrived from all over the world. Pinned onto the cellophane wrap was a card:

Thinking of you. Get well soon, Federico. I love you!
Madonna

That wonderful but bulky triumph of petals occupied a large part of the room. For space and air's sake, it was almost immediately diverted to the statue of the true Madonna who piously watched over the ward's entrance.

In the meantime, now back from his tests, Fellini was having lunch sitting on his bed, even though that semi-standing position caused his blood pressure to drop.

"We are taking unnecessary risks," quivered the chief physician at his assistant: "It's not prudent to please his every whim."

After Federico had finished his meal, most of the visitors had left, and Adina, one of his personal nurses, had straightened up the room, I went in to visit with him.

"I saw Vincenzone. He was elated to find you in such good shape."

Vincenzone, the reporter, had rushed from Rome to Rimini in between his shifts at the TV station. The night before he aired a brief report in which he politely urged the public and colleagues alike to respect Fellini's innermost feelings, and not to use them as a source for scoops and gossip. An Emilian cardinal had paid Fellini a confidential visit, which lasted more than an hour. In its wake, the sensational news of the filmmaker's conversion spread quickly throughout the press, despite the fact that Federico and Giulietta had been associated with the man for a long time and that the real content of the conversation never came out. The juicy tidbit, however, was picked up by newspapers and newscasts, and liberally adapted for the most shameless use.

Federico simply shook his head. He thought all that uproar surrounding his persona to be exaggerated, disproportionate. He even found it boring. Once he placed his head on the pillows, he couldn't keep his eyes open. Nonetheless, from time to time he still sought Aldina's care, if only to have his lips moistened with a few drops of water. Solicitous and calm, Aldina was always standing by. She was a short, big-bosomed woman from Rimini. Compared to her chest, her legs were very thin. She had a nest of teased blond hair and wore a perennial smile on her face. Fellini was very fond of her, and when she would draw near he unfailingly reached out with his good hand to fondle her buttocks.

"Well then... !" was her composed, cheerful reaction. She was resigned to contribute in that manner to her patient's health, to bring him that solace along with a cool glass of mineral water.

"She's the young housemaid of our childhood, of our first emotions, isn't she?" Federico told me as soon as she left the room, fishing for complicity.

Within a few days, he had almost fully regained his usual

authority. It was amazing to hear how peremptory and whimsical his voice sounded when he cried out for something, like when he would call out for his aides from his office. It was a stark contrast to his heavily impaired physical look, with his hand inertly lying on the folded white sheet, and his eyelids growing heavy as if made of lead.

Curious to know what had been said in the newspapers, he desperately tried to stay awake before succumbing to sleep. He had me repeat the headlines, along with a few passages from the articles about him. He listened holding back a smile, then he asked me to see his picture, while peeking at the other news out of the corner of his eye. There was a story from America relating Mia Farrow's venomous criticism of Woody Allen, who had became infatuated with their adoptive daughter. The actress had chosen a frontal attack, trying to destroy him.

Federico stared at me with his wide-open, stray-swift eye.

"She must be a real pain in the ass . . .," he whispered, knitting his brows.

He immediately sympathized with his colleague, and deeply felt his drama for having to contend with such an exacting wife. As he anticipated, I totally agreed with him.

The next day, the head neurologist from Rome was expected at the hospital. He had been away on vacation, but as soon as he came back he promptly followed up on Dr. Saraceni's invitation to Rimini. A consultation among all Fellini's attending physicians had become absolutely necessary. They had to decide whether to let him stay at the Ospedale Infermi, where he was treated with the utmost care but with no specific rehabilitation plan, or to transfer him to a specialized clinic, and, if so, which one.

It was their common opinion that a rigorous program of rehabilitation of his limbs was no longer deferrable. Giulietta was concerned, even terrorized by the idea of being left alone to face the task of reining in the imperious bridling of her impatient husband with her limited strength:

"If he goes back home, he won't budge anymore. I know how irritable he is. He simply won't listen. We need a clinic, a therapeutic center where he won't be able to butt in."

In the afternoon, the loudspeakers located throughout the Romagna Riviera carried the news that Fellini was out of medical danger. The music from *Amarcord* filled the air along the coastal towns of Rimini, Riccione, Cattolica, and Milano Marittima. Vacationers reacted with spontaneous elation, as if a burden had been lifted from their shoulders. The king was safe. Ilo Pulici, the president of an ad hoc "Committee for Fellini," proposed that "the day Fellini leaves the hospital should be declared a holiday." Pietro Ruffolo, the barber from Rimini who already had the honor of shaving the illustrious patient and thinning out his hair, told the following anecdote:

"I greeted him by calling him *Maestro,* and he replied to me: 'Look, I'm not a *maestro,* nor a professor. Here, I'm just a janitor.'"

It was August 11. The night before, the St. Lawrence shooting stars did not appear in the sky. The astronomers explained that the phenomenon would take place one night later than usual. Nonetheless, the giant comet Swift-Tuttle was making its pass near the earth–as it does every 140 years–and it was going to offer a true meteor shower, which was given the poetical and mythological name of Perseids. At the peak of summer, a profusion of shooting stars would be darting across the firmament.

"All you have to do is go outside," said noted astrophysicist Margherita Hack, "lie down on your backs, and gaze at sky toward the zenith, in the direction of the Constellation Perseus, almost perpendicularly above you."

Thursday, August 12, was departure day. There had been several visits to the patient and each followed the other at a brisk pace. Among them was that from Paolo Serventi, the promoter of his latest films, who had come all the way from Rome. Serventi was Fellini's friend and accomplice in all sorts of eccentricities. Despite being the cousin of a well-known communist party leader and a certified red himself, in *Interview* Serventi had accepted to play the role of a Fascist regional secretary. He was that inane and pompous character wearing the black uniform and boots, hostile to all "redskins."

In the early afternoon of that day, a salon was held on the little balcony off the corridor. People went there when they wished to take a breath of air–for in the ward there was no air conditioning–or when the team of doctors, who provided inexhaustible and meticulous care to the patient and monitored him day and night, confiscated his room and ordered visitors out.

Serventi seemed much relieved. As is usually the case from far away, things seem much worse than they actually are. In his diagnosis, the Roman luminary also emphasized the patient's slow recovery and gave a generally optimistic picture. The eminent clinician was a tall, emaciated, dark-skinned man: for all of these features combined he was nicknamed "Cypress." He looked down at the world from his unreachable heights, smiling aloofly at relatives and acquaintances. Nevertheless, in the name of their old party allegiance, he and Fellini greeted each other with a hug. They were on familiar terms, and the doctor would not lie to him: Fellini was truly on the mend, and one could reasonably rule out that he was in danger of death.

Meanwhile, journalists shifted their attention to Pamina, the pretty young nurse from Rumania who Federico had once compared to a Renaissance angel by Benozzo Gozzoli. They pressed her for an interview, hoping to wring from her who knows what secrets.

Federico asked me to take a few snaps of her for his archives: in his mind, he already had resumed working.

In an interview for *Il Corriere della Sera,* the reporter had intentionally asked Fellini the following questions:

"Many characters have entered this story. What is the script like?"

Federico launched himself into one of his fanciful replies:

"No doubt the main character is a film director in his seventies, who did not anticipate such an abrupt setback. Then there is the director's wife, many old friends, and a few new ones. And a nice merry-go-round of doctors and nurses."

"Which scenes will you remember the best?"

"All those about a lovely Rumanian nurse named Pamina, who, during my illness, through her beauty and charm, often made me believe that I had spent a little time elsewhere."

The published interview reported more of their conversation.

"Were you ever afraid of dying?"

"Yes, when my dear friend Titta Benzi, a staunch materialist and unrepented curser, after swearing a couple of times told me: 'Federico, do you know that I have prayed for you?' At that moment I was afraid."

"Maestro, did you pray as well? What is a prayer, for you?"

"It's a very smart and rational way to lay down your heavy load and entrust the weight of your pains and doubts to someone else."

"Someone has hinted at your possible 'conversion': have you ever thought of God's existence?"

"How can you not think about it?"

By five thirty that afternoon everyone had left: Loretta was going on a brief vacation with her fiancé and accepted a ride to Rome from Serventi. Once the patient was declared out of danger, Dr. Saraceni also decided to pack up and go. He promised to call everyday and keep in close contact with the hospital's medical staff. He fluttered away down the corridor, looking as if he was still wearing his white smock. He had done his part, playing a double role as doctor and press attaché. He performed the latter task admirably, well until the last hours of that morning. In fact, according to a rumor picked up by national radio and reported in the 12:00 p.m. newscast, Fellini was about to leave the hospital by helicopter for a top-secret destination. Saraceni had called a special press conference. I gladly agreed to be at his side as he faced a throng of journalists and photographers pressing against the glass doors in an effort not to be left out.

"We have no helicopters or submarines," the attending physician joked politely, with a clearly gleeful expression. "After a consultation with Prof. Braschi, it was decided that Federico Fellini should remain at this hospital for ten to fifteen more days. After that we'll see."

Fellini was the only one unable to escape the hospital during the mid-August holiday. He was condemned to stay where he was, albeit spoiled by his nurses, best of all Adina, who knew how to serve him his meals with the utmost care. And Pamina, who kept him company by reading the newspapers, mangling titles and content with her shaky voice made charming by her foreign accent.

From time to time, some unknown visitors insisted on being admitted. The medical staff and guards abided by their orders and would not let anyone in. There were no exceptions. When the visitors refused to leave, I would be summoned. One day an enterprising police inspector showed up to plead the cause of a lass who had clearly bewitched him. Her name was Lucilla. She purported to be an actress, temporarily residing at the *Pensione Luna* in Riccione.

"I will be there for a few more days, hoping that...."

"The doctors' instructions are quite clear," I apologized. "At any rate, I'll let him know that you stopped by, and if the situation should improve.... In the meanwhile, you can tell *me*...."

With her long, sleek raven hair, her lips marked by a purplish-red lipstick, her slanting black eyes ready to ensnare whomever incautiously gazed at them, she looked like Circe.

"It's a private matter between the Maestro and I. I'm sure you understand...."

"I understand, of course. I don't mean to be rude, but...."

Resigned, she wrote down her phone number on a piece of paper. She was going to remain in town, and counted on my good graces, even if only a phone call....

The next day, I equipped myself with a camera. In the early afternoon, while Federico was resting, I took a few snapshots of Pamina while she stood outside on the balcony, with the red oxide brick wall as a background.

When he woke up, Federico looked at me inquisitively, intrigued by the unusual photo equipment. He started joking in his usual fashion, taking pleasure in Pamina's excitement:

"We could try and sell the pictures," he proposed. "Do find out how much they are willing to pay for a photo of Fellini and Pamina together. One million? Two million? How about one of Fellini holding Pamina in his arms? We could try different poses, then put the pictures up for auction and see how much they go for."

Pamina looked on, enraptured. She had learned to play along. Now when the Maestro reached out to clasp her hand, she no longer hesitated and meekly relinquished it, while accepting a few other extemporaneous tokens of appreciation from him.

"How are the angels here?" asked Federico, touching her hip.

"A little thin," she replied wittily.

"And here?"

"A little better."

Federico laughed, looking at me with his one wide-open eye that no longer seemed tragic, but only infinitely amazed.

Pamina's life had been thrown in turmoil. Her sudden fame of being the Maestro's "darling" had placed her in the limelight. Every time she left the hospital, she was immediately attacked by reporters who hoped to extract from her a statement or some gossip.

"Are you protecting her?" Federico suddenly asked me in a serious, almost heartbroken tone, mumbling badly as he had not done in days, caught up in an emotional whirl. He was trying to pull me in: I had become his body, his muscles.

One of the guards, Roberto, tactfully knocked at the door, looking for me. He was a delicate young man, with a thin beard stretching from his mustache around his chin, which made him look as gaunt as a soldier at the front. Had he worn a gray-green uniform, he could have passed for a WWI infantryman. From the very beginning, we had come to a perfect agreement about the way to deal with all the various "beggars," whom he invariably treated with respect, unaffected by the power that derived from his uniform.

He had come to inform me that two ladies would have liked to see me.

I went past the accordion screen that divided the corridor from the hall, and found myself face to face with two blond ladies of different ages.

"My name is Maria Belloni," said the older one. "We left a note for the Maestro, with our phone number. I wonder if he's seen it," she said, smiling.

She had a florid face and an upright bust, reminiscent of her daring past as a soprano singer.

Chapter V

Mrs. Elena Diodati

Those two ladies were so polite, so discreet and graceful that I took an immediate liking to them. They were quite different from most occasional visitors, who vaunted a friendship with Federico or even hinted at having an intimate relationship with him. They exhibited none of that morbid curiosity and naïve ostentation of the others.

I gladly spent a little more time with them than I usually would, trying to reassure them. I told them that Fellini was given the names of all visitors. At that juncture, however, it did not seem prudent to provide him with a phone in his room, and that was the only reason for his silence. Anyway, I diligently took note of the phone number of the younger lady, Elena Diodati, who was presently staying in Cesenatico, and I promised to pass the information to Federico.

They both were heartened at my obligingness, and when I kissed them goodbye on their cheeks they shook my hand with warm gratitude.

"We've been coming here everyday since he was hospitalized," Mrs. Diodati found the strength to whisper, her eyes shiny with tears. Bashfully, she tried smiling. Her cheekbones barely raised, and her thin face turned more triangular, like that of a cat used to being petted.

"I'm sorry," I felt the duty to add.

"Oh, no, please, there's no need to be sorry. I'm not complaining for myself. So long as he knows that I'm here and that he can get a hold of me."

"I'm sure he'd be glad to do just that if he could, but he was positively ordered not to exert himself."

Now, why on earth did I take the liberty to make such a rash statement? Why did I arrogate the right to speak in Federico's stead?

Yet Elena found it quite natural:

"I see you do understand. I've been lucky to meet you."

"In my lengthy association with Federico, I'd never run into that lady," points out Rinaldi, pausing. "Her love . . . how should I say . . . her love pains really troubled me, I must confess."

A few hours later, in the late afternoon, the young guard approached me with an air of complicity.

"The lady you saw earlier today is still in the lobby, waiting."

I felt disconcerted at the news, unfoundedly pricked by a guilty feeling. I tried to find out something more from Roberto.

"She just hangs around in silence, without bothering anyone. She hasn't missed a single day since Mr. Fellini came here. Don't you want to talk to her?"

"Where is she?"

"Just around the corner, past the elevators."

I had barely reached the staircase landing, when she materialized in front of me, almost out of thin air.

"Were you looking for me? Were you able to talk to him . . .?"

"Not yet. And it's not because of ill will. . . ."

"I can't leave the hospital, I just can't. Here, at least, I can fancy myself being close to him. . . ."

"What's troubling you? You can trust me."

"Yes, but . . . certain things. . . . Excuse me, do you mind telling me your name?"

"My name is Rinaldi, Oscar Rinaldi."

"Oh, Rinaldi. I see . . .! I know you well, even though you don't know who I am. . . ."

"I'm sorry, I don't recall meeting you until today."

"In fact we've never met, but I have heard your name so many times when Fellini called you . . . from my house. Or from his studio in Corso d'Italia."

In a veiled way, she was sharing an intimate secret that had long eluded me. I was unable to hide my surprise:

"Yes, I don't doubt it, but. . . . Is there anything that I can do for you?"

She sat down on a step. The staircase grating separated us like a confessional.

"I think it's okay to tell you, I feel it in my heart. You see, Fellini was on the phone with me when it happened. . . ."

"With *you*!?"

"Yes. From his voice I realized that there was something wrong, and then all of a sudden he stopped talking. I heard the noise of the receiver falling down, hitting the floor. . . ."

She started crying again.

"I was the one who gave the alarm. I called him back at the Grand Hotel: I didn't know what else to do!"

I wondered if what she was telling me could be really true, or even plausible. I instinctively believed that it was.

"I left for Rimini that very afternoon. Luckily, I have a cousin who lives nearby. I'm staying with her now. I left my kids and my house to rush here, and yet I have not been able to see him, not even for a minute, to let him at least know that I'm at his side. . . . That's why I tried to give him my phone number. . . ."

"It's no use. Doctors' orders are to spare him any sudden emotion."

"I understand; it's just that I can't let go! But if he's better now, I don't want to upset him. . . ."

"I'll find a way to let him know that you are here."

As we stood up at the same time, I was struck by the feminine grace with which she harmonized her movements to mine. Putting them on and taking them off, she fidgeted with her sunglasses with which she hid her eyes swollen with tears. Her blond hair was elegantly rolled up into a perfectly controlled chignon. She wore a silk bush jacket, a pair of cigarette-pants and toe throng sandals with golden straps. An image out of the Sixties, à la Brigitte Bardot, more reminiscent of Saint Tropez than Rimini: the fashion style from her youth. She might have been fifty years old. She had a lean, hollow face, but with wide shoulders and large, copious breasts. The top part of her fluttering long jacket was left unbuttoned, revealing an evenly tanned chest. Through the décolletage, I caught a glimpse of the deep cleavage separating her lavish, turgid, and inviting breasts.

I suddenly felt a keen desire to rip off her blouse and sate my eyes with them, fondle them, hold them cupped in my palms.

Meanwhile, probably unaware of my internal turmoil, she continued her story, in her husky, burnished, and passionate voice:

"You know, we met on the set of *The Swindle*. . . . I fell in love with him at first sight, and I've been in love with him ever since. But what was I supposed to do? I wanted to have a husband and children. . . . I did start a family, but I never stopped loving him. Some eight years later we met again. I gave him the wrong phone number, whether by mistake or on purpose, I cannot say. And so, many more years went by without us even being able to talk to each other. But fate willed that we meet again, and this time I was careful not to repeat the same mistake. Back then, Federico was directing *The Voice of the Moon*. He had hired one of my young sons, Gabriele, to join his troupe, and on that pretext we were able to see each other almost every day. At night, I would drive Gabriele to the set at Pontina Studios, and that allowed Federico and I to spend many hours side by side, protected by our secret."

Her voice started to choke. She gulped for air.

"I'm deeply stirred. I don't know why I'm discussing my intimate affairs with you, but ever since I first saw you I felt this urge. I'm not making a mistake, am I?"

"You can trust me. Federico and I are close friends. We have been for many years."

"That I know. When I saw you emerge from behind the screen, I sent my friend to meet you first, just to use caution. You know Mrs. Belloni, don't you? Fellini gave her an acting role in a few of his films. I thought that if people saw me with her. . . . Most of all, I wanted to avoid Giulietta. Once Federico himself introduced us on the set: he passed me off as an old childhood friend! Can you imagine? How can a wife feel about such inexplicable presence of another woman? She seemed so uncomfortable. She knew perfectly well that he wasn't telling the truth!"

Elena was well aware of her charm, and she had no pretense of false modesty. She was still quite attractive, in that sort of way that Fellini found intriguing: a lady from the upper class, slightly spoiled, endowed with a sweet and captivating smile, and that impalpable fever that had consumed her face and spread to her eyes.

"You are very beautiful," I murmured.

"I wish! Just look at me! If only I were pretty, for him, so that he would still want me."

She aroused in me a sense of tenderness, a feeling of deep familiarity. I even put my hand around her shoulder, as a thoughtful, comforting gesture.

"Listen, Mrs. Diodati, don't leave yet. Let me see if I can talk to Federico in private. I'm sure I'll find a way to let you slip into his room for a minute. Can you stay a little longer?"

"Of course! This is what I've been waiting for!" She passionately threw her arms around me, molding her body to mine. "Can you feel how I'm shaking? I can't control myself. I don't know if I'll be able to go and see him without starting to cry."

"Please, for Federico's sake, get a hold on yourself: he shouldn't see you this upset."

Her jacket languidly loosened up, luring my gaze to her irresistible chest. There was no evidence of a bra: those tits–so attractive, slightly heavy, gently divergent–were in fact naked, defenseless! How tempting! Her amber skin, slightly spoiled by the sun, gave off a tenuous musky scent.

I was overcome by the same elation I experienced before, that uncontrollable desire to slide my hands under her silky blouse and cup those apples swelling with promise!

My covert fantasy of intimacy unwittingly led me to change my attitude toward her. "Elena, wait here," I said, ambiguously switching to her first name, on an unwarranted sense of complicity. "I'll come back. Are you alone? I noticed that you were talking to someone."

Was that jealousy in my voice? Was that a fit of possessiveness? How? I was assuming an unjustified tone with her, unless–the thought flashed through my mind–I had become the conduit of someone else's disposition, I was being inhabited with the feelings of someone who yearned for her: Federico!

"That was a stranger who was talking to me," Elena reassured me. "His wife is here in the hospital, and he needed someone to comfort him."

How come I suspected her of not being entirely true? What was I worried about? Was I behaving like the insecure lover of an overly seductive woman?

"Stay here: I'll be back as soon as I can."

Since it was time for his massage, Federico's room was crowded with hospital staff. While his physical therapist Maria Pia was intent on her task, others ran the hundred more tests, checks, and controls requested daily by the hospital administration, a fervent hustle and bustle that unfolded under the vigilant eyes of the head physician. I actually took advantage of his presence there to ask him how he felt about private visits.

"Generally speaking, the less the better," he stated without hesitation. "However, if the patient wishes to see someone in particular, he should not be denied."

That's all I needed to know. When Federico and I were alone again, I briefly mentioned to him about Elena, the attractive lady who had been pacing the hospital halls for days, crying all the while.

"Would you like me to give her a message?"

His eyes flashed. He knew only too well what I was aiming at:

"Where is she? Let her in to say hello."

I returned to the lobby. At the thought of finally seeing him again, Elena became prey to uncontrolled agitation. I gave her no time to think. I pulled her beyond the dividing screen, and she followed me meekly, in a daze. She made a final, feeble attempt to resist, trying to back out:

"Is there another entrance?" she asked in a pining voice, terrorized at the idea of being detected. But once we were past the folding screen everything went smoothly. Seeing us walk arm in arm, the guards and the policemen didn't seem particularly interested in the newcomer. Elena let herself be pulled along the corridor like an automaton, until we reached the threshold of the room, upon which Pamina, who had been advised to leave, fleeted lighter than a shadow.

Federico was lying on his left side, facing the window, away from us. They greeted each other like that, she from the doorway, afraid to go in, and he half-turned, in a twisted, uncomfortable position. Then at a signal from Federico, Elena flew across the room to his side: leaning over him, shivering, she pressed her hands over his.

Out of discretion, I set the door ajar. Through the narrow opening I kept an eye on the scene inside, while I also watched over the corridor, in case some unwanted visitor might show up, including Giulietta.

Elena bent down enveloping him, searching for his lips. With a modest, grieved reaction, Federico offered her his cheek instead. They kept their hands tightly clasped, their fingers intertwined, and exchanged words that I couldn't hear and didn't want to hear. I stood next to the doorjamb on the alert for them, pervaded by their emotions.

Their conversation only lasted a few minutes. They soon parted. Elena reappeared at the door, her face transfigured.

"It's some strange coincidence that I never met her before, that I knew nothing about her, wouldn't you say?" muses Oscar. "And to think that just recently, in Rinaldo Geleng's atelier, I viewed some drawings through which Federico had compulsively relived their torrid encounters. I seemed able to perceive the intimate nature, the nourishing depth of those images. You should ask Rinaldo to show them to you. He owns the color copies of the drawings. I can assure you, in all of Federico's copious production, I've never come across such a glorification of eroticism, tinged with so much love and abandonment: a depiction without compare. You'll see. When you examine them, you'll be astonished as well, and you will agree with me."

After Elena emerged from the room, we headed back down the corridor, and I protectively placed myself at her side. Once we were past the partition, she threw herself into my arms. A shudder ran through her body. She kept thanking me over and over, with what sounded like a relentless amorous wail, a pour of honey. I don't know if I can explain myself. It was as if she sought refuge in me, and I could feel her carnality, her naked skin. I warded off her thanks, but such was her agitation that she couldn't stop! I led her to the elevators, almost holding her up bodily, while she looked at me with a feverish glow on her face. Fallen prey to a nervous impulse, she drew me near and kissed me impetuously on my lips. Perhaps because I was caught by surprise, I imperceptibly stiffened. Receptive and vibratile, Elena detected it. She reluctantly restrained her ardor, limiting herself to brush her lips against mine, lingering at the corners of my mouth.

Several times the elevator stopped at our floor and left without her. Elena could not find the strength to stem that emotion, that wave of love that had swept over her. The steel doors opened once again: I forced her to part from me and helped her slide into the car. The two chrome doors curtained before her tear-streaked face and her undone blouse that adumbrated a lush bosom. In a split of a second I glimpsed the hem of a white bra. Ah, there was something restraining those generous protrusions, after all!

What bizarre ideas! What was I fantasizing? Never before did I feel such driving curiosity, such morbid lust!

I retraced my steps down the corridor and exchanged an evasive, complicitous smile with the guard.

Back in the room, I found Pamina feeding dinner to her patient: minestrone, chicken breast with boiled vegetables, cooked plums. Every once in a while Federico ventured to help himself, but he tired immediately and gladly welcomed the assistance of his good angel, trusting himself to her kind and solicitous hands. In the meantime, for the simple pleasure of listening to her, Federico invited the girl to talk about her native country, Rumania. She came up with a fantastic story that sounded more like a legend:

Ceausescu, Pamina told us, was a workless and penniless gypsy who used to roam the streets of Bucharest, living by thefts and swindles. One day he happened to be at the train station, in the midst of a teeming crowd and a bustling of nervous soldiers. All of a sudden, a gigantic brawl erupted. In the ensuing confusion, the gypsy eyed a suitcase that was left unattended, and at the most opportune moment he grabbed it and ran away. When he reached the street, however, some patrolmen stopped him and asked him what was he carrying in the suitcase. Seeing his hesitation to answer, they forced him to open it: the suitcase was full of propaganda leaflets for the Communist Party. Thus, the unaware drifter ended up in prison, mistaken for a militant subversive. The news spread rapidly in the city, and his name started circulating by word of mouth. When the Communist Party came to power shortly thereafter, Ceausescu's fame had grown so much that he had risen to hero status: he was inevitably bound to hold an office within the new administration. Due to a series of favorable circumstances, he quickly and painlessly moved up from his early post: a dazzling career that brought him the presidency of Rumania.

It sounded like a fairy tale but it was all true, Pamina asserted. Anyone in her country would confirm it: things had gone exactly as she had told us.

Federico listened to her, enraptured. When he had finished dinner, the young Rumanian straightened up the room. It was only then that I was able to resume my conversation with him about the beautiful Elena.

"She was shedding tears of joy," I challenged him: "She wouldn't stop."

"What a truly feminine and loving creature she is!" he nodded. "She kept talking about you," he added, immediately throwing the ball back into my court. "Did you feel her sensuality? She's like a magnet!"

A joyous and fairy atmosphere hovered around the room, while Pamina, radiant, kept going in and out with her innocent smile, tidying up, and handing Federico a glass of water tinged with a few drops of Coca-Cola.

When nightfall came, Giulietta appeared along with her sister and brother-in-law. She seemed better, a little jauntier, not so weary, perhaps thanks to the IVs she had been given that very morning, a tonic treatment more powerful and effective than the usual bland therapy of carnitine and Enervit. Nonetheless, she would not acknowledge that she was better:

"If you only knew how I feel!" she said with her hoarse, hollow voice, basking in self-commiseration.

Giulietta's arrival immediately sparked the doleful prayers of the hospital's patients and set in motion a pinwheel of notes, messages, and requests from those wanting to meet her. Some entreated her to stop by their wards, so that they could confer with her and entrust her with their problems and woes. Giulietta, however, did not have the energy to play the role of saint or queen visitant, nor to perform the duty of *mater dolorosa.* In order to spare her that toil, I went to meet the people who were waiting. I explained to them that also Giulietta was at the brink of exhaustion and was undergoing intensive treatment.

At my return, I found Giulietta sitting on the chair near the bed. Federico was turning his back to her. He had lost his joking mood and had resumed the role of the seriously ill, grudging patient. It seemed that I had no choice but leave. Out of sympathy, I patted him on his raised knee, over the sheet, kissed Giulietta goodbye and left.

As I was leaving, I was pervaded with a sudden, unjustified cheerfulness. Why? What was I happy about?

I walked to my car in the immense, now almost empty parking lot and drove off. The entire Adriatic coastline gleamed with enticing lights, its electric euphoria reflected by the black velvet sea. From Cattolica to Cesenatico, the renowned vacation funfair uncoiled like a tempting snake. I felt the unmistakable symptoms of hospital fatigue, that energy bleed that we suffer after a lengthy stay in an environment charged with so much pain. Three festive girls in a flashy convertible drove up beside me, waving their arms, seemingly intoxicated by nothing. Just to see their white teeth peep through their smiling vermilion lips, their eyes blaze with rash desire, their fine suntanned legs pulsate at the rhythm of their blasting car stereo, repaid me for all my lavished energy. I earnestly plunged into that life's wind, into that healthy contamination. Through my open window I happily reciprocated their jubilant waving, so grateful for simply being able to smell at such close range the intense perfume of their elation.

On Sunday, August 15, I arrived at the hospital in the afternoon, a little before five. As I entered the corridor, I ran into Roberto, the ever-present guard who looked like a swordsman. Drifting along and alone in that summer festivity, he walked over to me relieved to see someone. That day, Fellini had refused to meet with a famous film director who had stopped by to visit him. His colleague had caught him while he was being taken in his wheelchair to the lab for an X-ray. Feeling vulnerable and exposed to his look of commiseration, Fellini eluded his greeting. Therefore rumor had it that he was intractable that day. He was not in the least: in fact, he welcomed me with a merrier expression than usual, clearly gladdened by my presence.

On a small slide viewer that I had brought with me, I showed Federico the pictures that I had taken of Pamina. Flattered by our attention, the girl stuck her head in, curious to admire herself on the tiny screen. Her close-ups turned out expressive and luminous. She liked what she saw.

"What a slut face!" Federico commented, as he gazed at them. At being considered an angel with a slut face–the height of tenderness and sacrilege–Pamina got excited like a little child.

That calm, empty August holiday flew by like a light breeze. We were the only ones in the hospital room, three schoolmates in disgrace who were sent to stand behind the blackboard, and there they discovered the pleasure of playing together. We let our conversation roam magically. Over those comets, for instance, which had appeared in the sky two nights late: those match-heads that suddenly ignite among the fixed stars, and never fail to charm the viewer as if it were the first time.

"Where did you see them?" Federico asked me avidly.

"From a dark spot on the beach."

"In your country, do people express a wish upon seeing a falling star?" I asked Pamina, involving her in the conversation.

"Yes, of course!" she nodded dreamily, taking Fellini's hand into hers.

"Who knows what the primitive men might have thought on seeing a clear sky streaked with falling stars?" I wondered out loud.

"Or just a simple sunset," added Federico, lost in astonishment, gazing at the ceiling from his bed with his one wide-open eye. "Who knows how daunted Neanderthal man was . . . the sun disappeared and no one knew if it would ever come back."

On that August day, in that hospital room, Federico and I were once again united in our purposeless exploration of reveries. It was then and there that we began to see a glimmer of hope, thinking that we might soon unravel our dreams for work.

Able to use my cell phone, free from restrictions and controls, Federico indulged himself. He started calling all his friends who were vacationing throughout the Italian peninsula, picking up their voices from mountain and seaside resorts. His most secret *liaison* was staying at a hotel in Trento. Federico absolutely wanted to talk to her, however he couldn't recall her hotel number, unlike the other customary phone numbers that he knew by heart. His little address book was nowhere to be found, vanished along with his notepad and sketchbook. Rummaging through the pile of Federico's correspondence, I came across some exquisite booklets of poems by Metastasio, D'Annunzio, and Petrarch that Andrea Zanzotto had sent him. I also unearthed an affectionate letter from Geno Pampaloni, written in his tight, elongated, regular cursive, in which the literary critic expressed his sympathy with a few delicate sentences, imbued with a deep sense of friendship, and jeweled by a critical remark that struck me for its enlightening subtlety:

. . . because you, Fellini, possess the understanding of man's roots, joys and pains, all at once. . . .

"Let's call him right away," Federico suggested. "Do you have his number?"

During that enchanted afternoon, the only interruptions came from taking the patient's blood pressure–140/70, absolutely regular–and dinner. In the evening Giulietta stopped by. She seemed definitely more energized. While her face was still waxen, her eyes had lost some of their anguished, stunned look: it was the very same expression that Gelsomina exhibits in *La Strada,* when the Fool dies, killed by Zampanò. She had a rose in her hands, an elegant little gift from *commendator* Arpesella, an older gentleman who owned Rimini's Grand Hotel.

Federico would not rest at the idea of losing his address book, so Giulietta willingly started looking for it. She finally found it at the bottom of his locker. It had ended up, who knows how, between Federico's cotton undershirts that were recently ironed and neatly folded. Once her mission was accomplished, her relatives got her back in their care and took her home. The strict teacher had left the classroom. As soon as she was gone, we immediately returned being the undisciplined schoolchildren of before, in that rowdy atmosphere that Federico always fostered whenever he was free from responsibilities and roles.

The main focus of our attention was always the buoyant, incredulous Pamina. Used as she was to who knows what kind of boring patients and depressing wakes, she still found it hard to believe that she was actually taking part in a sort of outing. When Titta Benzi, Fellini's lawyer, friend, and notorious reveler, entered the room leaning on his cane with a sly look on his face, the atmosphere really heated up. Federico had a rousing good time. He lay on his bed with his belly uncovered, as if sunbathing on a deck chair at the beach. Titta was once again Federico's old school chum, "Fatty": the one willing to play the fool for him; the one who for half a penny would eat chicken shit, or the blackboard chalk that then got stuck to his teeth; he would also eat raw fish, at the harbor, when the boats came in. Over the years "Fatty" had become a well-known criminal lawyer, but for Federico his role had not changed; he still remained the all-too-condescending victim of the same jokes, only updated. At one point, Federico took one of his pictures, and with a felt pen he drew a balloon in which he wrote a cruel anathema: *blasphemer and whoremonger.*

"So now everybody will know who I am!" happily lamented his friend. "A statement like that written by Fellini in his own hand . . . who can possibly doubt it!? Now that my face is associated with his name, it will go around the world. They'll know me in the farthest corners of the earth as a thief and shyster."

The two kept on freewheeling, like strolling comedians, the white clown and the auguste, the couple into which Fellini inevitably divided the universe, the two eternal heroes of circus and life. Until it got dark. When the gang parted, Federico saw another endless, dreary night looming before him.

Fellini looked better every day: his face seemed more relaxed and his speech less garbled. Pamina would lavish him with attention at all times, so eager she was to prove herself up to the angelic role that first the Maestro, and then the media had assigned to her. She rejoiced every time a new gigantic rose bouquet arrived, a *corbeille* of flowers worthy of divas and soubrettes. She would immediately rush to look for the accompanying card and hand it over to Federico.

"You read it. What does it say?" asked Federico, involving her in his little game.

"It's from Greece. A producer named Manos."

"Ha! When did you meet him?" he said, feigning surprise, just to see her laugh.

There was a procession of flowers. The latest arrivals were two dozen giant, velvety scarlet roses sent by La Scala's *étoile.* Each new floral gift triggered Federico's by now set gag, and the flowers were then formally passed on to the angelic Pamina.

"They're all for you. Do you like them? Take them home tonight."

"But I rode my bike to work. I can't carry them!"

"Oscar will give you a ride home."

He assigned that task to me, his *ghost lover.*

The ardent Elena reached me on Roberto's radiophone. I immediately recognized her voice. She was so emotional that she was nearly speechless:

"As soon as you can, when you two are alone, please give a kiss to Federico for me," she pleaded. "Tell him that I think about him all the time."

With a jeering smile gracing his wrinkled face, Titta Benzi showed us the cover of the magazine *L'Espresso* featuring a curvaceous starlet. The girl was the result of a very successful interbreeding, which combined Romagnese and Finnish chromosomes. *Two perfect buttocks, so high, so round that they can cause a spiritual crisis.* There was then a spontaneous outburst of comments on the subject of the woman's ass, which always provided those overage "spivs" with an endless source of inspiration.

Fellini glanced through the magazine, looking at the pictures of the young actress. He himself had launched her career by using her in a TV ad campaign. That old fox, however, confirmed that he still preferred the charms of his young Rumanian nurse, and praised her incomparable gemlike features. He was even able to find suggestive onomatopoeic associations in the last name of that angel who had come from afar.

"Trif, Trif, Trif," he repeated, enunciating each syllable. "It sounds like a little butterfly flapping her wings: it's a flying name."

Federico asked us for a greeting card to go with the flower bouquets that he was giving to Pamina, and diplomatically wrote a dedication to her mother-in-law. A strategic move on his part meant to deflect suspicions, and reassure Pamina's puzzled and ferociously jealous husband, who in those days had unexpectedly risen to fame and had become the constant subject of local news reports and salacious remarks by Rimini's citizens.

To assuage his hostility, Federico convinced Giulietta Masina and Mario Saraceni to spend an evening with the married couple at the Grand Hotel. He was trying to make sure that he could count on Pamina's assistance in the future: he didn't want to ever lose her, even in the eventuality he was transferred to another city or hospital.

Those games he was playing reminded me of Fellini in his heyday: he was carrying out one of his most typical plots, trying to satisfy his knack for assembling characters and situations, according to a well-conceived design, as a film director, a *metteur en scene* of life. No doubt he was on the mend.

Giulietta came only for very short visits. She whispered in my ear that next Thursday she would go back to Rome. She was at the end of her strength, and the doctors warned her that she was inexorably pushing herself the point of collapse.

"Let's hope Federico doesn't find out," she said imploringly, as if speaking to herself. Despite all that, she never neglected going to her hairdresser, so eager she was to show up with her hair in perfect order: it was the indispensable condition for her to be at ease.

Her face, however, grew gaunter all the time, and it housed a hardened expression barely disguised by a grimace of pain.

Worry was rife among her relatives that while Federico was recovering from that ugly incident, it was now Giulietta's turn to relieve him and somehow suffer the aftereffects. Deeply worn out, Federico's irreplaceable companion had depleted her strength.

Tilde, the nurse in charge of the night shift, bore a striking resemblance to a mythic character from Fellini's pantheon: the pharmacist's wife. The likeness was especially evident in her picture pinned to her smock's lapel. Federico and I noticed it immediately. We recalled that legendary bather from *The City of Women*: her prosperous, ghostly figure in a swimsuit silhouetted against the bathing hut's door, which voluptuously moves over to the water's edge. The extrovert medical assistant exhibited the same contours of that unreachable enchantress, whom the group of childhood friends peeped through the holes in the bathing hut. The fact that she, too, was from Rimini further seemed to validate that auspicious, fantastic coincidence. Was there going to be a fruitful revival?

"Did you see this, Mr. Fellini?"–said Tilde getting all excited, while showing to him some old issues of *Gente* and *Oggi*. "You really got away with it!"

There were the pictures of Federico taken during his dramatic transfer from the Grand Hotel to the Infermi Hospital. A full-page photograph showed him on a stretcher, with his one wide-open eye, a blanket on, and the IV needle stuck into his arm, while the panting stretcher-bearers pushed him along the corridor of the emergency room.

Federico confusedly remembered the annoying flashes flickering around him, the various tests, checks, CAT scans, and the anonymous hands bustling over his already alien body.

"I wasn't able to ask for help," he told us, puzzled. "Did you ever try asking for help? It's impossible, your voice doesn't come out, and your words refuse to take shape, to be screamed. It's like saying *I love you.* Are you able to say it?"

"And before that?" I kept inquiring.

"There was that boy I already told you about. He was the one who saved me."

"Elena maintains that *she* was the one to give the alarm, that the two of you were talking on the phone when it happened."

"Is that what she said?" he pondered out loud, looking incredulous, disconcerted.

"But would you be able to recognize that boy's face?" I insisted.

"I could draw it for you."

"And you've never seen him before.... Does he look like anyone in particular?"

"No, he was a foreigner, just passing through."

"Did he look like the boy dressed in white, who leads the fanfare in *8 1/2*?" I asked, striving to find a possible precedent.

"I don't think so. . . ."

"And you, as a kid, did you ever wear a little red hat with a ribbon?"

"No."

If the boy who had stepped in to save him wasn't the little boy from his childhood, the boy always behind his inspiration, then what unknown presence had come to him when he reached the threshold?

Apparently Federico had assimilated his nearly final experience to a dream, or to the hypnagogic image of a *foreign* boy who, at the last moment, came out of the blue to save him; that boy was an innocent screen separating existence from nothingness.

Tilde would not chip in on the subject. She would come and go from the room, seeing to her chores, only paying partial attention to what was being said. But when the conversation shifted to the more concrete problem of the patient's rehabilitation, she did not shirk from the discussion; she knew exactly what she was talking about.

"You'll see, Mr. Fellini, when they put you in the pool. Guess who will be the first one to react to the treatment? Pippo!"

Federico gave her a stern look. "I want to have it in writing," he demanded.

"You can rest assured that I'm not mistaken. You'll tell me Tilde was right!"

The focus of our conversation immediately turned to that expression, *pippo*, and its numerous variations in Romagnese dialect that refer to a man's dick: most notable among them *bigolo*, the spigot placed in the bunghole of a cask.

The conversation inevitably veered from the bunghole to the fanny, with all sorts of local and ethnic variations: women from Ferrara were known as being more *carcadore*, better contoured in the rear than the women from Rimini. There even was a saying, as Tilde informed us, *Culo basso a mandolino, culo carcadore*, to extol the erotic virtues of the mandolin shape.

Who did we know who had a pear-shaped ass like that? At that point, our quest for specimens broadened to the hospital nurses in charge of Federico, who on his count fantasized about being able to welcome them–all at once–to his bed: blond Natascia, Maria Pia, and Manuela, funny and pretty girls, one fresher than the other, feminine gifts swirling around him all day long. If only they could feed him at night as well, by lying down next to him–"a practice that all highly-civilized societies should encourage, based on the example of the great elders from the Bible and of the wisest gurus . . . Gandhi, Mao Tse Tung"–they would have brought him to a speedy and complete recovery.

"Just think. To be able to admire Pamina's rosy cheeks on the pillow and absorb her breath, let the osmosis of fluids, the exchange of energy take place with true naturalness and generosity, in a precious flow and ebb of beings. Without malice or perversion, but rather as an exercise of kindness among kindred. Instead, when I propose it," he said pretending to be vexed, "those girls start laughing. They say there's not enough room in the bed, it's too small."

He displayed his dejection, while betraying an irrepressible sparkle in his eyes.

"You're right. We'd really need a big, big bed!" approved Tilde. "It would be good for you, Mr. Fellini!"

Federico looked at her and rolled his eyes. Then, knitting his brows he said to me:

"When people say 'Mr. Fellini,' I always think they are talking to my father. Don't you have the same reaction when they call you by your last name?"

He liked to be pampered. First he wanted to suck a lemon popsicle, then he wanted to drink some water with a little Coke, then he wanted the popsicle again, and then he complained about the catheter that was hurting him. The dear Tilde slid her expert hands under the sheet and fixed it, while trying to soothe him.

"By tomorrow they'll take it off, you know, Mr. Fellini? Try and be patient." Then she turned to me, speaking in a very competent tone:

"They turn off the catheter ninety minutes a day so that he won't grow lazy. He needs to get used to the stimulus again. It's meant to exercise the bladder. It's reacting very well."

The other nurses came in to get him ready for the night. Manuela, the youngest nurse, had blond, curly hair clasped into a ponytail; the other one, a girl from near Pesaro, looked like a neckless bullock, and had forceful, comradely manners: she was the kind who does not mind comforting the troops behind the front line. They approached him jokingly, and teased him jovially bringing up the names of their female colleagues, saying which ones were more or less pretty, what mischief they were up to, and what kind of reputation they had made for themselves. I left him in their good hands, with Tilde leading the younger ones:

"Come on, Mr. Fellini, now we're going to take care of you. It's all three of us, are you happy?"

"But what should I do?"

"Nothing. We'll do everything. Don't worry."

With those cheerful allusions worthy of a brothel, those kind, sincere, maternal, and indecent bursts of laughter, I left the room and set the door ajar behind me. Given that company and the atmosphere they created, my presence had clearly become superfluous.

Chapter VI

Enchanted Walls

The Pamina affair broke out. The dinner at the Grand Hotel with Giulietta did not have the intended calming effect; in fact, it did end up tipping the already precarious balance. Mario Saraceni attended the dinner in his multiple roles of doctor, family friend, and, to some extent, guarantor for the agreement. He was actually able to soften up the resistance of the angel's lawful husband, a simple, good-hearted truck driver. That meeting, however, unleashed a stream of malevolent comments from a part of Rimini's population. The next morning, the town's most circulated newspaper put the finishing touches with a nice gossip column titled: *Fellini takes off with Pamina.*

The pretty Rumanian was no longer able to stem her husband's fits of jealousy. As a result, she was once and for all prohibited from following the distinguished patient in his transfer to the San Giorgio hospital in Ferrara.

Federico was scheduled to move the next day. He was carefully kept in the dark about the newly arisen problems so as not to upset him beforehand.

A low-pressure system brought some rain. An August storm caught me while I was driving. The weather started pelting down on me around the town of Cattolica, and it continued all the way to the hospital. The sky emptied itself over the coast like an overflowing bucket of water. With good effect, since the rain also dispersed the oppressive heat and the static in the air: the newly dusted off countryside put on its bright green livery.

Given the heavy, torrential rain, as soon as I arrived at the hospital Federico insisted that I should give Pamina a ride home. In reality, it had almost stopped raining, so why the rush? I described the storm for him: the rain pouring down on the windshield, preventing me from seeing anything; the flooded asphalt. . . . He listened to my description as if absorbed in a fairy tale: for him, everything that happened outside his little room brought back life's essence and possessed a seductive atmosphere, a thaumaturgic quality.

He was in good spirits. If nothing else, his imminent move to Ferrara entailed some change, some progress. On the one hand, the rehabilitation program, the new environment, the need to familiarize with a new set of strangers and to win them over filled him with anxiety. On the other hand, the idea that the radical change was going to be assuaged by the presence of Pamina–that "good little girl," so pliant and intelligent, so solicitous and able to anticipate all his needs–appealed to him.

Pamina felt dreadful, as if she was guilty of deceit. Her heart nearly sank at the thought of disappointing him. She looked at me with imploring eyes, ready to burst into tears at any moment. She was tempted to confess to Federico about her forced desertion before he would find out from someone else. Their romantic little journey was to be no more, erased by the recent events.

Fellini seemed more protective of her than ever. He worried that she might get cold or that she might be caught in the rain on her way home. At the end of her shift, he insisted once again that I should give her a ride: "You take her home, Oscar: it's not prudent for her to ride her bike in this weather. Someone can come and get it tomorrow."

Fearing she might not find the bike again the next day, Pamina double-checked the lock before leaving, looking somewhat apprehensive. After setting a huge basket of flowers on the back seat, she got into my car. She guided me along the outskirts of Ferrara, through a concrete maze of gray apartment houses, with only a few garish road signs to provide bearings. I finally stopped the car before one of many identical entrances set obliquely on the side of a building, like theater wings.

I loaded my arms with the flowers and got out of the car to escort her to the elevator. Even though it was not particularly late in the evening, because of the clouds swollen with rain, darkness was setting in quickly. Pamina wished to tell me something, so I laid the corbeille down on the floor. In that impervious architecture, it was sufficient to take half a step to vanish from view. With a light twist of her body Pamina did just that, luring me into a sail-like triangular shade. Pervaded by an obscure, sinful passion, she leaned her back against the wall, in a neorealist pose:

"I know just how much he cares about you," she started saying, expecting some sort of reaction from me. With the flowers' smell wafting around us, I drew near to her figure, to her head enveloped in darkness. I could only see the glittering of her eyes, and then not even that, as her eyelids lowered and her lips hesitantly parted.

"I won't leave tomorrow, I won't see him anymore," she whispered all in one breath.

"You'll be able to reach him later on."

"No, I won't."

"Did you tell Federico?"

She stared down at her feet, whispering an imperceptible "yes."

"I must go, now."

"Let me carry your flowers to the elevator."

"It's all right, I can make it."

As she raised up the big basket in her arms, I picked a golden spike from it, as a talisman.

Even though she was stooping under the basket's weight, she offered me her lips for one last kiss, for Federico; and her eyes closed once again on her broken dream.

Then, almost without looking at me, she turned around and walked away with quick steps, looking tenderly clumsy with her burdened arms. Just before the elevator's doors closed, she turned around: her gaze, her pose, her smile were those of a fragile angel from a Quattrocento painting. Federico could not possibly be wrong.

Very early next morning, while I was still immersed in sleep, her voice reached me over the phone:

"Mister, come, you hurry up!" she said in her broken language. "He said come as soon as possible."

I got dressed and left right away, deeply concerned: what could have happened?

At the Ospedale Infermi I ran into a press throng: they were in full deployment mode in view of Fellini's transfer to Ferrara. I saw

Roberto stationing at the corridor's entrance, and I asked him what was going on. Not even he was aware of alarming developments, except the now official news that Pamina would not be following the Maestro.

When I poked my head in the doorway of his room, Federico gave me his tragic and lost look. His large bedridden body–similar to a stranded whale–fully expressed his nightmarish panic. Pamina's desertion evidently had scared him to death, and had left him to the mercy of the events. It had become necessary to select another nurse who would spend with him at least the initial period in Ferrara. The choice had fallen on the busty Adina, an efficient and affable woman, who, however, was devoid of angelic features.

Federico was about to go adrift without any real protection, without any throb of authentic affection: THE LOST OF THE LOST.

With the passing of the hours, the room came to life like a theater foyer. The cortege of hospital doctors came in to say goodbye, to pay homage to him, to express their great honor at being able to treat him.

At Federico's request, I had seized from the local bookstores all the available copies of his biography by Kezich. Before taking his leave, he intended to give one as a memento to all his friends, staff, and fans. Fellini autographed a special dedication for everyone, including the male nurses, the orderlies, and the guards, to express his appreciation and affection. By going through all that trouble, he revealed his deep grief in having to say goodbye to his childhood town. He regretted parting from Rimini, and in that moment of distress he asked us to draw up a letter to the mayor, an official message of thanks to be sent also to Rimini's newspapers so they could divulge its content. But he was overly upset: while dictating the letter, he stammered sobbing, his body jolted, so much so that perhaps out of decency he even asked Pamina to leave the room. Having me as the only one present, he felt dispensed from the need to control or to conceal his emotions. At the bare mention of his native land, his eyes filled with tears. I would never suspect such a sentimental, visceral attachment to his family roots, and so deeply disguised.

Federico F.

Dear Mayor,

As I am about to leave "my" Rimini to continue my therapy at a rehabilitation center, I would like to convey through you–as a personal friend and as the first citizen of this town–my heart-felt gratitude to all those people who have shown me their concern, solidarity, friendship, and affection, thus contributing to a positive outcome to my painful and troubling illness.

However, let us proceed in order:

First of all, I want to thank the Ospedale Infermi. In these days, when our national health care system suffers from dishearteningly chronic problems, with its efficiency, organization, and teams of doctors, this hospital has restored my faith in our country's capacity for recovery. A country that luckily is made of real and dedicated people like those working here, and not of abstract theories or wretched habits.

My kindest regards go to Prof. Angelo Corvetta, who not only has the highest knowledge, but also the reassuring look of an old schoolmate. My highest regards also go to his very young aides, all extremely solicitous, attentive, and reassuring.

I shall never forget the paramedics, the ward sister to the night assistants, all the way down to the cook, who is so excellent that he could be a chef in the most sophisticated restaurant.

I also would like to mention the municipal policemen from "La Fedelissima" corps, who with tact and discretion managed to curb the affectionate curiosity of our friends in the press and television.

In other words, when I decided to spend the period of my convalescence in Rimini, I definitely had a good idea. Demonstrations of solidarity and affection for me have been numerous. I also understand that when the Publiphono loudspeakers scattered along the Riviera announced that the doctors had retracted my reserved prognosis, many people about to dive from the springboards stopped at mid air.

This wave of affection from all over the world, especially from my own town, makes me think that I must have done something right to deserve it, even though I cannot really say what it is. In any case, I will do it in the future.

Given my nature and upbringing, I usually refrain from sappy rhetoric, but this time I will make an exception. I am glad that I was born here, and I would like to wish my fellow-townsmen to preserve, even in these hard times, their outburst of generosity and their appreciation for life and friendship.

In conclusion, as I leave, I bring with me a beautiful memory, and the hope of seeing you soon on a happier occasion. I say goodbye to you all, with love and gratitude.

Decoagulatedly yours,*
Federico

** Ask your family doctor.*

While we were drafting the letter, we were interrupted several times by the frantic to and fro of the various visitors who came in to bid him farewell.

Giulietta was the only one absent that day, and Federico chased her down with his cellular phone. She had decided to precede him in Ferrara to personally see that he found a comfortable accommodation. She wanted to make sure that everything was in order, and also to flood his room with a bunch of red roses, unfailingly accompanied by a card with her passionate note: *Your Giulietta.*

That day, Federico groomed himself carefully; he sent for a manicurist, a pedicurist, a barber, and a masseuse. He prepared to leave his Rimini like a Roman stoic readying for his final journey. Could he possibly have sensed that he was about to face an irrevocable sentence, an irreversible separation?

By the time I submitted to him the letter to the mayor that I had just typed, it was already one o'clock. Federico reread the letter and signed it, arranging for a copy to be sent to the local newspaper, a second one to the ward chief physician, and a third one to be forwarded by the hospital to Rimini's first citizen.

The content of the letter spread lightning-fast. Every public service department, every single person was afraid to have been left out from his thanks and, consequently, of the negative repercussions. Anxious to ascertain if they too had been dispensed the monarch's goodwill, people disquietedly questioned each other. One had indeed the feeling of witnessing a royal court's dissolution, a king's exile.

In concert with the state police, the hospital guards had planned a strategic sally to escape the press siege. At the agreed time, Fellini was placed on a stretcher and taken to some underground passageways leading to a secondary exit. The ambulance made off, silently and invisibly, in the fierce blaze of the midday sun.

THE LOST OF THE LOST.

Earlier, at dawn, Federico had sent me an S.O.S., a confused cry for help through Pamina. I will never know if I would have been able to hold back–even if just for the fraction of a second–the dark vertigo of his feeling *lost.*

Saraceni called me that same night. The patient's transfer had taken place smoothly, however he deemed it necessary for me to turn up in Ferrara as soon as possible. Fellini was very exhausted, very depressed: he needed to get his confidence back and to feel that he had not been abandoned.

Braving stifling heat and disheartening traffic, I left for Ferrara at three in the afternoon. Once I reached the freeway, I got stuck in the seething river of people returning from their vacations: millions of cars with Milan, Turin, Brescia, Bergamo, and Varese plates were pouring from the entertainment industry in the Romagna Riviera, back to the big industries up north. The party was over, the factories were about to reopen, and everyone was going home.

At one point I seriously thought that I was not going to make it. Traffic jolted along, with lengthy, unnerving stops. I was literally dripping with sweat, and I could not possibly envision a hundred more miles of that torture. Past the exit to Rimini Nord, a small fire at the side of the road, near the guardrail, made the situation even worse. The firemen's tanks were having a hard time clearing their way in the emergency lane, and the fiercely hot smoke spread onto the metal sea of cars.

Once I got to Cesena, the situation improved slightly. The three-lane highway at least allowed traffic to proceed without stops, albeit very slowly. As the electronic display warned us, we had to expect the congestion to continue all the way to Bologna. At six miles before the by-pass, we were still all lined up, bumper to bumper, moving at walking pace.

It was then that Federico reached me on my cell,

"Come, I need to see you," said his clouded voice.

"I *am* coming, Federico: I'm almost there."

All at once his voice took on a different tone and pace. "I'll let them know at the reception that I'm expecting you," he said, as if he was calling me from a grand hotel.

Luckily for me, most of the traffic continued on to Milan. Once I got on the exit ramp to Padua, I was finally able to leave that hell behind. I stepped on the pedal. With the wind whirling in from the open windows, providing some unhoped-for relief to the heat, I dashed through the Po Valley: Altedo, Ferrara.... I got there in no time.

When I arrived, the city appeared still and deserted, as if narcotized by the sultry weather. There was not a single sign to direct me to the San Giorgio hospital, and in that sweltering heat, people in the street were just a blurred presence. I stopped at the main pavilion of the town hospital. There they told me how to get to the San Giorgio, which was situated in an independent building, outside the city walls.

By now it was five o'clock. With a rather amused and astonished look painted on their faces, two young nurses on their bikes escorted me through the last stretch, pedaling off toward a solitary building off the main road. Once we got there, they directed me to the mezzanine, where the Maestro's room was located.

The hall was silent and empty: before me stretched a series of shiny floors and deserted corridors, and a number of wheelchairs lined against the walls. I went past the vacant nurses' glass booth. I walked to the second door on the right, and there I saw him, lying on the bed, and Adina bustling about, with that eternal smile on her face.

When our eyes met, we both startled, like two survivors who unexpectedly come upon each other–I am sure that is how it felt, even though I could not say why. Perhaps meeting again just a day later, but at a different hospital, must have caused us that irrational emotion, that shiver, as if we were two rescued soldiers who had escaped death in the trench. And thus, all of a sudden, it felt exciting for us to share once again the simple, soft coziness of a hospital room.

Adina withdrew discreetly, and Federico, with electrified eagerness, acquainted me right away with every single detail about his new accommodation.

The San Giorgio hospital was located almost at the outskirts of Ferrara, and it consisted of an unpretentious building encircled by a garden. A charismatic head physician, who had designed a special method for the rehabilitation of the brain damaged, ran it. He was entirely devoted to his mission, and he visited and treated patients only at his hospital; for which reasons he was held as a healer and a guru.

The facilities were very austere in appearance and were managed with unusual efficiency. The human landscape that populated it, however, was quite terrifying. Fellini liked to portray it as a circle of hell, a cave of horrors. The first time he asked to be taken outside in the garden, he ran into the other patients, who were for the most part poor things condemned to a vegetative life. He had encountered an especially high number of youths sunken into dementia, kids taken to that final shelter as a result of car accidents, reckless dives, and traumatic injuries, often ascribable to rash behavior, hastiness, and foolhardiness. The place housed a concentration of unbearable suffering.

Federico found all that fascinating and repulsive at the same time. He showed for it the same insatiable curiosity that he had all his life; a natural inclination to observe and dilate events; a "religious" sense of wonder even before the most excessive and wretched manifestations of mankind. He had already compiled an entire repertoire of stories and tales about it.

One day he happened to come across an old lady, who, like him, was being pushed along in a wheelchair, and out of politeness he waved at her. Apparently she took great umbrage. "Who are you!?" she hollered, in a paroxysm of anger. "I don't know you! Why did you wave at me? What do you want from me?" She would not quit it, demanding an explanation for such an intrusive and unwarranted gesture, distressing nurses and patients for that alleged offense.

"You should see the gym!" Fellini went on saying. "It looks like a Bosch painting." He unbridled his imagination, providing a meticulous description of the tragic and grotesque way in which the human body caves in after it is deprived of its central control unit, and it is unable to stem the massive biological and physiological landslide. It was as if a demonic hand had twisted the human body and had snatched it from the harmony of creation.

The patient that fascinated him the most, however, was a famous car tycoon who stayed in the room next to his. The man had suffered a stroke that seriously impaired his left cerebral hemisphere, the one that controls speech. Legend had it that he had tried treatment–unsuccessfully–at the most renowned clinics in Europe. In the end, when he finally berthed at that little hospital, he started improving.

From his room came a muddle of unintelligible sounds that reached incredible pitches. "He brays and trumpets all the time," said Fellini, embellishing and amplifying the event as usual. "I feel like I've landed in a savanna." Lending his ear, he invited me to pay attention: "Listen! What a concert!"

He was totally engrossed in spying on those atrociously incoherent, primeval sounds that lacerated the stillness of the nursing home like a witch's curse.

"What does he think he's saying?" Federico wondered. And he laid it on thicker by emitting a series of vocal arabesques, almost as irreverent as his sketches, as ferocious as his caricatures:

"I've been told that he wants to talk over the phone to his factory people. He demands to see the design for all car prototypes, all the new models that only he can approve. His wife and nurses struggle to interpret his loud brays and to translate them for his petrified employees. Just imagine, trying to give instructions at a board of directors meeting.... What a volley of raspberries, belches, and firecrackers it must be! Even better than a show by Totò, or by the vaudevillians at the Ambra Jovinelli! He likes to watch TV and comments upon it with piercing cries. Sometimes, when I doze off, I have the impression that the Togni Circus, with its menagerie of wild animals, is camping nearby. At night, I have the temptation to call Nandino Orfei, the beast tamer, and to make him come here with his whip and stick, so to silence that concert of brays, growls, and howls."

Tossing in his bed, Federico went as far as imitating the inarticulate sounds and broken noises of his fellow-sufferer.

"We met in the corridor, both of us in the wheelchair" he said, while becoming more and more excited and amused. "After I introduced myself, just to be funny I told him that what tormented me the most about being hospitalized was the utter impossibility to make love four-five times a day, as I was used to. He listened to me gravely, and at the end he nearly had another stroke. He burst out in such a loud and hysterical laughter, with such an accompaniment of sobs, hee-haws, and neighs that the nurses, fearing the worst, had to rush him away.

While having to rush to the tycoon's help whenever he howled, Raffaele and Barbara, the nurses on duty, did their utmost to serve the whole ward. For a tacit rivalry between he and the tycoon, not to be outdone Fellini claimed unceasingly the nurses at his bedside, for any real or imaginary ailment he suffered: his cervical vertebra was bothering him, his leg was tingling, his head was swimming.... They scrupulously took his blood pressure, also because every time he got up for his meals–he always requested to sit up in his wheelchair and eat at the adjustable table–his blood pressure would unfailingly drop, making him dizzy.

Seeing him from behind–sitting in a wheelchair, with his big head swaying on the thin neck, his round shoulders, his hoary tuft of hair–he really reminded me of the self-caricatures he had been sketching for a while. Just a few well-placed pen strokes, brilliant and cruel in their precision. How could he know himself so well even in back view?

He often returned to his dream from six months before: the letter to be delivered to Fellini at his studio in Corso d'Italia, and that gray marble slab engraved with his fate.

"Just think how precise that message was," he said with admiration. "THE LOST OF THE LOST." No writer, however genial he may be, could come up with an expression as perfect as that. An expression capable of describing the dreadful state of alienation, annihilation, and loss that I'm in now."

I tried playing down its importance. I told him that the dream was not necessarily about his illness: perhaps it could have lent itself to other less grim and chilling interpretations.

To Federico, however, everything was finally clear:

"It does refer to this condition of mine. Only now I can see it. At the time, I thought that the dream's message could relate to my work. I thought that it could be an invitation to reconnect with that part of me that was no longer active, with the Fellini at his studio, the Fellini who, in fact, was never there. Instead it was a premonition. The dream anticipated, in a wonderfully synthetic way, the condition I was about to experience. What I find amazing is the precision of the words: THE LOST OF THE LOST. It's hard to imagine another periphrasis that can describe the devastating effects of a brain stroke, in such a precise, dismaying, and pithy manner.

Those were the secrets of the dusk, when the dark grew outside the window and the shadows in the room shrouded us. Adina was getting ready to go home. After a whole day spent at the hospital, she eagerly awaited that brief time all to herself: a shower, a nice dinner at the restaurant, a carefree chat, without the constant reminder of illness.

Federico nibbled a little pasta, some chicken breast, a slice of boiled potato, a half spoon of chocolate pudding, but he soon started complaining of dizziness and nausea and asked to be helped go back to bed. The young doctor on duty, who had stopped by to wish him good night, tried to hearten him by calmly sorting out the tangle of his anxieties, and by advancing a rosy prognosis.

Federico's situation, however, did not warrant optimism. He might have been able to come out of his nightmarish condition only through an extraordinary effort, which required enormous persistence and trust. Impatient and spoiled as he was, could he possibly find within himself the necessary energy and determination?

Now it was time for the phone calls. Federico was finally granted the use of a cell, so that he could freely reach whomever he wanted, as he was accustomed. He remembered all phone numbers by heart–his infallible memory unscathed by his brain's upheaval. First of all he called Giulietta, in Rome. In the daytime, he would constantly track her down, always keeping in touch with her wherever she was. Then he called home. Their old housemaid Mariona answered the phone. She was the same age as her house masters and was slightly hard of hearing.

"Oh, Dr. Fellini! When are you coming home?" Mariona said, turning suddenly emotional, as she always did when he called. She elected to ignore the rude and ghastly remarks that Federico affectionately made to her, or perhaps she could not even hear them.

After talking to her, Federico spent some time over the phone first with Paolo Serventi and then with Mario Saraceni. After that, it came the turn of Pamela, Loretta, and whichever acquaintance of his that crossed his mind. It was like a propitiatory rite, a protective circle that he was casting around him, like an experienced magician. With all of them he joked, complained, and spun exhilarating yarns, inquired about their daily life, health, dreams, and work. Amid all that talk, I glanced through the newspapers. When he saw me linger unusually long on a picture, he became curious.

"What are you staring at?" he asked me between phone calls.

"Cavagna's tits."

"May I see?"

With an incredulous expression painted on his face, in the evening half-light he tried gazing at the image.

"I thought you said Cavani's tits," he said, realizing that I was not referring to the wizened woman director but rather to the piquant starlet.

He wiped out the astonishment from his face and sank back on his pillows, exhausted. At nine o'clock the night nurse came. She was a frail little woman, with a lean face and an empty smile, wearing a bell-shaped skirt that covered her calves. She looked like a lay sister, a creature straight out of a nunnery. Giulietta's brother and his wife had already paid their daily visit, a fleeting one as always, as they were afraid to disturb. They were people of rare kindness: unpretentious, meek, and solicitous. Having suffered the loss of a son who succumbed to illness when he was still in his teens, they were already accustomed to pain. They came over to the door discreetly, bringing Federico his neatly folded, fresh-laundered clothes, along with a few objects of everyday use and a ring-shaped cake that had the sweet fragrance of home.

I had not yet taken up residence at a local hotel, as Giulietta had advised me to do, and therefore, that evening, I had to go back to the coast: two more hours of highway-driving awaited me.

While Adalgisa was intent on getting Federico ready for the night, I kissed him goodbye on his head. It was then that I heard him mention Else's name for the second time in a day:

"Adalgisa, would you please call the beautiful Dr. Jacobsen and tell her to come? Just to make her happy," he added with a tinge of gratification, almost to belie his impatience.

Shielding herself behind an allusive and mischievous look, Adina had already told me about Dr. Else Jacobsen. The male nurses also pronounced her name with unmistakable enthusiasm. Wasn't that enough to stir my curiosity?

Nonetheless, I did not want to wait for her arrival and betray my interest for her so manifestly. I slipped out of the room and glided along the silent corridors. I hoped to run into her, needless to say.

In the meantime, Giulietta had been taken to a well-known private clinic in Rome. The doctors forced her to rest and tried to get her back on her feet with a powerful therapy: two IVs a day, morning and night. After trying to reach Federico on his cell, which was turned off most of the time, she called me, concerned that Federico, not knowing about her current condition, would try to reach her at home and not find her.

The second time, my drive back to Ferrara proved to be an uninterrupted, fast ride, marked by the frequent phone calls from Federico, who reckoned my miles:

"Where are you?" he wanted to know, and so I gave him my current bearings.

The highway was now all clear, and the air so red-hot that I had the impression of sailing the Canals of Mars, under a sky that looked like a blinding foil of molten gold. According to the large weather sign at the highway exit it was 103 degrees.

On my way to the San Giorgio hospital, I stopped at the first open café that I could find, to pick up a few cans of ice-cold Coke and some lemon-ice bars of which Federico was so fond.

When I got there, I found Adina sitting on a bench, in the courtyard reserved for the ambulances, smoking a cigarette. She welcomed me holding back a smile: having witnessed the various phone calls between Federico and me, she was expecting my arrival.

She had on a pair of golden slippers that immediately caught my attention. She wore a tight skirt, and a lightweight T-shirt sloping over her imposing breasts, which appeared disproportionate in relation to her short height. A bleached blonde mane towered her head, with not a hair out of place: in her affectation, she reminded me of Giulietta Masina.

"Dr. Fellini is having a 'private talk' with Dr. Jacobsen," she said to explain why she was there, enjoying that moment of freedom. Trying not to be melodramatic, she also alerted me that the hospital was swarming with reporters. Those scandalmongers often camouflaged or hid in the bushes, hoping to snatch a picture of a half-paralyzed Fellini.

"We are not even free to go out for a breath of fresh air," she lamented. "They should do something about it."

She stood up, put out her cigarette, and then started walking, leading me through the meanders of that building that held no more secrets for her. She was taking me to the neurologist's room, where Dr. Jacobsen was running a series of diagnostic tests on Fellini.

She headed toward the rear of the building, skirting the garden, so that I could inspect without being noticed those recesses and hedges where ambushes were more frequent. Then she went inside, leading me through a series of corridors, loops, and catwalks, to a large elevator. She kept a step ahead of me the whole way, almost vaulting along, tiptoeing. With her face often at three-quarter pose, and her everlasting ambiguous and elusive smile, she looked like Mona Lisa. It was a warning sign that I did not heed. Her fast gait made her protruding breasts stand out even more, revealing their unruliness, their irrepressible tendency to expand: they were two juicy and inviting melons ready to be picked.

I could almost hear Fellini's voice, that time we had talked about them:

"Did you see her boobs? They are bigger than she is! Rumor has it that she developed them overnight, when she had a raving fever."

And Tilde, who was a very outspoken woman of worldly experience, hastily pointed out:

"What's the saying you have in Rome? *She who's short has a big fort!*

What kind of strange ideas was I harboring? Why in the world that being, for whom I had never felt any sexual attraction, was putting an unknown spell on me, drawing me into her lewd coils?

We stepped into a service elevator, a very spacious one that was used for stretchers. The gate door closed, and the car started jolting up at a dreamily slow pace, enveloping us in near total darkness.

Adina pressed the button, then she leaned back against the side wall, bending one knee, letting her arms hang motionless near her hips, never taking off, not even for a second, her allusive smile.

Chapter VII

Lantern of Illusions

"I placed myself in front of her, whether through a deliberate or a fortuitous move, I could not say. Albeit there was plenty of room, erasing the distance between us I scurried to her side, seemingly driven by a blind impulse rather than a specific resolve.

Panting and swaying, the elevator slowly climbed up, lit by the blades of light that intermittently seeped through the door's staves. I had a growing sensation of being forced to obey an imperious and irresistible command. Unable to restrain myself, I grasped Adina's breasts, I squeezed them and fondled them under her T-shirt, and then I forced them out, subjecting them to a raging inferno of desire.

Those voluptuous bulges were definitely meant to be cupped and kneaded; yet they seemed to forgo their submissive and inert nature. Now independent, they kept flowing in and out of my hands, nearly coming alive; they took center stage, swirling with their lewd and slippery waves. They briefly feigned surrender to my frantic fingers and mouth, only to flee right away, like two riotous and turbid maidens.

Adina lowered her eyelids and lightly tilted back her well-groomed head. She stood there, with her lips half-parted, silently relishing that bewitched lust, that ersatz intercourse. Only the abrupt halt of the elevator put an end to my frenzy. Adina calmly regained her composure, and without saying a word about what had just happened, she put her smiling mask back on. She slid open the elevator's gate, and turning to a three-fourth profile she politely resumed her role of guide. With a spring step in her gait, she escorted me through another series of passages, arches, and doorways, to a staggered corridor. She then made a sharp turn and finally stopped in front of a glass door.

"They're here," she simply said in a clear voice.

Posted to the white doorjamb was a sign that read: Dr. Else Jacobsen – NEUROLOGIST.

I felt embarrassed about my childish and compulsive behavior. I wondered if the excessive heat that I suffered on the road had made me delirious, if perchance my brain had blown a fuse. My disconcertion, however, conflicted with the serene bliss written all over Adina's enigmatic face. I knocked on the glass door, and without waiting for an invitation to enter I opened it ajar. I saw Federico from behind: he was sitting in a wheelchair, slightly bent forward, with his elbows leaning on a desk, in a drawing posture. Across the desk, facing him and me as well was a beautiful young girl who raised her head. She was endowed with a luminous and expressive countenance, with clean and lively features. Her deeply golden hair was gently held back from her forehead: only a lock evaded restraint, tenderly hanging before her right eye.

The doctor smiled, surprised at that intrusion, but not visibly annoyed.

I was astounded. Could that little trench hospital willfully enlist such lovely women doctors? Was it part of their strategy aimed at improving their patients' recovery?

Looking for someone with whom to share my surprise, I turned to Aldina, but she was no longer thinking of me. Sitting on one of the wooden chairs aligned along the wall, with her little legs crossed and her golden slippers hanging down, she was intent on finding an errant cigarette in the pack.

"It's my friend Oscar," Federico explained without turning around, aware of the situation just by tracking the doctor's gaze. "Another fifteen minutes or so and we are done," he added now addressing me.

"I'll be waiting for you outside. . . ." I withdrew in good order, forgetting about the plastic bag with the Cokes and the ice bars that I had brought for him and still carried in my hand.

Cracking her immutable smile, Adina suggested that I knock again. I did so, more warily than the first time, and I hesitantly opened the door:

"I have an ice bar for Federico," I apologized. "It's so hot that it might melt."

Albeit slightly annoyed at the interruption, the doctor put a good face on:

"Then it's better if we take a break. What do you say, Federico? Would it be all right with you if we stopped for a while, so that you can have your ice?"

Were they on a first name basis? Perhaps it was one of the hospital's policies to create an impression of affection and familiarity for the patient's benefit.

The ice bar had started liquefying. Before handing it to Federico, I freed it from its paper wrap. Barely raising his eyes, he placed his lips on it, like an infant impulsively sucking on the nipple of a feeding bottle. I watched his hollowed cheeks, on which one could detect the growth of a white beard: he looked like a patriarch, a prophet. Was that intentional on his part? After three or four bites he had enough already, once again fallen prey to some inner urge. "I don't want it anymore."

Thoughtfully, Else got up to hand him a Kleenex. She picked up what was left of the ice bar from his hand and dropped it in the sink, where it could finish melting. As a result of her body's rotation, her unbuttoned white smock opened up, unveiling a tiny mini skirt that showcased her long, suntanned legs. With each move, other astonishing details were revealed. She looked more and more like a tall fashion model, a character out of cinematic fiction.

"All right, then. Should we resume?" she asked benevolently, returning to her desk.

Belying his usual impatience for commitments and tasks that were out of his control and direction, Federico did not try to wriggle his way out.

"Yes, let's start," he agreed obediently. "It's better if you wait for me in my room," he then said to me, with a complicitous smile. "It looks like it'll take us a while, here."

Apologizing for my intrusion, without further ado I backed out of the door, as the doctor's voice stated:

"Adina does not need to come and fetch him. When we are done, I will take him back myself."

Adina was temporarily unoccupied, and so was I. We had a

good amount of time to kill. We decided to spend it visiting those areas of the hospital with which I was not familiar–the cafeteria, the gyms, the labs, the meeting rooms–and so we headed back to the elevator.

This time I did press the button. As I slid in the elevator's striped half-light, I once again had the clear impression of being overtaken by someone else's desire, of being forced to act unknowingly, albeit not entirely against my will. Adina's bulging tits were eager to burst out from under her taut cotton shirt. They were longing to be freed, and they asked *me* to perform that task. Otherwise, why were we back on that elevator? Without saying a word, she pressed the halt button, stopping the car from its plodding descent. Then she stretched forward, causing her two soft moons to spread before me: they looked so large, so engulfing that for a moment I thought they would suffocate me. She was naked under her shirt. She did not even wear a demi-bra for support, yet those two marvels rose up turgid and firm like flesh domes.

Never before I had had such a clear, physical experience of the prenatal condition. I felt as if I was floundering in an eddy of whiteness, as if I was touching something warm, soft, smooth, and vital for the very first time. During that unforgettable, primeval experience outside the dark uterine cave, I became certain that sensual pleasure and existence were inseparable. Astounded and dazed, I plunged my face into those puffy confections, and started squeezing, biting, licking them incoherently. I let that irrepressible blind drive take over, and I obeyed it furiously, ravenously. Perhaps I even kneeled down–Adina was so small, after all, and that position would have definitely been more suitable. I can still feel today the warmth from her velvety skin against my face: through a vaporous epithelial exchange, that pliable, thin surface melted with mine.

I had the feeling of entering a milky universe, a soft cloud of whipped cream from which I didn't want to reemerge. During that ethereal experience, I actually longed to be swallowed up by it, to lose myself and disappear."

"To be honest with you, I have no idea how long we were in that elevator," Oscar candidly confessed. "I don't know how long

Adina kept the halt button pressed. But this I remember very well: reemerging required an exhausting effort. It was like coming out of a hypnotic whirl, a vortex of oblivion.

Nevertheless, despite that dazed, exalted state, I clearly heard a sentence shape out of Adina's lips, a name slip through her broken moans of pleasure:

"Suck them, my child, have all you want! I can feel how you like them . . . Federico!" she said, in her strong Riminese accent.

It was the same accent that now echoed in the room, as Adina answered the internal phone. It was a very agitated Dr. Jacobsen asking for our help. Due to the presence of photographers, the main hall was now impassable. Fellini did not want to have anything to do with them and obviously neither did she: the hospital was going to suffer bad publicity from that treacherous invasion. We rushed to the scene.

Carrying a bulky bag slung over their shoulders, some strangers hung about the hall. Nobody was able to tell me who they were, and they refused to identify themselves. Faking a doltish look, they mumbled the fictitious names of some relatives of theirs that they supposedly had come to visit.

Dr. Jacobsen had tried to dissuade them by invoking her authority. She had even threatened to call the police. "What's the crime?" they replied belligerently. "This is a public building."

I stepped forward to have a little talk with them. I decided to appeal to their understanding, reminding them that the respect for a person's dignity should never fail, not even in a pushy profession like theirs. My maneuver was successful. While the photographers and I were discussing the situation, shielded from our view by the folding partitions Adina and Else quickly wheeled Fellini past the hall, undisturbed. After the patient was released back to the ward nurses for his therapy, the doctor and I withdrew to the meeting room. Unexpectedly, she turned out to be well disposed. She went into lengthy detail about the nature of Federico's brain damage and his chances for recovery.

We sat on two small metal chairs, facing each other. The skirts of her open white smock were hanging down at her sides, leaving her legs on full display: while I diligently tried to follow her clear and precise exposition of Federico's clinical case, it was hard for me not to rest my gaze on them.

She explained that those who suffer from partial paralysis develop *misoplegia* syndrome, that is, a real hate of their lifeless limbs. Patients convince themselves that those limbs are not theirs, that they are prostheses, artificial devices. Or they come to think that they belong to someone else–to a corpse, even–and that someone, for some treacherous and gruesome reason, decided to place them there. They are so horrified and disgusted that their rejection broadens to their entire affected side, including their field of vision.

Federico tended to leave out the whole left side from his view, even though no functional disease affected his sight. His optic nerve being undamaged, it meant that he simply refused to see. His was an intentional blackout, called *neglect* in the medical jargon. As the lesion decreased, also his induced attitude would gradually lessen, until it disappeared.

It seemed to me, however, that the doctor's textbook treatment of the topic did not take duly into account the patient's peculiarity.

"I'm just a neurologist," Dr. Jacobsen pointed out. "I work on physiologic-anatomical data and nothing else. I'm perfectly aware that Fellini expects a different kind of help from me–psychological–but that's outside my area. He likes to talk about his anxieties, his dreams: he describes them in such a fascinating way that I could listen to him for hours. However, I wouldn't know how to operate on this kind of material. My expertise is lesions: I deal with reflexes, cellular regeneration, drugs efficacy. Beyond that, unfortunately, I'm just a simple listener."

Federico had told her as well about his premonitory dream. I took that as a demonstration of trust on his part, and therefore I provided a few more details that I felt were essential to her understanding of Federico. In any case, a psychological approach could only help deepen their relationship. I informed her of the Grand Hotel episode, in which Fellini had imagined talking to an eight-year-old English boy, or perhaps–I insinuated–he had really talked to him and was convinced that he had saved his life.

I was trying to turn her into a precious ally, making sure that

Federico could at least rely on an insider in that godforsaken little hospital. My tactics apparently worked.

"Oscar, who are you, exactly?" Dr. Jacobsen finally asked, calling me spontaneously with my first name. It occurred to me that we had not even introduced ourselves. Her friendly attitude gave me the opportunity to question her on what I cared about the most:

"How's Federico really doing?"

"He's seriously ill," was her simple reply.

We went back down the corridor, walking side by side. On reaching Federico's room, she quickly moved away, lavishing me with the vision of her long naked legs peeping through her fluttering white smock. I reported my conversation with the neurologist to Federico, trying to emphasize the positive side of her diagnosis, while omitting the rest:

" She assured me that they will get you back on your feet in a couple of months at the most." I knew Federico's aversion for the pompous presumption displayed by the hospital's doctors, starting with the charismatic head physician. Therefore, to sound more credible, I toned down my elation, discreetly hiding it behind a veil of irony.

"They believe that it's entirely up to you," I added.

"How so?"

"If you cooperate you can make it, and very soon."

"Who says that? Dr. Jacobsen? What does she know?" he flared. "And what does it mean, *very soon*?" The vagueness of the prognosis frightened him.

"She's enthused over your drawings. Through them, she's able to analyze the whole spectrum of your perceptions: she found that you're quickly compensating for the diminished visual input."

"Else is very intelligent, though," he added in a suddenly different tone. "She's a young scientist, very passionate and knowledgeable. And foxy, too! Do you like her?"

"Definitely she's not the kind of doctor that you expect to find at a hospital. I take it as a good omen, a lucky coincidence."

He soon regained his good mood. He was his old lively self again, eager to pick up his train of thought where he left it.

"Last night, after you were gone, I did call Geno Pampaloni.

Perhaps my opening was not totally appropriate: *'Tis the hour of yearning that touches the paraplegics' hearts,* I said paraphrasing Dante, as soon as he answered the phone. He got scared. 'Hello! Who's this?' he yelled. After he calmed down, he was happy that I called. He seemed sincerely concerned: 'I've been very sick too,' he said to comfort me. However, I didn't ask him what was actually wrong with him, as perhaps he expected me to do. I didn't want to suffer through the whole litany of his pains and troubles."

The howls from next door announced the tycoon's return. Sometimes, during the holidays and weekends, he was allowed to go home and spend a few hours with his family. Silence, then, reigned over the hospital. I then realized that Federico was actually waiting for him. With morbid fascination, he pricked up his ears, spying on any tone variation in those rattling, primeval sounds that came from beyond the wall, trying to capture who knows what messages.

That bizarre occurrence led him into a sort of comical euphoria; it brought back to life his naturally mischievous, disrespectful disposition, the iconoclastic spirit common to all Romagnese people, always prone to mocking, jesting, and caricature.

Hanging on the wall facing his bed, at man's height, was a sheet of paper that listed the weekly menu. I started reading it loud just for fun. Among the first courses was *ditalini in brodo.*

"What's that?" I asked Adina.

"It's 'little thimbles' in broth," she replied. "That's what they call that type of pasta 'round here. In Romagna, we call them *ditaloni,* big thimbles. But it's the same thing."

"You should add *Parmesan finger jobs* to the menu," said Federico, in a burst of juvenile humor.

"Amazing tits, eh?" he then remarked when Adina left the room, calling on my endorsement. "They look so soft, so milky that you could lose yourself in them," he added, questioning me with a sly look.

By then, Rimini was just a memory. We could now look back at what had beset him and rewind the reel of that film that saw him as protagonist. We reminisced how the Bard was among the first to rush to Rimini, with his large retinue of fellow citizens.

"My friend Federico is fighting like a lion," the Bard had commented in his epic tone.

"If only he had told me, I could have roared a few times, just to prove him right!" Federico sneered.

Our reminiscences inevitably led us further back, to his hospitalization in Zurich, and his three operations: the machines timely detected the onset of a new embolus, so Federico had to undergo a new operation, again and again. He went under three times. His doctors, including Saraceni, generally believed that the consecutive anesthesia was fatal to him, paving the way for the last attack.

Personally, Federico was firmly convinced that a sudden drop in his blood pressure was the reason for his ischaemia. "Because of the exertion," he kept saying. He related it to the moment he sat down on the bed to remove the elastic stocking off his operated leg.

I told him that when he was first hospitalized in Rimini, the doctors were quite pessimistic. There was no viable therapy other than the treatment he was already given, aimed at maintaining the blood as thin as possible to avoid the formation of a new clot. "He has Coca-Cola running in his veins," doctors said. Going below that minimum degree of fluidity was not an option, therefore they did not know what else to do.

Whatever the cause, the damage was done. Federico, however, would not resign himself to the idea. "It's like sailing without navigation instruments. I feel dismayed, like a skipper who sees that all his gauges have gone haywire, that his pointers spin wildly because the control center, the ganglion is blocked."

On saying this, he ran his hand over his head, as if that gesture could remedy the impairment.

He was deeply terrified, and there was nothing that could possibly lessen his fear. He even resorted to sarcasm, trying to turn his condition of helplessness into farce. When he saw Adina set the section-board for the dinner tray on his wheelchair's arm, he grotesquely transferred that image to another more familiar environment:

"Oscar, just think what it would be like going to dinner to *Toscano's* with all this paraphernalia, bumping into the other tables, knocking down glasses, dishes, and bottles. Or else going to *Giu-*

seppe's: that joint is even smaller."

He longed for his favorite restaurants, which now must have seemed like unattainable dreams to him. With great effort, the nurses lifted him up to make him sit on the bed, propping his back against pillows, while Adina briskly set the table in perfect compliance with his wishes.

The thought that his central control was a wreck was so horrifying to him that he had no confidence of restoration. His mind kept going back to his premonition, to the striking precision of that ill omen, those words engraved in the burial-gray marble next to his house door: THE LOST OF THE LOST:

I strove to find a glimmer of hope in that mortal dread:

"If you try and use your work as a shield between you and your illness, you will speed up recovery and will get back to normal a lot faster," I said, employing his own arguments. I was tritely feeding back the same words that he told me a thousand times, and that he was surely repeating to himself in his mind.

"It's also Dr. Jacobsen's opinion," I added alluringly.

I knew that the candid trust of the charming Norwegian was a comfort to him. He waited excitedly for the neurologist's visits, the same way schoolboys look forward to the class taught by the most attractive female professor, the one who makes your heart sink as soon as she enters the classroom.

"See if she's in the corridor: I think I've just heard her," he would say to Adina whenever a woman's voice echoed outside.

A girl like Else, the soul of beauty and health, only reinforced his favorite theory, according to which rehab centers should have sextuple beds and nurses willing to sleep with their patients: it was the only truly effective treatment, a powerful boost to life.

He shook his head, dejected at the thought that his suggestion would have been received as an outrageous paradox, as the pitiful raving of an old man captive to his deranged body, unable to accept the obvious.

Shortly after eight o'clock, when Adina was already getting ready to be relieved by the night nurse, Dr. Jacobsen finally appeared, showing her smiling and tender face that the summer sun had colored a seductive auburn. She was about to end her shift and had come in to tell the Maestro goodnight. Federico invited her to stay a little while and to have a chat. She sat next to his bed, she crossed her golden-brown legs, and she took his hand into hers:

"How are we doing today, Federico?" she inquired, sounding like a young fiancée fresh from graduation.

That was their private time: anyone else's presence would have been unnecessary. His face-to-face conversation with the beautiful neurologist, I'm sure, was for him the most soothing relief.

Eager to return to her hotel, Adina slipped out of the room. I followed her outside. I told her that there was no need for her to tarry any longer: I was glad to hang around until the night nurse arrived.

The next day Loretta reappeared, affectionate and enthusiastic as ever. The hospital was rife with excitement for the presence of Saraceni and the other luminary doctor from Rome. Both had been summoned to Ferrara for consultation: the hospital doctors had flocked in to bear their trains; also the local university professor had rushed in to peacock.

Loretta started sifting the mail that had piled up since her last visit. We both withdrew to the meeting room, away from that bustle. While we were there, the professor broke in, and out of the blue started yelling at us, making obscure threats. He especially grudged Loretta, who, in his view, was responsible for creating a mundane atmosphere that didn't suit him:

"This is the second warning," he thundered. "At the third infraction you'll be forcibly removed from the hospital."

At first, it wasn't clear to us what the target of his military ire was.

"This is all bullshit!" he then flared up, pointing at the countless envelopes strewn around in front of us. "The patient needs to see to himself, and nothing else. His whims have no place here. That Fellini doesn't exist anymore, he's gone, kaput! Now he's just a patient in our hands! His mail . . . forget it!"

THE LOST OF THE LOST. Was that still part of his ominous dream?

On delivering his clearly deranged diatribe, the professor adopted a rancorous and jealous tone. His eyes blurred, turning swampy and liquorish.

We didn't know how much importance to attach to his fit of anger. Loretta, in any case, didn't seem particularly impressed by his rant. Without ever raising her eyes, she stayed focused on her task and kept opening the letters with a paper knife.

Saraceni entered the room with a young chief-physician aide. Together they began a careful re-examination of Fellini's medical file, especially with regard to his drug therapy. At that point the professor, his chest thrown out like a tenor, strutted out of the room as if that matter didn't concern him anymore.

His wrathful theories seemed to me to be pernicious, especially when referred to Fellini, who now more than ever needed to be in touch with the outside world. His surprising recovery in Rimini, where he was surrounded with inexhaustible warmth, in a 'normal' atmosphere, only strengthened my conviction. Saraceni knew only too well about Fellini's fears and prophetic dream. Like me, he realized that all attempts at depersonalizing the patient were to be avoided, as they would be harmful rather than beneficial.

Fellini returned to the ward, wheeled in by the slender and graceful Dr. Jacobsen. The young Scandinavian turned out to be the true highlight of that medical symposium. Those eminent doctors conferred with their young colleague in her studio, treating her like an equal, and were impressed by her knowledge as well as by her unusual charms.

While maneuvering the wheelchair to push it through the door, Else turned her head abruptly and flashed a questioning look at me, as if in response to a voice she had heard. I hadn't said anything, but on seeing her jump like that, I instinctively winked at her and replied to her silent question waving with my finger, indicating that we could see each other later, after that hustle and bustle was over.

I can assure you that no sound came out of my mouth. The air had shaped out a question on my behalf, and I, by sympathy, formed my silent gesture in reply.

Federico was put back to bed, and I stayed in the room with him.

In the mail that Loretta had selected were a couple of letters that required a prompt response. One was from Italy's former President Francesco Cossiga, and the other one from Fellini's current film producer. We decided to take care of them right away, having a good deal of fun in drafting the answer, as usual.

I diligently wrote down Federico's response on a white sheet of paper from his pad, which was already crammed with his sketches and notes.

Dear President,
Two carabinieri came looking for me. Stating that they wanted to talk to me only, they refused to convey their message to the doctors, aides, or any of the other people that I had entrusted. I must confess that I got vaguely worried. Our Catholic upbringing forces us to always feel guilty when facing authority. When I found out that it was only a kind token of your friendship, I really sighed with relief. . . .

"I didn't know that in order to deliver a private message from a statesman it takes the cuirassiers, the police, the carabinieri, the special corps, and the counterespionage unit," he pointed out amusedly. "Also Giulietta in Rome got scared. We thought it was a court injunction, an ordinance, or who knows what. Better this way. In any case, I was delighted. Cossiga has always behaved like a friend: he is a respectable man."

Next we dealt with the letter to his producer.

Dear Leo,
The most eminent doctors told me that after working non-stop for 74 years, now I must take a period of rest at least twice as long. You can do your own math. We can talk again about resuming our project in 2041. See you in a century.
Love,
Federico

"I know, Leo won't be very happy," he remarked after seeing me sneer. "But Leo is spreading the rumor that we'll start shooting by Christmas; and here I am, still unable to stand!"

To rewrite the letters, I relied on an old electric typewriter in the meeting room that they let me use.

"Why don't you ask them to bring it here?" Federico asked stubbornly. With the typewriter, the pile of correspondence from all over the world, the books that cluttered the night table and even the windowsill, the room immediately started looking like an editorial office. It reproduced on a smaller scale the fervent activity, the wholesome, propitious atmosphere that he loved the most: his work!

Dr. Jacobsen and I crossed in the corridor. We fleetingly exchanged a few hinting words, like two conspirators. Secretly, we had already agreed on meeting later that evening, and I simply gave her an appointment at my hotel.

The "story" between us–if I can call it that–developed rapidly and inexplicably, like a plot in a movie, as if all we had to do was act out an existing script.

I stayed with Federico until Adalgisa, the night-shift nurse, arrived. A little before nine o'clock I kissed him goodbye.

"Are you having dinner with Loretta?" he asked me with curiosity.

"I think so. She and Adina are waiting for me at the hotel."

He looked pleased. I thought that by imagining the three of us together, he could ideally spend a little more time in our company. Instead, he was envisioning something that not even I had been able to foresee.

I barely had the time to take a shower and change clothes that I heard the hotel phone croak. Dr. Jacobsen was waiting for me down in the hall.

I headed downstairs with my hair still wet and knotted my tie in the elevator's mirror.

Else had decked herself out for an outing on the beach: blue shorts, azure and white blouse with an immaculate wide collar, leather sandals, and a sack bag. She looked like a winking girl out of the front cover of *Travaso,* or an illustration by Tamara de Lempicka: a cheeky flapper, a free spirit coming from a roaring past. . . .

Chapter VIII

Minerva Medica

Else wished to go out to dinner. She suggested a couple of places, a restaurant downtown and another one near the banks of the Po river, outside the city. We both liked the second option better. Personally, the fact that she had thought of an intimate little place, far from prying eyes, tickled me.

It was a sweltering night in Ferrara, and the air was still. We started driving, and in a few minutes we found ourselves outside the built-up area, on a towpath flanking the river, invisible to us in the dark. Else had brought with her an American textbook, *Cognitive Neuropsychology,* which provided a thorough description of the kind of illness that affected Federico. Even while we were dining, she kept showing me graphics and diagrams, coming with samples of writings skewed to the right, entirely lacking the left part: half a house, half a tree, half a cloud–and the patient was totally unaware of it.

In the aftermath of his brain ictus, Fellini presented that same type of dysfunction, but, amazingly, in his neurological tests he was able to identify his limitation without external help. Else showed me a piece of paper depicting various rows of objects. The patient's task was to cross out some of these objects; in that particular instance, some little bells had to be stricken. Usually, once they complete their test, patients do not have the slightest suspicion that they have omitted a few objects, since these are in fact located in an area invisible to them. When she asked Federico her customary question–"Did you mark them all? Are you sure?"–he picked up his pencil again and drew a few additional bells, with the anticipatory comment: "These are the ones that I didn't see."

He had realized that his field of vision was restricted and seemed perfectly aware of his impairment. Subjects struck by ictus commonly suffer from *anosognosia,* that is the refusal to acknowledge their pathology. They don't know and don't want to know. If someone drives them to the wall, they make up all sorts of excuses. A lady, who was not able to move her arm, openly claimed otherwise. When the neurologist invited her to prove it, she resorted to the most untenable excuses, claiming, for instance, that they had made her wear a jacket so tight that it prevented her movements.

The more Else continued her disquisition, the more I realized that her passion for the subject went beyond scientific interest. True, the doctors of the San Giorgio were generally flattered by Fellini's presence, but not to her extent. Just to be close to him, she disregarded her shifts; to keep him happy, she rushed to his bedside whenever he called her, day or night. She lived in a constant and feverish excitement.

After all, it was impossible not to succumb to Federico's natural charm. Sooner or later, the whole San Giorgio was going to revolve around him, just as it had happened at Rimini's hospital.

"He's a crocodile": that was the judgment that the jealous professor passed on him. "Be careful, or he will eat you up," he told his younger colleagues, warning them not to fall victim to his spell.

As for me, I spent the whole dinner trying to conquer the beautiful doctor Jacobsen, in the sense that I tried to win over her support for Federico's cause. I explained that to Fellini communication was vital. Mail, phone calls, and visits allowed him to elude his dreadfully prophetic dream: THE LOST OF THE LOST.

Else assured me of her tacit support. To allay my concerns, she graciously revealed that the old professor had a weakness for alcohol. He was close to retirement, and in any case he was not the one in charge at the San Giorgio hospital: the head physician was. Therefore, I could lay aside my concerns. Federico already enjoyed a very special treatment, and the rehab program had been carefully designed to accommodate his exceptional uniqueness.

That subject matter served to create a greater intimacy and understanding between us.

The very discreet waiter who was serving us kept bringing delicious dishes.... Ah, the round and sensual flavor of *cappellotti* filled with yellow squash! And the white wine from Alto-Adige, which glided down Else's Modiglianesque throat.... When drinking, she raised her head without taking her eyes off me or turning off her cordial, old-fashioned smile. The restaurant setting added to the illusion. Behind her was a window adorned with white crochet drapes, which provided the elegance from a faraway past: the same mysterious suggestion of a distant époque that I had sensed earlier that evening.

At past midnight, we were the only customers left in the restaurant. Silence reigned. Outside in the garden, a few night birds sitting in their iron chairs tarried on. When we passed by them on our way out, they cast an admiring look at the striking Norwegian, followed by hush-hush comments.

We drove back on that towpath suspended in darkness. Sensing the void at both sides, we felt like flying over a moon crater. I would have loved to wrap my hand around the tapering fingers of the charming and nervous lady doctor, but out of shyness and respect I restrained myself.

Back to Ferrara, I drove blindly through those still-unfamiliar streets, with no desire to stop or to put an end to our meeting. We first decided to go to a night bar and have a drink, but then Else suggested going to her place instead.

Her apartment was on the first floor of a modern building, in a neighborhood where streets bore the names of the old painting masters: Giotto, Cimabue, Duccio di Boninsegna.

"What does your apartment look like?" Fellini once asked Else during one of his morning phone calls. Now I could see for myself.

In the small living room, a little aquarium flickered with colored gems, like an iridescent crystal. The true surprise, however, came from the extravagant, obsessive presence of tropical fishes of all colors and shapes. They were everywhere. There were multicolored surgeon fishes displayed in glass cases on the walls; clown fishes, monkfishes, butterfly fishes, picasso trigger fishes, and parrot fishes. They were scattered everywhere, on the shelves and among the books, over the chest and on the desk, all of them endowed with fine striped livery. It was a total explosion of colors–bright yellow, green, blue, orange, purple, red, turquoise, black, white, azure, pearl. Fishes with slender bodies or bulging bellies; with half-moon tails, or fantails, or rainbow fins. Some had managed to glide onto the computer; some had even invaded her bedroom, in the guise of a radio alarm clock, a phone, a kite shaped as a devilfish or a dolphin fluttering from the ceiling. It was some sort of Nordic devotion to the sun, to the South Seas, to the polychromous light split into an endless series of dazzling, orgiastic colors, of mind-boggling hypnotic shades from the submersed world. It was, in other words, the intriguing revelation of her subjection to Poseidon, the water deity, and to his ever-changing throne.

I sat down in the living room, amid a number of large pillows strewn on a cast-iron couch. She settled in a nearby armchair, displacing a plush white ape, which she sheltered in her slender arms. She told me that the ape was the souvenir from a rejected suitor. "At least you'll embrace *him*," he told her, after finally giving up all hope.

When she moved to Italy, the first thing that she took from her old family home was that chimpanzee, which was by then consigned to the attic since Else's mother could not stand it.

"His arms are as long as mine," she said comparing their lengths, thus revealing her complex through that defense mechanism.

I sat there tensely alert, like an antenna stretched out, straining to pick up any signal from her. I was lending my senses and my ears to someone else who was listening–I was certain of that. But I didn't mind: my curiosity just grew bigger and bigger with each passing moment.

Else was in a relationship with a lusty mulatto–a French chemical engineer living in Brussels–but it was winding down, nearing its end. They consumed their passion during the weekends. Every month they took turns visiting, but the distance was prohibitive and the time spent together insufficient. So Else's lover ended up getting back with his former Flemish girlfriend, whom he had left for Else, but he did so on the sly, keeping her in the dark.

A dream revealed to Else what was truly happening. One day, when she was in Belgium, in her boyfriend's apartment, all of a sudden she felt the presence of that other woman between them: a figure with no identity, an unrecognizable face. Else did realize that it was her rival, and started loathing her.

I dared risk an interpretation. The intruder was perhaps a figment of her imagination, the personification of a disturbing aspect of her personality, a role that she rejected, that in fact she loathed. She used that mirror image to censor her unbecoming behavior, in order to engage herself in a controversy. Was there any reason for her to reproach herself? Was she perhaps involved in a double-crossing of her own?

Else admitted that out of solitude and need for tenderness, she had seen her former Italian boyfriend of many years, and slept with him. Therefore, it was possible that by deploring the actions of her current lover she was actually censoring her own guilty behavior: her secret betrayal with a man from her past.

Wasn't it through dreams that Federico penetrated the meanders of the human soul, both in his life and films?

"The only way for you to be faithful is to be faithful to yourself," I said, repeating to her the absolving words that the Maestro had taught me.

At two o'clock, we were still lingering outside on the balcony, talking in a low voice. The street-lamps in the square shed vapors of light that glowed against the black-ink sky. When I drew Else to me, her lithe body thinned in my arms.

I kissed her on her neck, on her face; I explored her naked skin under her light shorts. She pressed her body against mine, arousing me. Back to the living room, we lay down on the couch pillows.

"*Hvorfor*? Why?" she asked, trying to decipher what role she was supposed to play in that script.

Her proportions recalled those of the ancient goddesses immortalized in marble. The small and firm breasts, the athletic back, the high round buttocks, the lithe legs were those of Artemis the hunter. I undressed her, as shudders ran through her body. My fingers grazed her naked thighs and reached her bush, where her tender, slithering stem lay. Her open fount made her pliant to my hand: she meekly let herself be fondled and then she delicately took me in her hand.

"Tell me a fairy tale," she cooed, half-closing her eyes.

"Should I tell you the one about the closed door that one must never open?" I teased her. "It's a story from the *Arabian Nights*. . . . A poor fisherman was sitting on his rock, dejectedly, when an eagle swooped down from the sky seizing him with its talons, and it flew away with him, taking him to a royal palace faraway."

Else listened to me, harmonizing her amorous movements to my words.

"The fisherman was brought to the presence of the monarch and the court warriors. When they took off their armor, a number of beautiful women appeared before his eyes. In that land women were the rulers, whereas men were assigned the meanest jobs. The queen, however, fell in love with the fisherman and proposed that he stay with her as her spouse. He would become the lord of the castle and would rule over the servants. He would have full control of the land's riches and could manage the coffers as he wished, making liberal use of gold and gems. In exchange, he was given only one prohibition: he was not to open the secret door at the end of the palace corridor, on no account; he had to resist that temptation at all costs. The queen and his lover lived in perfect harmony and happiness for a long time, respecting the agreement. But then the fisherman started thinking, 'Since the queen has made available to me such astounding treasures, I wonder what kind of amazing marvels lie beyond the forbidden door.' And so, one bad day the temptation had the best of him and he opened the door. Outside there was nothing, nothing but the eagle, lying in wait. Once again it seized the fisherman with its talons and flew away, taking him back to his wretched rock, and it left him there, sad and unhappy as it first found him."

By the end of the fairy tale, the petals of Else's flower had opened to pleasure. "You have his same voice . . . Federico's voice," she muttered.

I whispered something indecent, so that, like a morbid child, she would fully give herself up to that mysterious and overwhelming instinct, as alluring as fish bait.

In the sultry night, our bodies were dripping with sweat. Slippery and listless, they became enfeebled from the protracted pleasure.

At five o'clock in the morning I headed back to my hotel. I got lost driving in the deserted town. Streets, crossings, buildings, everything looked new to me: it was like gliding through a dream, like dazedly wandering the rooms of an enchanted castle. I beckoned a young man on a bike to ask for directions. He stopped to listen to me: his angelic face, ravaged by drugs, was beaded with sweat. In those days, Ferrara was hosting a gathering of buskers, and street musicians had been flocking in from all over Europe. The young man must have been as lost as I was. He mechanically repeated my words, staring in the void. Then he suddenly roused himself, as if in disbelief, pointing the way. It was the right direction.

Federico gave Else a copy of his biography. Touched by his gesture, she took the big book in her hand and asked him: "Did you read it all?"

"Yes," Federico replied, "but I won't tell you the end."

Later that day, before going into the wards, Else and I met in the little garden outside the hospital. She still had the book in her hand.

"Are you leaving?" she asked.

"Yes, after saying goodbye to Federico."

It was a gorgeous day; the radiant light shed everywhere, from the bright green pine trees to the blooming oleanders, deep into the air molecules.

"I found him much better today."

"Perhaps he's recovering. By being next to you."

"As soon as you left, he called me."

"What did he say?"

"He talked to me as if we had just made love."

"And you?"

"I simply listened to him, sharing the same sensation."

Giulietta fell ill during the night. She went into hypoglycemic coma and nearly died: the doctors were able to save her by a hair's breadth. One thing was sure: she could no longer take care of her husband in the same way.

"What a cruel fate!" Maria Maddalena, Federico's sister pitied them, when we talked over the phone. "All that renown, all those awards, and now just look at them!"

Else too was given the bad news. She reached me on my cell while I was driving back to Rome, and she advised me not mention it to Fellini:

"In stroke patients, emotional upsets can have calamitous effects: they could thwart the limited progress we've been able to achieve so far."

Besides, when I heard Federico earlier that day, he seemed particularly elated, highly spirited, like he had not been in a long time.

As soon as I got home, Elena called. She was crying, muttering that she couldn't bear the thought of being away from him.

That night, I had a dream involving Else and Federico, together of course, in the hospital room. Federico was wearing an elegant dark suit, and he was standing on his feet as normal. Unwilling to see to himself as a sick, defeated person, he contentiously refused to go back to bed. Even though he was very tired, rather than lying down on the hospital bed he decided to squat on the floor, sneaking between the headboard and the wall. I tried to make him comfortable by improvising some sort of makeshift bedding. I laid a wool blanket and a sheet on the floor, and he immediately settled down, curling up like a dog. Else and I also found a quilt to cover him up and keep him warm.

What was the meaning of that night visitation? What was the reason for Federico's silent refusal to lie in bed? Why was he so surly and yet so sweet at the same time?

I knew he was not just being capricious. There was nothing ostentatious in his behavior. He simply showed an innocent desire to stop playing the patient, a role that he found offensive and mortifying.

Perhaps it was the presence of Else, so young and so pretty, which brought about his resentment. "Don't we all behave like that, when we're kids?" I reasoned in my dream. "When we want to attract the attention of an adult that we like, and we want him or her to stay with us and satisfy our longing. . . ."

In the dream, Else and I exchanged imperceptible glances and winks. Could he possibly have realized what was going on between the two of us? Could he possibly be touchy because he suspected our betrayal?

"For a Riminese fanny, the cock spends every last penny. For Loretta's ass, the cock just hopes to make a pass."

How many of these epigrams on the cock and the ass did Federico compose? I wish I had collected them! In *Ginger and Fred,* it was Pippo Botticelli-Mastroianni who recited them, to the inevitable disappointment of the bourgeois Amelia Bonetti-Masina.

On that subject, Else faxed me a drawing that Federico had sketched for a neurological test. "Draw for me a table set for a feast, as elaborated and detailed as you can," Dr. Jacobsen had asked him. And Federico, in his usually grotesque and dramatic style, diligently obliged. With a few strokes of the pen, he sketched himself sitting at head of the table in his wheelchair, with a carving fork in his hand, his head adorned by four hairs, and a ravenous expression on his face. On the draped tablecloth, he placed a woman with a nice fat ass and a cat face, lying on her stomach.

"Did you forget anything?" Else urged him.

At which point, Federico did complete his fantastic creation by adding two lit candles to the array, one on each buttock, as a masterful finishing touch. Now it was a full square meal.

I thanked Else for kindly keeping me abreast.

Unable to visit Federico for a few days, I kept in touch with him by phone:

"I am depressed, demoralized, dismayed," he grumbled, thus proving that he had yet to come to terms with his new abode. "When are you coming?"

On returning from the Venice Film Festival, Marcello Mastroianni had stopped by to pay Federico a visit, making him very happy. With his amiable graciousness and kind disposition, his beloved Marcello-*Snàporaz* always managed to delight him.

As soon as I returned to Ferrara, Federico enthusiastically gave me a full report of his visit.

During their meeting, to please his unfortunate friend and to show solidarity with him, Marcello unbuttoned his shirt, revealing the rigging of straps and buckles that he was forced to wear around his chest. He had a herniated disc, and his back pain gave him no respite. He couldn't even bend anymore.

"So forget about screwing . . .," Federico teased him. "Well, in any case you never really cared about that!" he added in a familiar tone.

"Federì, you know what? This cage that I'm wearing kind of arouses me," he candidly confessed.

"Who knows . . . maybe he's right" Federico pondered out loud. "Perhaps, as always is the case, the presence of an obstacle to overcome, a problem to solve produces in us the most propitious condition, the most suitable creative tension, and it makes us achieve what's difficult to achieve. . . ."

Marcello's visit had really electrified him. Since he was first hospitalized in Rimini after his stroke, Federico kept thinking of him. "Marcello promised he'll come and see me after the Film Festival!" he kept saying. He cherished the idea of being happily reunited with his "boyfriend"–that was the tender definition that Marcello, his eternal buddy, favorite actor, and alter ego had coined for him.

Many were the people who went to see him and meet with him, almost like pilgrims. That near veneration, however, did not allay in the least his sense of solitude and loss into which he had plunged.

"You should come more often," Else softly exhorted me. "You should move to Ferrara: he wants you here."

I had the inexplicable sensation that the two of them were consorting to satisfy their mutual longing through me. Was it crazy?

Despite the prevailing pessimism, from a medical standpoint Else was quite upbeat:

"Federico has asked to have his meals in the cafeteria with the other patients," she told me, stressing his progress. "He wants to lead a normal life, like everybody else."

She wanted to prove that my worries, definitely caused by a sense of overprotection, were unjustified. All the better. Ultimately, life was asserting itself.

"He has even chosen who he likes to have at his table," Else went on saying with a pleased voice. "It's an old lady who's unable to speak, but her eyes speak for her. If only you could see how lovingly she looks at him! She makes every effort to express her admiration, her infatuation. She often even bursts into tears, so much so that Federico ends up crying with her!"

Else came to pick me up at the station. She was decked out like an upswing manager determined to make an impression: wearing an elegant suit with a short skirt, she looked sexy and refined at the same time. Without first stopping by the hotel, she drove me straight to the hospital.

I stayed with Federico till late that night. I wanted to see for myself if Else's enthusiasm was justified. I found out that, like her, the other doctors were also reasonably confident.

Time went by fast as Federico and I screened the many requests for an interview that he had received. Besides the national newspapers, also many local newssheets, radios, and TV stations had submitted pages and pages full of questions and were waiting for an answer. As a result, we had to decide what to say to whom. Federico, however, kept digressing; he preferred to dwell upon his forced stay in that hospital:

"It's like being in jail, or serving in the army," he explained. "In order to survive, you are forced to make friends. I don't mean just with the people who buzz around–doctors, nurses, or the other patients–but with the institution itself, with its own laws, logic, and apparatus. The patient is inexorably bound to become a part of it, one with it; to be absorbed by it and caged in.

I asked him what was for him the most intolerable thing about that reclusion.

"I now realize that my way of thinking has changed," was his frightened conclusion. "Therefore I've changed too."

He never harbored any illusion that his therapy would bring about real improvement. He always showed hostility towards the physical exercises recommended by his therapists. I tried the best I could to soften up his testy resistance and opposition.

"The sooner you get yourself on your feet again, the sooner you will be able to get out of this place and regain control of your life."

However, he had a lucid, grim view regarding his hemiparesis:

"My body has lost its static equilibrium, its structural mechanics. The delicate system of thrust and counterthrust, the complex framework supported by the skeleton has become unbalanced. Now that the body architecture is out of plumb, just to be sitting is a deed of prowess. The equilibrium of millions of muscles, nerves, and tendons propping up the framework is broken. As long as everything works fine, we do not realize how miraculous the body's functional capacity is. When we are wholesome, none of us thinks 'Oh, gee! Look how well I can stand, bend, and move to one side.' This loss of a reassuring stability, of a leveling center undermines a person's general balance and place in the world."

While talking, he kept massaging his left hand that was lying listless and useless on the sheet. For the first time, I witnessed his exasperated outburst of rebellion against his own body:

"This son of a bitch has let me down."

In that offensive language, in that fit of anger I noticed the agony that we all experience when we are faced with a betrayal, of any kind, because it always surprises us and finds us unprepared, helpless.

Taking advantage of a moment in which the night nurse was out of the room, he asked me to look into the bedside table's drawer. I found a crystal in the shape of a parallelepiped, with a pointed top, no bigger than a perfume bottle. It was a gift from Osho Rajneesh, the Indian guru who had made headlines in America for his habit of going around in his Rolls Royce. He had a fleet of more than ninety of them, bought with the money from his followers.

"A microscopic being came to see me," Fellini said. "She entered the room and I did not even notice. All of a sudden, I saw her standing there, next to the window. She wasn't any taller than the bedside table. She had a dark, withered face: she looked like a being from goodness knows where. 'Osho is sending you this', she explained while handing me the crystal. 'Who's Osho?' I asked, repeating the name to myself, and finally I remembered."

While he was recounting that incident, he placed the crystal on his forehead and on those parts of his body that had stopped responding to commands from his brain.

"It's supposed to release the blocked limbs from their spell. Osho also sends word to me that I must leave the hospital and put myself in the hands of a pranotherapist. But how can I do that? Here they treat me: they are efficient, scientific.... Besides, where could I go?

It was a gorgeous evening in Ferrara. The taxi that took me from the hospital to the hotel drove by Palazzo Diamanti, accompanied by the wheels' soft rumble on the cobblestones, then it entered the San Giorgio Cathedral square, which was leavened with lights.

Even though it was very late Else was waiting for me.

At that hour, the only place we could find open was a small unpretentious trattoria, the food however was quite genuine: *cappellotti,* baked melted cheese, wine, and a ring-shaped cake. It was a sweet and relaxing break. Once again, I didn't even know in what part of town we were. I liked the idea of entrusting myself to Bradamante's horse, without questioning where it would take me. Take me and that fairy woman, half doctor half lover, who belonged half to me half to a magician. Weren't we in Ariosto's town, after all?

On the way home, Else stopped her car in front of a two-story little palace, clearly well preserved.

"The lead glass windows are still the original ones," she daydreamed, as if she had just rung up the curtain on an enchanted view.

It was the Poet's house: the windows, the gratings, the bricks, the little front door, all retained the simple, austere harmony of a medieval building. Did Orlando's *octava rimas* echo in those rooms? Did the Paladins face each other under those vaults?

A shiny brass plate informed us that the building now hosted a library. The outside walls, however, were the same from those bygone days: in that narrow, flagged street, they still conjured a powerful sensation of boundlessness.

Else and I stayed up all night, talking and chasing love without ever surrendering to sleep. Her tales were like her, innocent and perverse.

CHAPTER IX

Labyrinth Of Mirrors

Else lavished me with flattery. Smiling to herself, she noticed how my body evoked erotic fantasies of her girlhood. It reminded her of those Greek warriors, from her ancient history books, who were entirely naked except for their footwear and helm.

Which image of me was she relishing? Which unresolved emotion, which figment of her imagination got caught in her memory's taut net?

She had shaved almost all of her pubic hair; her vulva, aiming to resemble that of a little girl, was nonetheless capable of swallowing me into a vertiginous, dense abyss.

She indulged her secret weaknesses; she yielded to the lure of her vices, chasing them until satiated; she enjoyed the animal thrill of clasping my hardened penis between our stomachs, she squeezed her clitoris against my testicles until she came with an agonized whining. It sounded like the yelp of a prematurely born cub; it resembled a desperate life lament.

Her ardor quenched, she wanted me to stay close. Lapsing into drowse, she soon stirred, hugging me and holding me tight, giving me random kisses. Lying like that all night, clinging to each other on a French bed that was too small for the both of us, we tirelessly courted daybreak.

At seven o'clock the phone rang. Else answered it half asleep. It was Federico. I could hear his unmistakable melodious voice blandishing and caressing her, as if the two of them were cradling together in an alcove. Trilling like a siren, he clasped her into his tightening coils and savored her abandon, sip by sip. She reveled in his languid grip: I could clearly see it from the way she stretched out purring like a petted cat; from her listless expression when, after finally hanging the phone, she drifted off into sleep.

Did she drift into a dream?

At seven thirty, I got up and dressed quickly. Else was soundly asleep. With her statuesque naked body reclined on the bed, she looked like a water nymph, a provocative unarmed warrior: Bradamante without her armor, Diana without her quiver. Her fair hair at shoulder's length left her neck uncovered. Grazing her bare skin with my lips, I laid a kiss there, arousing a secret thrill.

So pure was the morning sun that its liquid gold trickled all over the town's walls. From Via Garibaldi, I walked to the loggia of Palazzo del Municipio, with its steep elegant staircase, covered by a barrel vault, climbing next to an overhanging wall. That sophisticated backdrop featured the clear geometry of a Quattrocento painting. The stalls of an antiques market had invaded the harmonious little square, and a curious crowd was strolling around, giving life to a fictitious Renaissance scene. The old-fashioned objects on display added to the illusion of having fallen back in time, among pageboys clad in motley tights and ladies attired in brocatelle.

I passed under the solemn high arch and entered the San Giorgio square. Immersed in that goldsmith light, the cathedral quivered with unfathomable lightness. With its striped white and powdery-pink wall stones, it brought to mind the softness of a comfit, of a marzipan creation. The bell tower at the corner displayed a similar alternation of soft hues, as enticing as strawberries and cream. Confectionery animals garnished the church façade, which was divided horizontally into three parts. Above the entrance one could see Saint George defeat the dragon; at the sides were a number of run-on biblical scenes. The lions mounted the last guard at the front of the cathedral, which was protected at the parvis' edge by two frowning and massive griffins.

Out of religious scruples and vague apprehension, I decided to go in. I entered the cathedral through the front door and moved aside the heavy curtains of stiff morocco leather, repeating a gesture from a long forgotten past.

Coming out of the cathedral, I was welcomed by the sight of a young girl idling on her bike in the sunny square. Her little stretch dress rose with her movements, impudently unveiling her naked thighs. At each spin-around the saddle slipped through her buttocks, like a trapped dark mouse: it was an image created by Fellini for *Roma, Amarcord, The City of Women. . . .* He used it again and again. I recognized his trademark, his artistic copyright.

With that throb in my heart, I headed back to the hospital. I crossed reluctantly the magic mirror of timeless illusion and returned to the realm of time and place.

When I arrived at the hospital, Else was already there. Her presence had been requested repeatedly by her exacting patient, who would not accept being separated from her. Nor would she from him. Fellini coaxed her into coming at impossible hours and constantly tried to make her stay; and she willingly fell into his irresistible snare.

Like every Saturday, most hospital activities were suspended, including gym rehab exercises. Many patients did go home for the weekend. Federico could not adjust to that holiday emptiness. Else told me that sometimes, in the afternoon, he would start calling out her name, playing the fool:

"Else!!! Else Jacobsen!!!" he yelled.

Federico proclaimed that the effigy of the gloriously good-looking Norwegian doctor had to be painted on the ceiling of every room and corridor, where went the gaze of those patients who were forced to lie on their backs: they would all have a speedy recovery.

"Did you see her thighs?" he asked, expecting me to vouch his claim. "Long, strong, endless . . . they look like two highway stretches, two consular roads!"

I spent all that day at the hospital working on the unattended written interviews, trying to expedite as many of them as possible. The local gazettes, the town newssheets, the regional chronicles, all were awarded the same consideration as the national newspapers. Federico felt some sort of professional solidarity with all reporters and did not want to disappoint any of them.

"Perhaps we can first divide the questions by topic, and then we can choose a couple of answers to give to each one."

All queries came with respectful letters of accompaniment; most of them, however, were extremely long and detailed. Not everybody realized how really weak Federico was. At that juncture, he needed every ounce of energy left in him simply to stay alive. Generous to the last, each time he tried to come up with an original theme, a different title, or an amusing episode. The reason for his magnanimity sprang from his own past as a journalist and his recollection of an overly authoritarian editor:

"If those reporters show up without their articles they'll be given a scolding."

Among the many queries submitted to him, the one asking him to define the difference between Rimini and Ferrara intrigued him the most. Federico invited me to share with him my musings on the subject. I told him that when I arrive in Ferrara, I have the impression of entering an invisible sphere, a different territory with an uncertain geography and an arcane boundary. It's not a mere literary affectation: it's a palpable sensation. In Ferrara, life pulse seems to slow down, time stops ticking; the palaces, the walls, the streets, the old houses, the aristocratic architecture of the courts . . . all concur to create the illusion of a suspended city. A city built on metaphysical abstraction, on psychic creation. Knowing that Ariosto once lived there makes you think that Ferrara is a borough born out of his imagination, materialized through a powerful alchemy, like the enchanted castle where Merlin lured knights and ladies to make his beloved Ruggiero stay.

In Ferrara, the illusion is not just confined to the night, to the plays of light, to the phantasmagoria of shaded battlements, to the reflections of the street-lamps on the deserted pavements. The sorcery takes place also in the daytime, in the blazing summer sun, when the landscape, veiled by an impalpable mist, shimmers like a fata morgana.

"The countryside is flat, boundless," Federico reminisced, "with all those missiles pointed at the sky!"

He called to his mind the cyclopean silos used for storing grain, scattered throughout the plain as far as the eye can see.

A journalist had submitted that Ferrara is a city of fog, as opposed to solar Rimini: the stronghold of meditation and thought versus the fair of hedonism and fun.

An even more fascinating hypothesis, in my view, was to consider Ferrara an emanation of Rimini. On reaching Ferrara, the sea mist thickens into fog. Here, atop a tower, in a secluded cell, a wizard breathes out the ghostly vapors from the sea and gives them shape. Doesn't something similar happen in a film theater, where, amid spirals of smoke, the hazy products of the imagination take shape?

Page after page, we systematically responded to all queries. The answers were then sorted out and placed in the envelopes addressed to the respective interviewers, all ready to go.

It was dinnertime already. As always, Federico jovially invited me to join him, as if we were at the restaurant.

"Food is good here: tell them to bring you a tray," he would say.

That was one of his greatest passions: to get together with his friends and enjoy with them the simple pleasure of savoring food, of sharing comments and stories. It was his way to relax at the end of the day, in a lively atmosphere of light-hearted conviviality.

That evening, like every evening, Federico received the visit of his lady admirer, a rosy and buxom blonde who showed up punctually with her large bag brimful of delicacies. The woman loved spoiling him with unusual treats: a jar of strawberries in liqueur, a small bunch of gooseberries, a jam made from special fruit.... Feeding him with the tip of a teaspoon, she made him taste those rare dainties right away. Then she left them on his night table, as an enticing viaticum for the night, a soothing remedy to the endless hours of anxiety looming ahead. Those dainties proved more effective than any drugs or doctors, and decidedly more effective than Adalgisa, the private nurse who started her night shift at eight o'clock. Because of her giddy halting gait, Federico had nicknamed her Mrs. Hen. He could not stand her: he deemed her too dull, too strictly observant of the rules. Federico felt they had nothing in common and therefore they could have no conversation. The moment she arrived, the night turned for him into a vertiginous void. She was so rule-governed that she forbade him to savor his favorite cookies, she denied him the use of the phone, and she turned down all his eccentric requests by invoking hospital regulations: with infuriating obtuseness, she invariably sided with the institution.

"Her life must be so hollow that she compensates by identifying herself with the hospital," he said, seeing through her like an X-ray machine. "She *is* the hospital. She knows the timetables for all activities and abides by them willfully, fanatically."

He came to hate her. Adalgisa in turn tried to justify herself with me, invoking common sense:

"He wants to go down to the gym at four o'clock in the morning; he demands to have breakfast before seven and that's not possible; he grabs the phone to call around his friends when people are asleep. And so I have to tell him that at those hours certain things can't be done...."

All she could bring to her own defense were strict logic and rigid social conventions, that is, those arguments that were the least compatible with Federico's nature. From her, Federico expected the exact opposite. He wished that they could face those long hours of crucifixion together, as nurse and patient; he wanted her to help him swindle his fate as a cast out. He easily managed to do that with Paola, the daytime nurse, who had come to appreciate his witty remarks and had learned how to play his sidekick: he as the White Clown, she as the Auguste, like at the circus. Hadn't it always been Federico's favorite game? He spent his whole life as a schoolboy, who rebels against an authoritarian principal and treats him to raspberries and sneers. Yet at times Federico traded places with him: he himself played the principal, becoming the target of his own sneers. It was not by chance that he chose his friends among the worst students, the "smart dunces." He loved the dropouts rather than the chevroned admirals.

What could Adalgisa possibly know about all that? In the end, she had to give up her position in favor of a colleague of hers, Maria Veneria. With her complicity, Federico was able to weave his secret web of sorcerous spells.

Federico lived vicariously through me a number of emotions, encounters, and adventures that he would have liked to experience directly. By evoking those sensations, he recovered some semblance of a good mood:

"Have you seen any nice *mighnott* at your hotel?" he asked, wondering if I had run into any whores. That pidgin word, *mighnott,* which mixed Roman and English, was for him a propitiatory jargon, a childish witch-spell similar to the *asanisimasa* in *8 1/2,* a magic formula able to take you to a different dimension, a fantastic and imponderable one.

A nice *mighnott.* . . . Could Nordic Dr. Jacobsen fit the description? Tall like Bradamante, with legs long like highways and inviting like *consular roads*: could she be his embodiment of comfort?

It had been pouring rain all afternoon, so much so that in low areas around the hospital there was some flooding, and the temperature dropped.

After dinner we retreated to Else's place. She strewed her apartment with flickering candles and turned off all lights. In that glimmer, she came to me in bed where I lay already naked. But she did not wish to lie down. Ready to romp, she straddled me like Hippolyta with her deer. She wanted to look at me, to touch me. Her long tapering fingers ran over my whole body, as if she were reviewing an anatomy lesson: she performed a sort of medical examination, a palpation that reminded me of Asclepias' vestal, the holy whore keeper of health and senses.

"I can feel all your muscles," she cooed in her hoarse voice. Deriving some ineffable pleasure, she mapped each fiber of them and reshaped them with her fingertips. From that we soon slipped into love playing. We stoked love's fire with our talk, thus producing sparkles that further ignited our lust. When the raging flames finally started to abate, Else lay at my side and kept caressing me. She caught my mouth with hers, desirous to capture every little throb of pleasure. For a long time I lay like that, breathless, next to her smooth, Amazon-queen body.

In a twinkling, I strayed from her and found myself in another dimension.

I was in Tivoli, in Hadrian's Villa. Not the collection of ruins that it is today, but the Emperor's sumptuous residence in its pristine form. I silently roamed about the pavilions and the pools, the Portico and the Baths, the Nymphaeum and the Canopus with its oblong reflecting pool, framed by trabeated columns and statues arranged in a hemicycle: the Caryatids and the Sileni, Ares and Mercury with their impudent glutei. I wandered through the Library, the Triclinium, the Hospitalia, and the Terrace of Tempe. My subconscious reconstructed all that my eyes could not see during my several visits there. It was a hypnagogic travel that even allowed me to smell the wild fennel and mint that grew along the sunlit paths.

Some time before dawn, I returned to my hotel room. I had just fallen asleep when the phone rang: it was a journalist friend of mine from Rome: *Il Messaggero* had just published the news that Giulietta had been taken to the hospital.

How could we keep Federico from finding it out? The news was going to spread like wildfire. I got out of bed and quickly I left the hotel.

The sky had dropped all its rain the day before, and now, on that Sunday, it flared up in dazzling sunlight. The Po di Volano–the canal running through the city–shone in golden slivers, and the air flaunted its crystal-clear purity.

Contrary to my expectations, I found Federico still in bed. He lay under a thick wool blanket, shivering. Trying to get out of the cold's grip and win that tremor, he was sipping a cappuccino from the cup that Paola handed him. He looked deadly pale and slightly confused: his brain waves were out of tune, buzzing with static.

"Oscar! When did you get here?"

He addressed me as if he hadn't seen me for days, oblivious to the fact that the night before we had stayed up late, working. He was happy to see me, of course, but he seemed weighed down by inhuman exhaustion.

Paola, his private nurse, tried reassuring me. "He slept for over an hour. He's always weak when he first wakes up: he needs some time to get his bearings."

His paralyzed hand lay stone still on the bed, as if in rigor mortis. Else rushed in to check his blood pressure, which was very low. Federico's conditions slowly improved, so much so that he was eventually able to follow Else to her office for their usual private conversation. I stayed there to finish what work was left from the day before; for the most part it entailed placing the typed answers in the relevant envelopes. When Federico returned, he insisted going back to bed. He did so against the opinion of the doctors, who tried all possible arguments to convince him to stay up so to improve his muscular tone.

Else retired to her office. We agreed to have lunch together after she was done with work.

In the meantime, Federico had regained part of his strength and even his good humor. Some of the questions he was asked inevitably provoked his goliardic jeer, especially those referring to the progress of his convalescence and to the alleged improvements after physiotherapy, when in fact he was totally hostile to it, disenchanted with its results:

"Let's say that things are going much better. I pee myself only twice a day and I shit myself every time I feel like it," he sneered rather dismally. "I wonder what the newspapers would make of an answer like that!"

A journalist and priest maintained that Catholic religion could quite rightly boast a long tradition of irony.

"I didn't know that" was Fellini's surprised reaction. "Just look at that little lamb up there!" he added, pointing at the crucifix hanging on the wall, across his bed. "Irony, perhaps, is part of Eastern religions, perhaps of the great Greek mythology, but it is nowhere to be found in a transcendental religion that identifies itself with such a cruel and inhuman sacrifice."

When I finally sat in front of the typewriter to jot down the ideas that had emerged during our conversation, Fellini had dozed off, tired again.

When I left him, Federico was fast asleep. Since I was leaving for Rome that night, I trusted Paola to have him sign the cover letters and to see that the envelopes were mailed. I intended to spend with Else what time I had left before my train's departure. I needed to recharge my batteries with some sun, a good meal, and the sight of Else's harmoniously long legs, which Federico liked so much and ideally shared with me.

Else was waiting for me down in the courtyard, sitting in the car. As soon as I slipped inside, I bent down and brushed my lips against her naked thighs, relishing the smoothness of her golden skin against my cheek.

We stopped along the canal banks, to have lunch at a little

restaurant renowned for its fish. From the large windows we could see the flowing glittering water, strewn with sun specks.

During all that time, Federico was with us, between us; he was practically sitting at the table, enjoying with us the flavors of that meal. I didn't know how to separate myself from him, nor did Else, who was fatally falling in love with him.

"He takes up all my energy, all my time," she confessed. "I can't explain it."

During their morning conversation, that day, Federico had chatted about Marguerite Yourcenar and Emperor Hadrian.

"I'm not quite sure . . . ," Else continued. "He seemed to be talking about a dream . . . a dream in which Hadrian's Villa Tivoli had become his own residence, as if *he* were the Emperor."

I felt speechless and helpless, drawn into a void, as I faced that uncontrollable encroachment of brain waves, that emotional upheaval within the deep well of the unconscious.

After lunch, we didn't go back to the hospital to see him. Instead, we retreated to Else's apartment, like two secret lovers fearful of being discovered.

At mid afternoon the phone rang: it was Federico looking for her. "He always calls me when you are here," a disconcerted Else whispered to me.

The beautiful doctor then continued talking to him in a low voice for quite a while. During all that time, I perversely kept enjoying myself, fondling her on the sly. She tried holding out, but her senses reacted against her will, as if they were charmed. As soon as she hung up she came immediately, breathing heavily like never before, as if she was giving up the ghost, and her shivering body was covered in goosebumps.

Holding her on top of me, I caressed her velvety round twin curves enfeebled by pleasure. I started spanking her gently, a buttock at a time, then I smacked her harder and harder, laying it on thicker when she complained.

"Do you want to punish me?" she asked in her hoarse voice.

"Why would I do that . . . ?"

"Because I let the two of you fuck me, like a mignotta. . . ." She used precisely that word, *mignotta,* a word that she could hardly pronounce.

How long did we squeeze love from our bodies? When we finally snapped out of it, we realized that my train was about to leave in a few minutes. Yet, Ariosto's princess Bradamante took me on her hippogryph and dropped me off at the station in good time.

Our lips brushed in a quick kiss goodbye. The train started rolling silently on the tracks.

The sun was a flaming coppery disc that cast its liquid, incandescent rays on the plain's edge, creating a backlit embroidery on the orderly rows of trees, an elegant black lace on the fading limbs and leaves.

In the countryside, flat as far as the eye could see, the silos stretched up toward the enameled sky, like launching pads, looking altogether faithful to Federico's description. Finally, the horizon became imbued with yellow and purple. Before the train reached Bologna, the sunset burned down its languid light.

Evening came quickly across the Apennines; the shadows kept stretching and thickening, and became more enveloping with each passing moment.

CHAPTER X

Runaway Lover

The chances that Federico could at least partially recover from the effects of his stroke were getting better by the day. His doctors reported meaningful improvements and were now reassuring.

But not Federico! His voice on the phone sounded invariably broken, listless, resigned:

"I can't stay here anymore: I can't stand it! I want to go back to the Grand Hotel."

Else's voice, on the contrary, exuded pragmatic Nordic enthusiasm and candid love. We talked every day on the phone:

"With the help of his physiotherapists, today Federico took his first steps. It's an unbelievable progress! Everybody present applauded him!"

On hearing that, my heart sank. Poor Federico! I tried viewing that grotesque scene with his eyes, imagining what it must have felt being exposed like a puppet in a theater. I could only share his gloomy depression and dejection. When I talked to him, however, I made sure not to betray any of those feelings. I tried striking the right notes, naively resorting to those arguments that seemed to me the most vital, foremost his encounter with the beautiful Dr. Jacobsen.

"How about Else? Isn't she of comfort to you?"

"It would take a hundred like her to free me from this evil spell!"

I beseeched him not to give up, to strive with all of his might. All my exhortations, however, sounded hollow, and I was the first to realize it.

The weekly magazine of a major newspaper published a large photo report on Fellini. Photographer Alessia Matiz Saffi expressly went to Ferrara to immortalize him in various postures. Fellini willingly obliged, even though he refused posing in his usual clothes–tracksuit and jogging shoes–choosing instead to sport a pair of jeans and a light blue denim shirt, which gave him a manly and a refined look.

Else told me that Federico was even able to hold himself upright for a few seconds, without help, and that almost immediately he started directing the shots as if he were on his set, instructing the photographer on how and where to aim the camera. To get a better angle he even convinced her to perform some acrobatic maneuvers, making her climb on the windowsill and on a rung-ladder. In short, he would not relinquish his old profession.

Yet, when he called me that evening, he sounded as dejected as ever. More than ever. In his mind, the weeks and months that awaited him in that jailhouse dilated becoming an annihilating eternity. He realized that he could no longer delude himself with the idea of leaving the hospital for the Grand Hotel, as he fancied. Despite what anyone else was eagerly saying, his stay was not going to be a simple convalescence. This was not a limbo where he could lazily spend hours in bed, with his phone at hand, and his friends flocking in to visit. On the contrary, he faced an extremely hard task; he had to try and restore his lost balance through techniques that he had to learn day by day, moment by moment, an inch at a time, with no end yet in sight: a titanic effort. It was like setting a puppet back in motion, a puppet whose strings had become incredibly entangled, twisted, knotted, perhaps beyond repair.

Poor Merlin, prisoner of a nightmare!

It was as if his big old body–so stout and imposing, so soft and feminine, so captivating and friendly–had collapsed into rubble. And Fellini was falling into ruin with it. What survived of him was his thought, his expression, unscathed by the disaster. Fellini was still able to weave his verbal embroideries; to flash out his inimitable word play dazzling like magnesium lamps; to perform his metaphoric acrobatics, those spectacular swerves capable of breaking through the listener's mind and conscience.

We all cherished the vain hope that nothing really irreparable had happened to him. His voice perhaps had become a little hazy, but his speech was still sweet and strong to our ears, as in the mysteriously unearthed story of the great magician narrated by Friedrich Schlegel:

Gawain was riding his horse, lost in his sad thoughts, when a sudden voice came from his right. He turned his head, but all he could see was a light vapor scattering in the air; yet, when he tried passing through it, he was unable to do so. Then he heard that voice again, now saying:

"Gawain, Gawain, do not vex yourself, for all that must happen will happen."

"Who's talking to me?" he cried. "Who's calling my name?"

"Why? You no longer know who I am, Sir Gawain? You once used to know me very well; the proverb must be true: 'out of court, out of mind.'

Gawain then recognized Merlin. "Master Merlin!" he shouted, "I now recognize your voice. But I beg you, come forward so that I can see you."

"You will never see me," Merlin replied. "And I will not talk to anybody else, after you. You'll be the last one to hear my voice. Furthermore, nobody shall ever come near this site, including you. For all my regret, I cannot leave this place. I must stay here forever. Only she who keeps me here has the will and power to come and go as she pleases, to see me and talk to me."

"My dear, sweet friend!" Gawain exclaimed. "How can you be so bound that you'll never free yourself? How such a thing can happen to you, the wisest of men?"

"I'm also the maddest of men," Merlin replied, "because I love a woman more than I love myself. I taught my beloved how to fetter me, and now nobody can set me free."

"O, this saddens me greatly," Gawain exclaimed, "and it will also sadden King Arthur. He has people looking for you all over the land. That's also the reason why I'm here."

"He must learn to find himself again" Merlin said, "for he will not see me anymore, as I will not see him. Go back, now. . . ."

Else was in love. I could feel it from her words, from the hesitation that crept into our conversations, from her constant need to reveal her disconcerting secrets:

"When he slyly caresses me I like it," she was anxious to confess. "I appreciate the liberties he takes with me, even though my infatuation for him is not physical."

Sometimes Else and I would talk on the phone till the wee hours. She would call me from the little studio reserved for the night duty doctor, after slipping into her cot, and she would bring me up to date:

"Today a young film director and great admirer of his came to see him. Federico, however, didn't let him in right away. He subjected him to some sort of vigil at arms, which the other one accepted with respect and perseverance. After *three* unsuccessful attempts, he was finally allowed in, and the two of them talked for over an hour without anyone else present.

Federico didn't want to leave his bed. He didn't want to conceal the seriousness of his illness by receiving him in his wheelchair–why would that make him look better, anyway?

'Won't you get up?' I asked him while I prepared him for the visit. 'Are you going to receive him in bed?'

'I do it so not to embarrass him,' he replied. 'When *he* was in the hospital, he received me in bed.'

He never ceases to surprise me. I feel helpless, exposed, at his total mercy. I could even stop working and seeing other patients. I feel like spending all my time with him. And he with me."

Since I agreed to provide my body to satisfy Else's passion, I had become an integral part of that triangle. But how much longer was she going to accept that tender dream, that pleasant confusion?

Federico called me Sunday morning:

"I've decided to leave this place: I can't stand it anymore."

Depression kept its hold on him for most of the day. Not even his medications were able to raise his spirits, except for negligible periods of time. The thought of Giulietta being in the hospital tormented him:

"I must go and see her," he agonized.

He was very much concerned about her. Instead of reassuring him, Saraceni's prudent reticence had the opposite effect, making him fear the worst.

"I know that they keep the truth from me" he complained to Else.

In his aggravation, at times he flared up, railing against the nurses and yelling out of control.

His crises became more acute when Else was not present, so she now fretted about that too:

"I feel guilty if I take even just one day off. I don't even know what my shifts are anymore. I try being at the hospital all the time: I practically don't have a life out of here."

When she burst out like that, I unfailingly replied by telling her that she would never meet someone as special as Federico, both on a personal and professional level. It was a once in a lifetime opportunity, a fate's gift not to be wasted. She had been entrusted with the last days of an extraordinary man, perhaps the greatest genius of the century. Otherwise, for what reason–or fortuitous coincidence–would a charming Norwegian neurologist have crossed all of Europe, to land at that little hospital in the Italian province right when Federico arrived? Our lives often rely on an invisible map for direction. We all have a map, but we must be able to see it to get to the treasure.

I indoctrinated her. I flattered her. It was essential that she would not give up her task, so that Federico's ill omen, THE LOST OF THE LOST, would not come true.

The encounter with Fellini had left an indelible mark on the heart and mind of the Norwegian girl. I could feel it. But, in the end, wasn't the dry logic of everyday life going to prevail over her irrationality? Wasn't it going to foster their unavoidable separation? Like a modern Ariadne, Else was holding the thread that could allow Federico to find his way out of the labyrinth. If that thread broke, what could keep him from being swallowed in darkness forever?

"At this juncture, for him to interrupt therapy would mean to erase all the progress made," she was the first to worry.

Fellini had already stopped listening to those who tried coaxing him, whoever they might be. He kept saying that he wanted to go back to Rome, to the point that it had become an obsession. He knew only too well that he was condemned to being a paraplegic for the rest of his life: he had no illusions.

"I've regressed to the stage of infancy. I'm like a little child who must learn everything, from how to stand up and walk to controlling his gestures. I've collapsed like a house of cards. My illness affects the center governing my balance. Since that center does not respond, every little area of my body slips over the other, leading to a major landslide."

"September 18 was a Saturday, as you might recall," Rinaldi continues somberly. "The news was all over the Italian papers. Against doctor's advise, Federico finally took action and made a foray to Rome. Dr. Jacobsen obtained an authorization from the hospital's head physician, who granted her to accompany him as his personal doctor, a quite unorthodox role. She brought with her a whole pharmacy, and a map detailing all the resuscitation centers between Ferrara and Rome.

Federico had organized the trip on his own. He was determined to see Giulietta and to verify her physical condition, whatever the cost. The newspapers came out with the sentimental headline: RUNAWAY LOVER AT SEVENTY YEARS OLD. In Rome, the paparazzi were lying in wait outside the hospital where Giulietta was. Federico was so vexed by them that he lashed out in anger:

"Why don't you take a picture of my d***?"

The media faithfully reported his remark the following day.

The next weekend, it was I who went to see him in Ferrara. Bad weather was raging all over Italy: the summer was taking its leave.

Federico seemed somewhat resigned, however, his intolerance of the hospital and even of the medical staff had reached an all-time high.

Despite his grievous physical and emotional discomfort, in the week preceding his trip he had been able to do some work and had filled his sketchbook with notes.

When I arrived, I found him propped up in bed, with his glasses on and the sketchbook in his hands. He was planning a film about his misadventure. A story was taking shape: the stroke, the Grand Hotel, the hospital in Rimini, and finally his current segregation, which afflicted him the most. Clearly, the prospect of returning to Rome had stirred his creative juices. On handing me his sketches, he hastened to play down their importance, resorting to arguments that I had heard him use before:

"These are not sketches in the traditional, literary sense of the word. I never work that way. With my sketches I go a different path–I don't need to explain that to you–since you perfectly know what my method is. Personally, I'm not able to produce writing meant as a sequence of events. My notes refer to the color of a tie, to the shape of an eyebrow, to a person's mannerism, look, or gait. . . . In order for these notes to arrange themselves into a real picture, I must feel a sense of urgency around me. Without urgency I couldn't work. To set in motion the film apparatus, I must feel the pressure from the troupe, the obligation of contracts and deadlines. The subject matter only takes shape in an inescapable situation, in a hot environment. I can't think in the abstract, otherwise. I can't envision a film full of stock characters, places, and events, all mixed up, with the only goal to produce some little story. Narration becomes clear to me at the very moment that the story forces itself upon me, and by then it's too late for me to back out."

Talking again about his work, albeit in such a discrete manner, as a remote and farfetched possibility, was apparently beneficial. He immediately regained his resolute look and authority, his usual ability to translate ideas into creative projects and mechanisms.

After lunch, he lay down on his pillows, visibly exhausted. Yet, he indulged in conversation, as usual. To him, informal discussion was an impalpable expression of friendship to be nourished with offhand inspiration. Earlier, while he was having lunch, I had taken advantage of that time to glance through the newspaper and read it aloud. I lingered on those subjects that could arouse his curiosity: books, politics, society news. And so, after a while, it came naturally to him to pose this existential question:

"For you, what comes first? Cinema, literature, cunt, ass, tits?"

"Cunt, Federico," I answered with no hesitation. "Without it, all the rest wouldn't even exist."

He half-closed his eyes, nodding. A pleased smile appeared on his face. It was the kind of answer that he expected from me.

In those days, Federico had a passionate admiration for the radiantly sensual soubrette Valeria Marini. I was telling him that if it weren't for her inability to speak English, I would have considered her for a femme fatale role in a film that I had scripted. At that, he burst out in pyrotechnic flares of disapproval:

"Who cares if she doesn't know how to speak English, if she doesn't know how to act, or if she can't do some other bullshit that the producers can think of! A cunt like that doesn't need to act! All she has to do is show up! All she needs is an audience cheering for her! What else is there? I'm surprised at you."

When it came to the buttery and curvaceous starlet, whom he had personally met, he would not admit any doubt. The only attitudes toward her that he allowed were enthusiasm, gratitude, and total trust.

"Did you meet her?" he kept asking after that. "Did she accept?"

The starlet notwithstanding, paramount in his thoughts was always Else, the heavenly nymph Egeria who had materialized from the fjords. She was devoted to him like an affectionate daughter, like a thoughtful lover. With her long naked legs, her ever-ready smile, her softest touch, she was the most successful female incarnation of his celluloid dreams, a wonderful loving addition to his harem. She aroused such enthusiasm in him! She re-ignited his *élan vital* by simply walking by! He demanded the same unconditional ardor from me: he spied on my gestures and looked at me in the eyes to see whether I shared his fire for her.

"She's a combination of power and grace. She's Hyppolita, Diana, Minerva, and the heroic female from the Nibelungs, all in one! And then she's so smart, so witty. She understands everything! Around here she's best, a true scientist. All her male colleagues have their eyes on her! Do you like her? Are you madly in love?" I obviously denied it, even though I admitted to share his passionate admiration.

As their relationship grew, their respective roles of patient and doctor reversed. Federico had become her irreplaceable confidant. She told him everything about herself and made him partake of all sorts of trivialities and mischief.

One day Else showed him a fax, illustrated with uninhibited images, with which she had been invited to attend a "Slut Party," a themed Rave at a countryside villa near Ferrara. When I arrived at the hospital the next morning I found Federico in the common hall, sitting in his wheelchair, drawing on his sketchbook: he was designing the clothes that the attractive neurologist might wear at the party. To convince her to attend, he decided to portray her with her costumes on, following a method normally used on the movie set to provide directions to the various film units. His creations looked like sketches by George Grosz: equivocal, aggressive, pronounced, and totally expressionistic like his films. With their vivid colors–deep blue, red, yellow–and their darting lines, some of them called to mind the work by Oskar Kokoschka. The soft roundness of forms gave way to angular, soaring shapes: the soft chin, eyes, and face of Dr. Jacobsen were pointed like those of a lovely bug.

Else was immediately fascinated by those felt-tip pen portraits; she was both upset and happy at seeing that unimaginable explosion of inventiveness, humor, and sensuality.

How could they call him an "ill man"?

In her office on the second floor, the doctor kept a folder with a number of drawings produced by Federico for his neurological tests. They were astounding fireworks of imagination, wit, and expression; they were dense with associations, self-irony, and subterranean drives. Those genial hasty sketches closely resembled the illustrations of his dreams, which he collected in those big, leather-bound folio books, jealously stored in a desk drawer, under lock and key. They were an inexhaustible reserve of radioactive uranium, a high-density magma on which he drew to fashion the stories for his films.

At seeing so copious a production, so high a peak of imagination, one might have thought that his vitality was still intact, that he could start all over again, as if nothing happened.

His spirit seemed indomitable. His playfulness, his wittiness, his verbal acrobatics over all topics were as nourishing and contagious as in his best days. Those who had never been exposed to them before were dumbfounded. Like Paola, the day nurse. Still unaccustomed to his crackling sparkle, she never ceased to be amused and surprised.

In the evening, before being relieved by the night nurse, one of her last tasks was to make him inhale a drug meant to free his nostrils and to make him breath better.

Naturally curious, Federico checked the label on the medicine-bottle where the drug's name was spelled out in capital letters: LIBERBAR.

"What a fantasy! We could create a whole series of names like that. What can we call a drug that gives you an erection? HARDOLIN!"

When the rush of emotion swept him, however, one could detect the vague cleft left in him by the stroke, the effects of some mechanical breakdown, of a faltering control system.

The noted leader-writer of a popular weekly had published an affectionate, vibrant editorial on him. Federico already knew its content, yet he wished to hear it from me all over again. His journalist friend had concluded his article saying that he wanted Fellini to be named senator for life: "Not because he's fallen ill, but because he's a genius!"

"What a blunderbuss!" Federico exclaimed, bursting into deep sobs that shook his chest.

He also got emotional for the wonderful article published in the Sunday's edition of *La Stampa,* which remembered Roberto Rossellini and Anna Magnani. When the great actress passed away, Rossellini didn't allow Giannetto De Rossi to put the make-up on her body, but he insisted doing it himself, with great care and devotion.

Listening to that story, Fellini became engulfed with sadness, and a tearless wail racked through his body.

Then, there emerged a fond memory of his actress friend, whom he loved very much:

"Anna was afraid of Totò. She feared him because she knew that if they were together on stage he would steal the show. In part she was right. If an actor and a seal are onstage together, all eyes are for the seal. Totò possessed that irresistible, *elemental* magnetism, which animals, fantastic creatures, and dreams all have. Totò himself once told me that when he and Anna worked together, she would go and see him in his dressing-room before the show to plead him: "Prince De Curtis, I beg you: tonight try not to be so funny. . . ."

His reminiscences broadened to include other actors and actresses that he knew:

"I worked with so many of them. . . . Yet, I did not talk about myself with any of them; almost never. A little bit with Peppino De Filippo, Benigni, and Marcello, of course. Also with Anita Ekberg, but only to explain why I kept postponing our inevitable encounter. And Terence Stamp ... with him too I shared rare moments of confidence."

In the first days of October, gathering what little strength she had left, Giulietta ventured by car to Ferrara accompanied by professor Saraceni. Like a film diva from the Thirties, she adorned herself with a turban-like hat to hide her incipient chemotherapy baldness: she was losing her lush fair hair, always perfectly groomed, that she loved so much!

Rather incongruously, Federico appeared to take her visit almost distractedly. He continued tending to a project he advocated, which would endow his hometown with a rehab center similar to the one in Ferrara; and so he was busy organizing a meeting of doctors and sponsors to be held at the Grand Hotel in Rimini. In short, he pretended not to realize how serious Giulietta's illness was. However, after that day, if they wanted to keep him there they had to chain him up.

He could no longer sleep at night, even with tranquilizers. His state of depression, combined with his systematic refusal of treatment, irremediably hampered his program of rehabilitation. When they took him to the gym, he put up such strong psychological resistance that he fell into a lethargic sleep. He would not listen to anybody, including the charismatic hospital's head physician, for whom he still felt some camaraderie.

And so one day he called me:

"Don't come this weekend. Tomorrow I will come there."

He would not have any objections. Once again he organized the complicated move all by himself, over the phone. He rented a Mercedes with driver to go from the San Giorgio to the Policlinic in Rome. He was moving to the ward run by the distinguished neurologist who looked after him when his circulation problems first manifested themselves.

"I can't take it anymore," he said in anguished, broken voice. "I've been bouncing from one hospital to the other since April," he said exaggerating the length of his ordeal, albeit not by much. "Giulietta will have our apartment ready, remodeled to my needs.

In the meantime, I'll stay at the Policlinic. In any case, if I stay here I'll never recover. If I don't leave now, who knows how much longer they'll drag it out! They force me to stand up like a robot. If I keep my balance for more than ten seconds they clap their hands: you can't imagine how stupid, grotesque, and humiliating all this is. I am not making any progress, anyway. The use of my arm is gone, that's already out of the question. And my leg is gone too, despite all the massages, physiotherapy, and electric stimulation. . . . To make a movement I must perform twenty exercises at the same time: tighten your butts, lean your stomach out, bend the spine, move your arm forward, raise your head, make a raspberry! All this just to move half an inch. I don't believe in these methods. They might work for other people but not for me. When I'm in Rome, I will hire a male nurse, a good physical therapist, but at least I'll do as I think fit. Here I'm forced to sleep when I'm hungry, to go to the gym when I'm sleepy, to wait every time for my turn because the hospital has its own rhythms, its own needs based on schedules, staff, programs, customs. . . . I have my rhythms too, and it seems to me that it's more important to meet the needs of the patient–the one who's supposed to recover. . . . The San Giorgio is a good little hospital, slightly better than others. Actually, people here are kind, skillful, caring, enthusiastic, but I can't stay here anymore: I've stayed too long already. They said a month, forty days, and there's no light at the end of the tunnel yet. Anyway, I don't want to bother you with my troubles. I'll call you as soon as I get there, so we can meet right away. Actually, you know what? I'll call you from the car, before leaving. Did you meet with Marina Valeri? Did she accept? Look, if you want to see me next time, you must bring her with you as a laissez-passer!"

Else had tried to convince him to resist a little longer–a week, ten days at least–in order to consolidate what progress he had made, but nothing and no one could crack his determination.

"I tried to encourage him, but to no avail," she said over the phone, disheartened.

To make things worse, the friendship between the Scandinavian doctor and the Italian director, that unusual alliance, that fanciful match, apparently annoyed some people. The hospital received anonymous defamatory phone calls about Else, and the nurses were unable to avert them.

Else found a love message on her answering machine from someone who clumsily tried imitating Fellini's inflection. A threat was mounting against her. One day a man called asking for her, passing himself off as Federico's brother-in-law. In a threatening tone, he warned her that it was more prudent for her to leave the Maestro alone, and he advised her to hit the sidewalk if she wanted to scatch her itches.

Else found threatening messages even on the windshield of her car. Who were these people? What were they trying to unveil? Why were they afraid of her?

In the meantime, Fellini was planning to give his official farewell to Ferrara with a lunch-party at a renowned restaurant. He invited the whole medical staff who had cared after him. He wanted everybody to be there: doctors, nurses, and physiotherapists. The only one excluded was his night nurse, Maria Veneria. How come? According to Else, Federico had grown impatient with her because he found her to be whimsical.

Maria Veneria, a passionately pious woman in her late thirties, had replaced Mrs. Hen. For what I could tell, she had done so with sensitivity, efficiency, and savoir-faire.

I have known for quite some time that contact with a wizard can never be innocent. Nonetheless, I could not really figure out what was going on between the two of them. Their relationship hid an elusive secret. She was gratified at the opportunity to be close to such a prestigious and influential personality. She glowed at being near the overheated mental circuits of a genius like him, perhaps too much so.

"We never sleep at night," she confided one time that we were alone, late in the evening. "It doesn't matter to me. I'm also used to going all night without rest. I sleep a couple of hours during the day, after school, and that's enough for me."

Teaching was the main profession of that pious woman, who devoted herself to hospital nursing more out of Christian love than interest in money. Looking after Fellini, she inevitably neared the mouth of the volcano, getting dangerously close to the edge of the seething crater.

"I listen to him gladly," she continued. "To escape anxiety, he talks and talks. He confides also his own personal, intimate matters. He keeps nothing from me. Sometimes he urges me to get close to him: he has such a need for physical contact, for a warm healthy body that he drags me into certain situations . . . and I. . . ."

She broke off her story. I realized that as a woman of faith she was reluctant to reveal those kinds of secrets, but at the same time I also sensed her eagerness to share them with me. Only a few bluish guiding lights illuminated the corridor. Even though we faced each other, I could hardly discern her fearful eyes moist with temptation.

"Do what you feel is right," I assuaged her. "Your mission is to bring comfort, isn't it?" I sugar coated the pill, in the familiar and authoritative tone that she expected from me.

In that cloistered semidarkness, she nodded assent. I hugged her with gratitude. I must confess that I found it somewhat disturbing and arousing: perhaps it was her vaguely monastic air, or an ambiguous blasphemous desire. . . . She became aware of it. Instead of moving away, she overcame her innate modesty and pressed her generous firm breast against me, adhering her body tightly to mine.

We stayed like that for a long time, exchanging slight shivers and sudden jerks–oh, how enticing and masterly they were! Those burning embers yielded a forbidden scent:

"I'm always afraid that someone might come in and find us," she whispered in one breath. Her sibylline statement was neither an admission nor a denial. She blazed up. Her body heat came through her light summer clothes like fire.

"Does Dr. Jacobsen know about this?" I inquired tentatively.

"If she does she didn't find out from me, that's for sure. You're the first one to hear it."

"We must see each other again," I proposed. "Not here, though."

This was not a stratagem of mine, I can assure you. In spite of everything, I wasn't sure of what I had heard. I was afraid of misinterpreting, of letting my fervid imagination lead me astray into the hazy, extrasensorial territory where Federico lured me. By then, in fact, I was convinced that I was living his unconscious drives, that I had become his physical body, the wholesome terminal of his desire.

Maria Veneria simply slipped the pen out of my shirt pocket and scribbled her phone number on my hand.

"Call me!" she whispered brushing my mouth with her incandescent lips, and she vanished into the room like a faint shadow.

The ensuing events took a rapid turn, and I was not able to see her again.

The restoration of Fellini's films kept me busy in Rome the whole time. The deadline for the New York retrospective was coming fast: to the American organizers, a delay on the scheduled projections would have been unforgivable.

Maria Veneria and I talked on the phone occasionally, but we never got to the heart of the matter. And then Federico left Ferrara.

Perhaps, to fathom the mystery, the only way would have been to take a look at Else's notes, at what she wrote after her sessions with Federico. However, mindful as she was of the deontology code, would she ever agree to open her secret Ark for me? My veiled suggestions to do so fell on her deaf ears. Yet I was certain that I could decipher the mysteries contained in the Ark better than she could, that in there I could find the clue leading to the core of my quest.

Chapter XI

The Last Exile

That Friday afternoon, Federico finally acted on his intention to leave, and he moved to Rome. His new room at the Umberto I Policlinic resembled a camp. Since no one had thought of looking for a private nurse, his painter friend Rinaldo volunteered to spend the night with him. Federico settled for the bed by the window, leaving the one by the door to his friend. On the modest Formica table against the back wall stood out a gaudy bunch of red roses. It was Giulietta's token of love that marked each of Federico's moves. Unfailingly, among the roses' leaves, was her card with the touching message: *Your Giulietta.*

Apart from that, the whole setting conveyed a sense of desolation. The room's closet was so puny that it couldn't even hold his basic personal items. Bags, clothes, linens that would not fit in the closet lay scattered on the floor, heaped on the chairs or the radiator. The table was cluttered with all sorts of sacks and food containers. The counter of the tiny night stand and its two open shelves were crowded with glasses, medicines, water bottles, personal items, sketch-books, block-notes, a phone-book, a pair of eye-glasses, all jumbled together.

But Federico didn't mind: he was just happy to be back in Rome, as he wanted. He recognized that room as the same one where his brother Riccardino was once hospitalized:

"You know, Oscar. . . . This is the very room where Riccardino died," he revealed as soon as he saw me.

How did he know? Based on what signs? Yet, he was absolutely sure that the room was the same. When he told me that, a surprised smile flickered on his lips, tender and sad like a return home. An almost identical coincidence had taken place in Rimini's hospital, regarding Room 1 in the General Medicine Division.

"This is where my mother died," was the first thing he told me.

His Lares seemed to be showing him the way to the shades below.

Federico had arranged to stop by his apartment in Via Margutta before being taken to the hospital. He relished being home again, inside a familiar geometry of lines and objects. He even sat down at his favorite spot, on the couch by the phone and the lamp, with the mail tray at his side. He would settle there for our many work sessions, royally clad in his velvet damask robe–a present from a costume-designer friend of his–while I took my place in the embroidered red cloth rocking chair, facing him, with the Olivetti 32 resting on my knees.

He was once again in the healthy embrace of his home, from which he had been exiled for months after his illness.

His current precarious situation did not seem to alarm him that much, or at least he tried not to show it. Federico, however, spent the night on tenterhooks, experiencing severe attacks of dyspnea and smothering depression. "How can I get out of this?" he kept whispering, without expecting an answer. His return to Rome had not been carefully planned. His apartment had not been readied to accommodate the needs of a hemiplegic like him, and it was not going to be ready for a while. Nobody could take care of it. In fact, Giulietta was also crossing over into the river of no return. That was the most painful concern for him.

"It hurts me so much seeing her like this because of me!"

He didn't know: nobody had explicitly told him that his lifetime companion was battling death, just like him.

Thus Federico would have to stay at the Policlinic for who knows how much longer, and he could not rely anymore on the zealous and tireless assistance he was given in Ferrara.

A big-shot politician in similar condition would have been lodged in a princely nursing home, even though less deserving of it for his services to Italy. An undiscussed genius of our century, like Fellini, was instead abandoned to the hurried care of an overworked public health system, and left to languish in the indifference of the mighty.

It didn't seem fair. I have always dreamed of a country where an extraordinary artist like him is given the proper honor, a nation that takes care of its most prestigious representative by pampering him and lavishing him with attentions, like a head of state.

"Look in the night table, there are some notes. Please put them in the closet."

In that room, there was no place with a lock where his personal papers could be saved from prying eyes and grasping hands; there was no privacy or protection for the last fruits of his mind. The notes consisted of three pages tightly written. Each line was dramatically slanted downwards towards the end, as if he were fatally running out of charge.

"Would you like to go over them?" I asked him before putting the block notes away, seeing that he was still holding his reading glasses in his good hand.

Dropped back on his pillow, Federico simply shook his head without the energy to lift it:

"When is Giulietta coming?" he asked.

Else Jacobsen had followed him once again in his hasty and reckless transfer to Rome. From the time of his departure to that of his arrival, she kept me constantly informed of his moves. However, due to the day's events, we did not have a moment to ourselves until ten o'clock that night.

Raffaele, the accompanying male nurse dispatched by the San Giorgio hospital, was staying at her same hotel. Federico had made a reservation for the two of them at a popular restaurant. Wishing to escape Raffaele's "custody," we purposely ditched it in favor of a quieter and friendlier little joint.

Since we were both concerned about Federico's condition, after dinner we thought advisable to stop by the Policlinic and check on him.

When we arrived at eleven thirty, we were the only ones to roam through the deserted pavilion and the silent ward where Federico was. Unable to stay awake, his friend Rinaldo had settled on the bed next to his. Lying motionless like that, the two of them composed a rather disquieting image, an ominous morgue-like sight. Yet the doctor on duty with whom Else consulted was quite reassuring.

After we left the hospital, Else deserted her hotel to spend the night at my place. But the good and wise giantess who lay in my bed was not there for me. Her shapely forms were more than ever "his," like the many Hyppolitas and Minervas that he had fancied as a young child discovering the opposite sex. The indisputable femininity of that blonde Valkyrie was the same to be found in the fountains' naiads, in the public statues extolling the Italic patriotic virtues, with those bronze, cannon-ball-like buttocks that schoolboy Federico admired with his nose up in the air, as he marvelously fabled in *Roma* and *Amarcord*. A remote womanliness carved out of marble or granite and turned into polished flesh. A mix of burning lust and cold frigidity, resistance and wantonness, stiffness and smoothness, which concealed a world of seething passions and secret delights to be unleashed after she finally gave in to pleasure. Her feminine essence could be seen in the many marriages of Ares and Aphrodite depicted in the high-flown paintings by Titian, Tiepolo, and Poussin; in the unreachable nymphs chiseled by Bernini, Giambologna, and Ammannati; in the carved figureheads, caryatids, and demigoddesses of springs and grottos. . . .

While bound to vanish, for the time being Federico's alchemy seemed to be working, still intact.

In the early morning, Rinaldo called me to say that during the night Federico had suffered a bad attack of anxiety and dyspnea. Else and I hurried to the Policlinic, speeding through a sunny Rome without traffic on that pealing Sunday. By the time we arrived at the hospital, however, Federico had totally recovered. In fact, he was surprised at our concern.

Else had to leave for Ferrara. She spent the morning with him, till breakfast time. Being Fellini's official escort doctor, she wanted to make sure that the ward staff would do everything possible for the welfare and safety of "her" patient.

Raffaele, the sturdy male nurse who had been assigned to her, was waiting for us at the station. His face was an expressionless mask of politeness, but as he welcomed us his openly unpleasant and weary smile betrayed his discontent.

In the early afternoon, I returned to the hospital to see Federico. He was alone, more alone than he ever was in Ferrara. He was in a state of utter dismay that neither my reassurances, nor the greetings from his friends were able to dispel.

"How will I come out of this?" he kept asking himself.

We went on talking about it till dinnertime. A shadow was hanging over him, like a sinister omen: it was his encounter with Nannarella. While he was being taken back to his room after one of his numberless check-ups, Anna Magnani materialized in the corridor, right in front of him:

"Ah, Federì, you took your sweet time to get here!" she reproached him, as if she were waiting for him. As she was leaving, she turned around, and in her hoarse voice she said:

"See you later, Federì!"

"It's not a good sign!" He wrinkled his brows disarmingly, trying to tame that gloomy warning.

I couldn't get used to the idea of seeing him prisoner of a useless body, confined in such a cruel bondage: it seemed a great injustice.

Of all the things that I stuttered, Federico singled out that word.

"Injustice, you say.... Why? What does justice have to do with anything?" he countered inflexibly, absolutely immune to self-pity. He even accepted adversity as a creative stimulus, which was his indispensable philosophy of life. And yet, at the same time, he rejected the gloomy notion of an irreversible, harsh fate.

At dinnertime, Giulietta came surrounded by her relatives. She had a lost gaze. When I hugged her, I was struck by her weightlessness: she felt like a little bird with hollow bones.

Else had sent me a letter–via courier–containing an envelope for Federico. She was charging me with the task of delivering it in person, and making sure that he would read it.

Unfortunately, that weekend I absolutely had to go out of town. Before leaving, I tried to drive to the Policlinic, but some antigovernment rally forced me to take several detours, and I got caught up in an inextricable traffic jam. By the time I finally got out of it, it was very late: going to the hospital would have meant not leaving. I wish I had gone anyway!

And so I decided to stay on course to the highway, and not to veer to the hospital to see Federico. He called me on my cell.

"I have a letter for you from Else," I informed him immediately.

"When will you bring it?"

"I'm leaving now, but I'll be back this Sunday. I'll swing by the hospital on my way home."

There was a pause in his voice, a void that is still eating into me.

"All right, I'll see you Sunday" he suddenly ended the conversation, disappointed and impatient as usual.

THE LOST OF THE LOST.

I was never to see him again. I was never to deliver the letter to him, nor to read it for him.

It was a moving love message.

By the time I got back to Rome, Sunday night, Federico had already been taken to reanimation.

The crisis came at six thirty, during dinner: apparently Federico choked on a morsel of mozzarella that obstructed his throat. At least, that's how the person who was caring for him at the time described his fit of suffocation.

It didn't take him long to lose consciousness, but it took the doctor from reanimation a whole thirteen minutes to show up in his room: it was a death sentence.

Just a few hours earlier, at noon, Federico had gone out to lunch with Giulietta at a restaurant in Porta Pia. His executive producer and a male nurse accompanied him, two strong men who were able to see to his complicated transport. Giulietta, who was absolutely worn out, wore her amaranthine turban with which she hid her baldness. Perhaps for the first time, Federico had a chilling realization of how seriously ill she was. Given his conditions, what would become of him without Giulietta?

After lunch, he asked to see his new office in Via Capo Le Case. His faithful friend Rinaldo had found it for him, just a staircase away from his own studio. After fifty years, the two of them would reunite, so they could "mess" with colors and canvas once again, like in the old days. Federico spent that Sunday afternoon sniffing around the site of his new life. Then the executive producer took him back to the hospital in his spacious van. At six o'clock, dinner was served: broth, mozzarella, and a side dish. Federico ate sitting up in bed, his back propped up by pillows. His private secretary, who just happened to be there visiting and was the only other person in the room, assisted him. While Federico was swallowing, he rolled his eyes. The sudden fit was so violent that it almost cast him at the foot of the bed, half-paralyzed as he was. He was choking. The doctor on duty was a freshly graduated young girl. She came in, perched on her stiletto heels, but she was not able–or not capable–of providing timely help. Federico lost consciousness. The ward had no resident reanimation specialist. One was urgently summoned from another ward, but in order to get there it took him a quarter of an hour ("thirteen minutes," the hospital administration specified in the following days, which just made their heavy responsibility official). By then it was too late to do anything. The prolonged hypoxia had already caused irreparable damages to the patient, who, by now at death's door, was taken to reanimation. Federico was given external cardiac stimulation and attached to a respirator. Despite everything, he never stopped breathing and his heart never stopped beating.

On the eight o'clock news, it was simply announced a sudden worsening of Fellini's clinical conditions, without going into further details. Scrappy information came in from my journalist friends, and actually many of them called *me* to have further details, updates, and encouraging news. What could I know?

Tuesday morning, I woke up with a start: it was the early hours, five minutes to five. I had heard Federico's voice calling me. At that point I was sure that he had passed away. I turned on the television again to check the news ticker but I found no confirmation to my premonition. The situation had not come to a head: Fellini's conditions were unchanged from the day before and remained serious.

It was only later on that I found out that his electroencephalogram became flat during the night. Fellini was in a coma and clinically dead, even though he was still breathing thanks to the iron lung: his body was surviving him.

How much longer? A few hours? A few days?

Almost all of his coworkers and closest friends rushed in to the Policlinic, and I spent the whole day with them. The TV-crews started gathering outside the hospital. With their equipment already in position, at dusk the cameramen turned the discharge lights on, aiming their powerful white beams at the outer walls of the pavilion.

Bivouacking at the entrance amid the neoclassic columns, the journalists mounted guard, poised to capture the smallest news, tip-off, or indiscretion. They screened all newcomers, whispering their names to each other, wondering whether they might be potential sources of precious information. For the most part, they were inexperienced girls recently assigned to cover the news, very conscientious but not in the least aggressive. In a story a la *The Big Carnival* by Wilder, they would have cut a poor figure.

Federico's cell was off-limits. He was locked up behind a milk-glass door, at the end of a corridor. We buzzed to get in, however, first a plainclothes policeman, then a green-coated doctor barred our way. Nobody was allowed to visit the patient, let alone non-relatives: orders were strict.

The on-duty doctor was not in the least touched by our distressed pleas:

"Tomorrow Fellini will be in the same condition as he is today," he replied with utter arrogance, thus disposing of us.

The next day, professor Saraceni was going to decide whom to let in at visit time, between three and four in the afternoon.

An ever-growing crowd gathered outside the entrance gate to the Umberto I, then strewed along the hospital's fences, waiting for the impending event. In dealing with Federico, however, the media, and as a consequence the public–who influences whom?–were hopeful of a miracle. Which just confirmed my theory: Federico was a saint, a witness, an awakener; he was some sort of martyr in whom people could identify themselves. Through his work, he bore witness to each of us. That was the distinctive and charismatic gift bestowed upon him, as a Prince of the Church was to state in his learned homily inspired by St. Paul.

Saints are worshipped for their supernatural interventions.

Fellini's miracles are his film stories. They contain a spark, which can help viewers overcome life's obstacles, unlock unknown powers, and find the right path. At a metaphysical level, poetry can be as redeeming as religion. All prodigies overflow with creativity, which can reveal itself in a miracle of faith like in a work of art. In either case, creativity spills its beneficial effects over the viewers. With his genius, with his universal language, Fellini was able to interpret the hearts and minds of people all over the world. He gave them the solace of being less alone, less misunderstood, less judged.

Rinaldi's tone becomes more and more excited.

"That explained the electricity in the air, the flocking crowds, the widespread confusion, the spontaneous camping outside the hospital walls, the immediate quartering of journalists and photographers, the sway of faces obedient to his occult directorship, like in a sequence from one of his films. *The Nights of Cabiria, La Dolce Vita, The Voice of the Moon.* What would have been the next title?

The day after at the Policlinic I saw Elena again, elegant and distraught looking. She was obsessed with one idea: she wanted Federico to listen to Nino Rota's music through a headphone. In her view, that expedient was the most direct way to reach his heart and brain, to make him feel our presence, to reconnect with him and perhaps cast a ray a hope.

Elena intended to use a tape that Federico himself had given to her son. As it had happened with other comatose patients, she was sure that those familiar tunes could break into the dark wall confining him, that they could penetrate into some cracks, sending in a light probe, throwing in a life-ring. Naturally, I agreed with her, but unfortunately the doctors were opposed to the idea. Also in this case, we had to present our request to Saraceni, who had become the most authoritative link between the patient and the outer world. His arrival was expected momentarily, but he was late.

In front of the reanimation ward, camouflaged among the awaiting small crowd, was Gerta Blumen, wife to one of Fellini's publishers. Tall, spindly, ash blond hair, black clad, she just stood there, stock-still against the wall as if to support herself. A weary smile lit her hollow face, her eyes looked dewy and dazed, like those of a fawn before the hounds. In a state of befuddlement, she had taken the first available flight out of Berlin without telling anyone, not even her husband. She too was hoping to arouse the pity of the doctors on duty, so to spend a few moments with Federico. The doctors, however, would not listen to any argument: the prohibition regarding non-relatives was irrevocable.

In the end, the experiment with the audiotape was also turned down. Dr. Braschi and his medical staff believed that an auditory stimulus might actually set off a fatal epileptic seizure.

Fellini had been lying in a tube for four days connected to an artificial lung, without any contact with the outside world: THE LOST OF THE LOST.

None of us wanted to leave the hospital. We were under the illusion that by means of electromagnetic waves, invisible ripples in the air, mysterious assonances, and heart pulses our presence would get through to him and would bring him comfort.

For the largest part our group was made of the women who loved him: it was some kind of "choir," whose composition became better defined by the day.

One of them was Angelica, a young Greek actress. She kept calling me from Athens since that fateful Sunday. Finally, one early morning, she called me and woke me up: unable to restrain herself she had decided to come, and she was due to arrive in Rome that afternoon.

A cynic and wretched episode further exasperated people's mood. Saturday October 23, at 1:10 a.m., the TV news ticker reported the following update:

FELLINI REMAINS IN CRITICAL CONDITION

The release of a picture of a dying Fellini has created a stir. Prof. Saraceni, Fellini's personal doctor, denounced the vile episode. The Ministry of Health, in conjunction with the Policlinic administration, has started an investigation. Giulietta Masina, the Maestro's wife, has warmheartedly thanked those newspapers that have not published the picture.

Someone penetrated the aseptic cell where Fellini was kept, removed the bandage that kept his eyes moist, lowered the sheet covering his chest and took a picture of him. The helpless dying patient was forcefully exposed to the camera, his image to be offered to the highest bidder. A despicable action that would have been impossible to carry out without the help of an inside accomplice, the compliance of the medical staff, and the guilty negligence of those in charge.

They had sold him out.

With a spontaneous and unanimous decision, all Italian newspapers refused to publish the pitiless image and to partake in the loathsome exploitation. RAI did not broadcast it in its news. The first one to show was Swiss TV followed in quick succession by Canale 5 and Retequattro of Berlusconi's network. Those who saw the picture found it unbearable to watch. Federico was all skin and bones, his face wasted, and his big chest gaunt beyond recognition: a dreadful sight. *Ecce homo!*

"It's a kind of image that remains indelible," the loyal RAI reporter confided to his friends.

He felt personally offended and indignant with Berlusconi, the media tycoon. On the spur of the moment, he put together a collage of old interviews with Fellini to be aired that same night. In those interviews, recorded back in unsuspected times, Fellini painted a disquieting picture of his little noble adversary.

Angelica abided by her decision to come. Her plane landed that evening at Fiumicino, in a torrential rain. She called me right away from the airport. While in Rome, she was going to be a guest of an old Russian soprano, and I rushed to meet her at her house.

The young actress was even more attractive than I remembered. All of a sudden, I felt as though I had been waiting for her since we last saw each other. By "we" I mean the three of us: she, Federico and I.

In our presence, the elderly opera singer indulged in nostalgia. She unearthed some old records of her performances. Sunk in her armchair, she listened to them ecstatically with her eyes half-closed.

I felt like being plunged into an old Russian novel. Under the influence of that charming *madam,* expert of life and love, Angelica's enchanting beauty easily dulled my senses. Despite the inclement weather, she insisted going to the Policlinic without further ado. She picked up her cream-colored duster, made of a soft, draped fabric, and she put it on her shirt that kept coming unbuttoned, unable as it was to contain her bewitching breasts–oh, Federico had extolled their praises so many times! And so we went out, diving into the night.

We proceeded down the deserted corridor of the hospital. There was not a soul left but us. Holding our breath, we stood in front of the lit glass door that led to the forbidden ward. Angelica had brought with her a love letter for Federico that she never had the courage to mail, and now she was clutching it in her hands like a votive offering.

Her body's proportions were reminiscent of the goddesses sculptured by the immortal Lysippus, Praxiteles, and Phidias. With her thick chestnut hair flowing on her broad shoulders, her exuberant breasts tempting beyond the wildest imagination, her lithe muscular thighs and rounded glutei, she was a true vision, a dweller on Olympus.

Federico had purposely drawn her down to his set, and he was asking me to take his role.

I know that what I'm saying may sound absurd, but it is not, I assure you. And Angelica was the first to realize it.

"Do you really think all these things about me?" she asked me later on that night, laughing incredulously, while rolling her fairy body in my bed. She cupped her velvety breasts and squeezed them, making them brim over; they looked like white puffy meringues of sugar and cream. I plunged my face and waded through them by way of kissing, biting, and licking. "You are crazy!" she kept saying, astounded. "You are even worse than he is!"

She was morbidly intrigued by that arcane game in which the two of us chased each other on her sumptuous body. As she explored the meandering path that brought her there, back to Federico and me, her skin grazed the other ethereal female presences hovering around the dark room, causing her unconfessable sensual shivers.

"I forgot that you're such a dirty old man!" she added, shuddering with jealousy and delight.

The tepid sun warmed our skin, in an artificial spring pulse. The diaphanous air was likewise deceitful. The vividly colored Capitol in front of us, with the bright green hill and the floodlit staircases completed the illusion.

Was it possible not to suspect Federico's light touch behind that amazing incantation? Was it possible not to imagine that he was still having fun and had no intention of quitting anytime soon?

Angelica and I spent a good portion of the afternoon at the hospital, mingling with other friends, sitting on the corridor benches. At night, by tacit mutual consent, we let ourselves be consumed by a compulsive tertian fever.

The gifted actress indulged in her innate narcissism. She let herself go without restraint in front of my video camera, blinding the lens with her voluptuous forms and prodigious breasts. Still cupping those spectacular creamy puffs in her hands, she reclined on the couch in a lascivious pose, like a pinup. Keeping my eye on the viewfinder, I zoomed on her most intimate parts. Unable to take her eyes off the screen, she gazed excitedly at herself, lapsing into frenzied licentiousness. In front of the impassive camera we even made love, standing or clinging to each other in the armchair. As the night went on feverishly, we moved our intertwined bodies to the more hospitable double bed.

The elderly opera singer finally gave up on the idea of claiming back the young Greek guest, with whom she intended to revive the time-faded glories of her roaring years.

Else Jacobsen came back the following day.

We really counted on her–a highly esteemed neurologist and a foreign one to boot–to bypass the sanitary cordon that kept us from Federico.

When she arrived at the Policlinic, escorted by Mario Saraceni, she was able to cross the forbidden threshold without problems. She came out one hour and a half later, with a dazed, tense expression on her face. She had seen Federico and had been able to consult with her colleagues. The patient's general condition required an extremely cautious approach, no different from the course already taken.

I sensed her hesitancy. She was emotionally disturbed and torn. In the end, though, like all of us, she too was willing to resort to any method capable of alleviating Federico's "lostness"; to anything that could rescue him from the state into which he plunged since his stroke, and that was tragically unfolding before our eyes.

In the few moments that she was alone with him, Else was able to sense the unbridgeable distance that separated him from the world. She managed to convey to us, with her eyes more than with her words, the dismay that she felt during her visit. Other than that, Federico's real clinical picture was like the official one. He was in an utterly precarious situation, and anything could break the tenuous thread that kept him alive.

Once again, that Sunday it rained cats and dogs. Going to the hospital, we got soaking wet. Not even the umbrella could protect us, shaken as it was by the heavy storm.

Else had an appointment with Dr. Saraceni. This time she was going to be with Federico, alone, for a while. I figured that she could, at last, whisper to him those words from her undelivered letter.

In the afternoon, the hours flew by distressfully. And then there was Elena . . . with her softly curvaceous figure and quivering passion, with her nearly-feverish eyes and taut face. . . .

Oscar interrupts his narration hesitantly, and he looks at me in the eyes. He feels it necessary to provide some explanation for his confidential tone. Even I, his avowed confidant, could mistake it for indulgent decadence.

"I'm using this type of language because I know that you can understand me. I'm not searching for vulgar indiscretion or trivial effect. The truth is that through Elena's behavior I finally intuited, once and for all, what was going on. Thanks to her, we were finally coming to the point."

CHAPTER XII

Oracle

"I find it natural to use a tone as vaporous as Elena's . . . 'amorous liaison.' I don't know what else to call it," Rinaldi says in self-justification. "It's like a slightly faded perfume, better suited to her elegance, her high-society charm, her rustling raincoat, her blond sausage curls, her delicate ringed hands, her obscure raging passion that seemed to be consuming her from the inside out.

It's not up to me to judge her, and at any rate it would be pointless, as well as inappropriate. I just want to say that what was happening belonged to the realm of sensory illusions. And that was the only certainty.

During those long afternoons that we all spent waiting at the hospital, Elena was an assiduous presence. Often she would linger into the evening and the late night. One felt that her subterranean communication with Federico had never been severed. Whatever she did, one could sense that a part of her was absent, swallowed into the other dimension, beyond that impassable door. Not being allowed to see him or touch him, she had thought of the stratagem involving Nino Rota's music: at hearing those notes, perhaps Federico would know that she was the one who sent them and would welcome her at his side.

When you will have the chance to look at the drawings that I mentioned earlier, you too will be stunned at their sensuality. I'm really talking about Eros here, that kind passion that makes you lose yourself in your loved one. Of all the drawings of his last period, perhaps these are the most dramatic and fascinating: they're so exuberant and colorful that they just scream at you. They look like hymns to the woman, to her body, to her sex, to her infinite ability to make us happy or to destroy us. Only when they are before your eyes, you can grasp their real power; the irrepressible tension, the clash of archaic forces, the sublime charge of play and pain that I am extolling.

When she was at the Policlinic, she glowed with a special radiance. She was surrounded by a halo, as if she were endowed with special powers, like a priestess. There were moments when I had the absurd notion that if she had managed to penetrate Federico's cell, she could even resurrect him, as in miracles. And in any case, life and death stream from the same energy: the origin of life, the first source, is conceived in a woman. The woman intercedes for us, and our Savior Jesus Christ was made flesh in a woman's womb.

"Just think of the string of attributes that have been ascribed to the Madonna," Rinaldi points out. *"Heaven's Gate, Sick Healer, Ivory Tower....* No man has ever possessed so many supernatural qualities."

Elena, wonderful woman and lover, gave the impression that afternoon of being at the center of a powerful magnetic circuit, the conduit of high-voltage current. By looking at her eyes, you could even sense that she was in a light trance state. Just by being near her, you immediately felt her charge, her fluid.

Just past the entrance to the pavilion, between the hall and the corridor, there is an indoor cloister, a peristyle enclosing a scanty lawn, and in the middle is a bronze bust of Lazzaro Spallanzani. It was a transit area where people rarely stopped. The reporters had requisitioned the outdoor atrium, and the visitors gathered in small groups or scattered along the aisle, depending on the time of day.

Right before we reached the small cloister, Else and I intentionally veered off, looking for a secluded spot. I leaned my back against the openwork balustrade, and she stood in front of me, undecided. As I drew her close and held her, I felt her body mold to mine. She had that seductive ability, which comes naturally to certain women, to ply their whole being to you, to give and receive at the same time. Her full breasts, pressing against my chest, conveyed that unmistakable warmth that makes you feel helpless. As she lowered her eyelids and rested her head on my shoulder, her hollow face turned almost colorless. Indifferent to the rare passerby who eyed us with surprise and curiosity, we intertwined in intimate embrace. What could we do? Break up our indecorous posture? We lacked the will. Eventually, we returned to the corridor and camouflaged in the crowd. But then, as if obeying a mysterious, irrepressible impulse, we joined again before the sacred door, near the forbidden threshold. Leaving all caution aside, Elena melded again her body to mine. All our actions were driven by desire. Prey to the same irrational and invincible lust of that summer day in Rimini, I bared her silky curvy breasts.

Oh, being able to grasp them, to fondle them! Oh, how greedy I was! What I did not dare do back then I did now, in that public place, risking a scandal. I groped blindly those puffy clouds, those soft doves: bare, they felt slightly enfeebled, which made them all the more attractive!

That was madness, of course, an unknown frantic heat! And how voluptuous it felt! Federico was only a few feet away, beyond that door that we were virtually crossing: Elena's body was so aglow with passion that it radiated all the way up to him. I turned her around to face the milky iridescent glass, I grabbed her by the shoulders and pulled her to me. Her tight and slippery skirt easily lifted, exposing her silk garter belt. She writhed at my intruding, groping hands and endured their excruciating linger.

How was it possible that people just stopped coming by? How was it possible that the door remained closed all that time? That not even one person would come around the corner, past the jutting wall where our niche was? Doctors, nurses, guards.... Where were they? Had they all disappeared as if by magic?

In that dimly lit enclosure, in that silent limbo there were only the two of us, consumed by an obscure drive, joined in an explosion of senses. Elena was so tense and excited that her waxy face became even thinner, subdued by the keenest pain, a harrowing lust: she had the countenance of a medium.

Like her, I too was drawn into that powerful whirl and was bereft of lucidity. I unveiled her overflowing breasts as in an offering, and while I fondled them with one hand, with the fingers of my other hand I harped on the creases of live flesh that I freed from her silk garments. Enervated, she surrendered:

"You have his hands!" she whispered, shutting her eyes tightly.

Molten lava flowed unchecked from her, a scorching magma that soon swept her away.

I penetrated her like that, standing against the wall.

"Federico, honey, can you feel me?" she said, running her hand over my face and my eyes.

After a dazzling dance of phosphenes the miraculous portent was over. It only lasted for a brief spell, during which the wizard suspended life around us.

Then the love whirl spirited away, life soon flowed back, and the everyday dimension resumed its course. As the spell dissolved, our protected limbo became once again the anteroom for restless souls that it had always been.

With her elegant ringed fingers, Elena tugged her loosened fair hair back on her nape.

Else was given permission to visit Federico once more in the capsule where he was artificially kept alive. This time she was finally able to talk to him alone, to whisper the words she had wanted to tell him, those same words laid out in her childish and shaky handwriting in the letter that was never delivered.

As soon as the neurologist came out of the door, I stared deeply into her eyes, searching for the truth.

"He's fine. He's even better than yesterday," she whispered. "He reacts to pain. He has feeling even in his paralyzed limbs, which is an unexpected response."

"And what do the doctors say?"

"They are puzzled. Federico never ceases to surprise them. His pupils react to light, and instruments still detect neurological activity."

She told us that his tongue kept moving restlessly between his half-parted lips, as if he were sucking or he were trying to speak.

I deluded myself, finding some arcane meaning in it: reality becomes the Word, and the Word comes true.

That was the last time they met. Else left in the early afternoon for Ferrara. At the train station, she had with her several copies of a comic book that had just published a good number of Fellini's sketches. They were autographed drawings excerpted from his hitherto inaccessible big book of dreams: each sketch was enriched by a commentary expressly written by him. With that load of coated paper, her handbag was a heavy burden over her athletic shoulder. Bowed down by its weight, she walked along the track to her Intercity car. Standing on the platform, while the railway men secured the train doors, she hesitated shaking her head:

"I don't really know why I'm leaving," she recoiled with a disconsolate smile. "Now that he's not there anymore, going back to the San Giorgio does not seem to make sense."

That night Angelica and I had dinner with some friends of ours at a crowded and smoky Chinese restaurant.

Feeling wired up and restless, the actress deserted her Russian friend once again. She wanted to share with me the ambivalent emotion that was tearing her apart and that she futilely tried to resist.

That night, her demigoddess body made love almost independently of her, as if it had fallen victim to a spell, to a sorcerous potion. While she was brought to a spasmodic climax, her body was rocked by furious pangs of pleasure. Her overflowing breasts–which were her pride and her crux–enveloped me, and they nearly crushed me and suffocated me under their weight. She took delight in that unusual lust. She savored the dry, bitter taste of splitting herself into two, of pleasing her senses but not her soul, of succumbing to her guilty weakness and morbid depravation.

The next morning, the clear sky and blazing sun enveloped Angelica, displaying the glowing colors of her native land, providing the perfect set for her bursting figure and luminous complexion. Her lavish and shiny dark hair, her voluptuous curves, her slanted green eyes bore the heraldic mark of royal stock; they conjured the elusive charm of the Parthenon virgins.

At the Policlinic, the press now lay a tighter siege. Their swelling ranks moved from the atrium outside to the cloister inside the hospital. And as time went by, from there they moved directly to the visitors' corridor.

Fellini's condition had worsened.

The Bard was among the first to call me that early morning. He insisted that I work with him in drafting the funeral oration for Federico. While sounding protective, his mellow voice betrayed some trepidation. Rimini's mayor and Federico's sister, Maria

Maddalena, had repeatedly asked *him*–as a friend and a fellow-villager endowed with inimitable diction and moving eloquence–to deliver the memorial speech. After the funerals in Rome, Federico was to be taken to his native town on the Adriatic coast, and there, at the City Palace, was to receive a second farewell.

The zealous Masters of Ceremonies were anticipating the event, as they customarily do.

I warded him off, firmly determined to shun his caustic invitation. I would have never been able to talk about Federico with the grievous expressions reserved to the dead: it would have meant giving up hope!

That night I woke up suddenly, startled at hearing Federico's voice. I felt cold sweat trickle down my spine. The tone and inflection sounded rather like those of an elderly woman, perhaps even my mother's, but it was definitely he who spoke:

"You know, I'm locked up in here," he complained.

Where was he locked up? And why wasn't he telling me how to free him?

Angelica was forced to leave for Greece. The producers threatened to disavow her if she would not return to the set that she had abandoned when rushing to Rome.

As for the reprint of Fellini's films, the chemical plant kept delaying the delivery date, thus seriously jeopardizing the New York retrospective. That afternoon, photography director Dario De Palma and I final proofed and released *The Clowns*. . . .

Oscar halts his narration, as words clog up in his throat in a whirl of emotion. In order to overcome it, he tightens his lips and smiles at me, looking for my complicitous understanding.

Do you remember that film's ending? The music and all other sounds suddenly stop. The empty trapeze swings back and forth under the cupola of the *chapiteau*, and in the background you can hear the barely perceptible rustle of confetti falling down like colored rain!

The clown's funeral, that mad chase at breakneck speed closing the film was shot right here, at Studio 5, in the same area where Federico's coffin is now displayed. Hardly a coincidence, is it?

Friday night, as soon as he emerged from the aseptic cell where Federico was kept, Dr. Saraceni approached me.

"The fact that he's still alive defies everything I know about medicine," he mumbled brokenly. "He breathes unassisted, his heartbeat is strong. Unfortunately, his temperature is rising. It is not a matter of days anymore, but of hours."

Rumor had it that Giulietta, on her part, refused all treatment: she saw no reason to keep on living.

They had reached the milestone of fifty years of marriage. Their wedding anniversary was the next day. All newspapers emphasized the event. One even published the wedding announcement drawn by Federico himself on that distant October 30, 1943.

Giulietta did not have the strength to visit her spouse, and she asked to hear mass at home. She spent all time kneeled in prayer, with bent head.

In the meanwhile, back at the Policlinic, a number of famous and not so famous characters from Fellini's colorful universe alternated on the Formica bench. Some of them were mythical figures. Like Vanina Olcese, elegant and distressed like a Czarina, with her tall busby hat, her cream-colored cashmere mantle, her powdered face coated with chalky rouge that accentuated her already aloof lunar look.... The visual effect was priceless.

With polished art she played the sincerely afflicted and then left.

As soon as she evaporated in the dimly lit corridor, we all returned to being obscure extras.

Feeling an undefinable change in me, I realized that I was gathering more and more sensations that were not mine. I was lending him my senses. I was registering for him stimuli from other people. Mila Rutovic's doleful reaction, the bursting tears that filled her orphan-like wide-open eyes, the light vanilla fragrance wafting from her hair.... They called for Federico's gentle caress: I just knew it.

Stefania was the latest addition to Fellini's circle of acquaintances, and for this very reason her feedback reaction was even more phosphoric, her passion more manifest. She was Neapolitan, and therefore naturally inclined to wear a widower's mask, a thoughtful puckered smile. She was dressed almost entirely in black, a color that magnified her shapely body and beautified her stately, tragic grief. She was a staunch believer in esotericism and in the occult powers that it could unleash. Making her heart beat in unison with his, she never left Federico's vigil, not even for a second.

She wanted us to form a chain, so that we could charge him with our strength and help him resist death. But where could we do it? While we were all in favor of the idea, we hesitated out of modesty. Concerns of appropriateness and perhaps also fear of ridicule held us back. Someone suggested we go down to the basement through a little door just around the corridor, and look for a suitable nook amid those winding tunnels. Another suggestion was to settle ourselves right in front of the notoriously impenetrable glass door, ignoring the bustle of doctors and nurses. In the end, we agreed that the best thing was for us to go outside and stand below Federico's windows. A stage designer and architect in our group who was used to drawing plans and topographical maps was able to locate the windows in almost no time.

Maria Kolosimo was also one of us. She was the harp player in *Orchestra Rehearsal*. . . . Do you remember her? Her hair was still blonde back then, and she was wearing an egg-colored soft coat with a large scarf-like collar. . . . She consulted the *I Ching*. The oracle's response was hexagram 8, UNION: Holding together brings good fortune. Then our plan was right. All the more so, because the hexagram had a moving line, by which it changed to hexagram 1, THE CREATIVE. The response couldn't have been any more clear.

We moved under the shelter of a lush oleander, overlooked by an imposing palm tree, as oriental as the moon in the ultramarine sky, shining through endless waves of silver clouds. Around us a whole family of restless cats moved about silently. Joining our hands we formed a circle. In the trembling silence, we focused on the yellow glimmer from Federico's small windows. Could we reach his heart? Could we bring a spark of light where the darkness fell? We all prayed in the secret of our hearts, invoking him for nourishment and protection.

The evenings were cold and humid now, November was at the door. The many of us who obstinately refused wearing winter clothes shivered against the bitter chill seeping into our bones.

The evening report didn't bring us any news. Federico the wizard had one more trick in store before fulfilling his final destiny.

"In any case, *he* will decide when it's time to 'stop the action,' Serventi warned me over the phone, as if we were on his movie set. "I don't feel well, I'm already between the sheets," he said, prostrated by that ineluctable event. "And I hope to laze in bed also tomorrow, provided that Federico does not make me get up," he concluded in his arhetorical and cynic soft drawl, typical of all Romans.

Federico died Sunday, October 31. His heart stopped beating a few minutes after noon. "Cardiac arrest," said the laconic medical bulletin circulated by ANSA, the Italian news agency, at 12.52 p.m.

All TV stations interrupted their regular programming to provide viewers with the breaking news. The newspapers–I don't know if you remember–that morning had merrily announced the fiftieth anniversary of Federico and Giulietta's wedding.

Rome was celebrating her Indian summer with one of those glorious October days that Federico loved so much! The golden sky lavished a spring like warmth on streets, buildings, pine trees, and it reached into people's hearts.

Outside the hospital railings, the caravansary of TV crews stamped the ground agitatedly, as in a military camp.

At the reanimation ward, someone informed us that Fellini's body had already been taken to the morgue and gave us directions on how to get there.

The Umberto I Policlinic was a city unto itself, vaguely built in the style of Piranesi and Art Nouveau. The visual graphic of its sign system, however, was unexpectedly modern: a stylized coffin on a plate informed the visitors where to find the morgue.

We crossed sumptuous halls and art deco galleries flanked by slender and elegantly fluted cast-iron columns; we walked along meandering paths, amid pavilions whose domes were leavened like minarets: it was an unexpected décor, worthy of a film set.

Finally we reached the morgue, the palace of the dead, already besieged by the crowd.

The news-hungry reporters ran to meet us. Even though we did not know each other, all those days spent together keeping vigil over Fellini had brought us close.

For a week already there had been discussions of bringing Federico's body right here, at Studio 5 in Cinecittà, for the lying-in-state. Giulietta suggested using a wall-size picture of Federico as a background to the coffin. It was that famous shot where he stands alone in the big empty theater, his figure brushed by the light blade of a 10,000-watt projector.

It was decided that the funeral rite was to be officiated at the *Basilica di Santa Maria degli Angeli e dei Martiri* in Piazza della Repubblica, where State funerals customarily take place. For the moment it was impossible to pay him homage. The prohibition to see him coming from his family extended beyond reason.

Monique Larouche, the unruliest of Fellini's followers, found out that it was possible to get to Federico through the underground passages of that vast morgue, thus bypassing security. At the point where the gardens grounds are below street level was a travertine stone portal, as imposing as the entrance to a pharaohs hypogeum. There was no living being in sight, except a cat standing still on a whitely tympanum, in profile, like an Egyptian divinity. We crossed the threshold without giving it second thoughts, and we quickly found ourselves deep down in the bowels of that unknown city. With our steps echoing on the slippery grès floor, we started our journey in that net of galleries that extended for miles and miles, as far as the eye could see. The galleries' walls, lined with yellowish ceramic tiles, reflected the chilly light from the neons on the vaulted ceiling. We ventured deeper into the labyrinth without the faintest idea of how to get back.

The subterranean network of the Policlinic extends to the whole university district. It is like a vast, buried metropolis, a tireless intestine seething with the bolus of the surface city. We got lost in that maze, as one could expect. Fellini was hidden someplace over our head, but where, exactly? Would he help us find the way?

The most direct way to stealthily get to the morgue was the

service elevator used to carry the corpses, but we had a hard time locating it. We walked in single file, strewn along the endless corridors, looking like a bunch of lost souls on their way down to the Avernus. We finally caught sight of an odd-job man in the distance and we immediately approached him.

"Follow the red arrow, that will take you to the outside," he directed us, vaguely suspicious.

None of us had the boldness to ask him about our original destination, which made us lost in the first place. We meekly followed his directions and regained the exit somewhat relieved, even though we were not willing to admit it. The wizard did not let us violate his last cell. Perhaps we were simply unworthy.

Pictures of Fellini flooded the TV screens all day long, on all channels. Montages of interviews, vintage special reports, movies, film clips, tributes, and the Oscar ceremony played over and over as a leave-taking.

As to the commercial TV stations, *Retequattro* quickly arranged a Fellini film-marathon, with the words *Ciao Federico* superimposed on the images. Every fifteen minutes, his films were interrupted with endless commercial breaks: the law of the jungle still prevailed.

Angelica called me from Athens, sobbing. She was upset about a dream that she had "seen" the night before: that was the exact wording she used in her native language.

In her dream, she was making love with me, in a place that looked like an agonistic arena, an open-air amphitheater. The tiers of seats were packed with spectators, who accompanied our sexual encounter by following a pre-arranged choreography, as if they were an integral part of the show. Fellini was all around the scene. She felt that his presence was real, albeit incorporeal. As our intercourse went on, my penis grew smaller and smaller, and her vagina started bleeding, so much so that her blood soon flooded the soil beneath us and then the whole arena.

"I'm coming to see you at the hospital, at the Policlinic," she told him at that point.

"I'm not there anymore," he replied. "You know where to find me."

Angelica had "seen" her dream Sunday night, at the time when Federico was departing this life.

November 1 was a Monday. Viale del Policlinico was covered with a flaming red carpet of leaves. The sky was solid gray, with a thick layer of clouds. Contrary to the reports in various newspapers, no one was allowed to see Federico at the morgue.

His coffin had already been sealed, anyway. None of us would get to see him one last time.

His body was laid in state here in Cinecittà, at Studio 5. Where else?

The sky backdrop with the hanging clouds is the same one used for *Interview.* That was the scene where the two painters sit on their suspended scaffolds, and they alternate weary brush-strokes with scurrilous contumelies. Antonello took care of the set design. Do you like it?

The delicate limbo-like hues, ranging from the light blue of the draperies and the passementerie to the gray of the floor carpeting, are both appropriate and suggestive. The remaining space is left empty, unadorned like a cathedral nave. Ambulance and first aid services have been planned so as to minimize possible problems deriving from a massive participation of people. For safety's sake, two separate entrances have been set up, one for the authorities, the politicians, and their bodyguards; the other one for friends, aides, and colleagues: his longtime work companions.

His most affectionate assistant director willingly took care of it. Trying not to forget anybody, he jotted down a list of names of all the people, who, out of respect ought to be placed at the coffin's side, next to press area.

The lighting design is by the photography director of Federico's last films. He created a Mithraeum like whiteness spreading down from the trusses, enhanced by the sky-expanse. The beams of two mobile projectors placed on top of the towers intersect over the coffin, creating a dramatic effect that in theatrical jargon is called "cross-eyed lights": it is the radiant halo used to welcome the artist on stage.

The coffin–Oscar reminisces–arrived from the Policlinic shortly after midnight. Problems arose when they tried hoisting it on the stand: they miscalculated the length of the supports: they were too short, uneven, and unstable. It was like a gag directed by Fellini himself: a wobbly circus act, a clown-like entrance greeted by clapping and catcalls. They fixed the problem, however, and then everything went smoothly.

Adriana, the dressing-rooms custodian, armed herself with thread and needle and sat down to sew a golden fringe to the blue velvet drape. After so many years of attending to the Maestro, her tranquil expression made you think that she was simply performing her usual job.

The canons from the basilica that had accompanied the coffin left. In the huge theater there was just a few of us, sleepless and restless.

Nobody felt like leaving. Stefania, Milenda, Lorena, Giannella, Florita, Marvisio.... We set up shifts to cover the first night of wake, but the thought of abiding by them never crossed our minds!

Elena arrived in the heart of the night, sobbing, and she asked to join us. She crouched beside the coffin and leant her forehead against the wood: we tried to make her move away but it was impossible to deter her.

Unable to stay in bed any longer, at four o'clock in the morning Rinaldo decided to come to the theater. With a black blindfold covering his eye, he looked like John Ford. He was dressed to the nines, wearing a corduroy suit, and sporting an eccentric bow tie and a mackintosh; he also carried a rolled up umbrella to use as a cane, like an old English gentleman. He brought a big leather-bound album, with rice-paper pages, for collecting signatures. He wanted it to replace those provided by the basilicas' funeral services, which were too plain looking.

The big book looked like a missal. It was so imposing that none of us dared sully the immaculate first page with a comment or a signature. We wanted Rinaldo to be the one to christen it with a phrase, a sketch. The painter dallied with the idea, then all of a sudden he pulled a pen out of his breast pocket and, while standing, with a few strokes, like a magician, he sketched a portrait of Fellini as a young man before our astonished gaze. Two big embers in place of his wide, magnetic eyes, his hat pushed back, and a scarf wrapped around his neck. Underneath it, he penned his dedication:

July 1939, four croquettes. Do you remember?
Rinaldino

And he burst into tears.

In those few words he fully described their fateful first meeting. Still unknown to each other, they were standing in front of a deli's window, famished and cold. They found a common cause right away. Looking in their pockets, they scraped together enough change to buy those four croquettes. The two of them had been inseparable since then.

I found it quite peculiar that their teeth were chattering with cold in July. But I also found it unnecessary to question that story, because that is how Federico related it to me. He conjured from memory that Charlot-like scene, which unfolded exactly as he would have filmed it, if only that story could have found its little niche in his fictional art.

Perhaps it could have found its little niche also in his *Block-Notes* project, a series of freeform stories modeled after Simenon's *Dictée,* a work that Federico kept reading over and over again, in the original French version, and that he greatly admired.

Following Rinaldo's lead, we all signed the book, almost joyously. All of a sudden, a lighter mood emerged, quite similar to the playful atmosphere that Federico was able to create.

The coffee jugs started being passed around, along with the warm croissants, pastries, and cakes brought by the owners of the *Osteria del Curato.* Monique held tightly in her hand a lively colored mechanical bird, which chirped at the slightest touch. She hid it inside the pillow of red roses resting on the coffin. When they removed the coffin from its stand, the quivering would set off the goldfinch's shrill call. The bird would still be there if the guards had not found it and flushed it out.

During all that time, Elena kept clinging to the coffin, numb and shivering from the cold. "You know, I'm a little ashamed to confess this. . .," Rinaldi says, shielding himself. "But by now I'm sure you've got the general picture, and I can't hide anything from you about my altered state. When the others went to the dressing rooms upstairs to freshen up, I went up to her. I sat on the platform, next to the bier, and with the excuse of warming her up I held her in my arms. Instead it was she who set me on fire. She offered me her lips, which, withered by her pain and tears, appeared to have lost their firmness. They felt like grape skins, but were hot nonetheless. She calmed her sobs in that kiss and I didn't know how to withdraw from her embrace. Her eyelids sealed down, and her already pale face went as white as alabaster.

I don't think that the others noticed it; they didn't see the absurd excitement that grabbed hold of us. My heart pounded with indecent delight. It was like tasting her again, still warm from our previous encounter. What kind of perversion was that? I didn't know her, she didn't belong to me, I swear. It was like being possessed: that was true for the both of us.

Only once was I was able to break her away from the coffin. As uncontrollable shivers went over her body, I lifted her up so that she could go upstairs and drink something warm, a coffee or a milk. Reluctantly, she let herself be drawn away. Perhaps because of the chill in her bones, or perhaps because she just remembered what was in her mind when I interrupted her thoughts earlier, she told me about a Danish down comforter that she had bought for her and Federico. She described how the two of them lay down on the carpet, on their improvised alcove made of couch pillows, and embracing each other they enjoyed its warmth. "Who knows who's got it now!" she grieved.

She is right, that warmth belongs to her and to no one else.

By then it was six in the morning: the rain seemed to taper off for a while.

The gates opened at nine. The first blue government cars with their contingent of escort cars arrived, followed by the photographers and the early-bird visitors.

The intimate wake morphed into a crowd bath.

Chapter XIII

Portents

Oscar's story remains unfinished.

Else Jacobsen and various other people come looking for him, and so he says goodbye:

"See you tomorrow at the church," he adds vaguely

The tone of his voice seems to suggest that our conversation might not be over yet. His story is only suspended; his confessions will resume. Or perhaps I simply hope that to be the case, so infatuated am I with his morbid tale.

The next day, at the funeral service in Piazza Esedra, I see him from afar. He's with Else and the mythical Angelica, the Greek actress.

Since I am late, it is unthinkable for me to try and go inside the basilica. The square has been packed with people for hours: just pushing my way through the crowd to get to the portal would be impossible

Going around the barriers, I somehow manage to move closer to the side. When the coffin appears, carried out of the church by a handful of Federico's friends, like the surrounding throng I, too, am moved: I raise my arms and start applauding.

Someone holds a white polystyrene heart-shaped banner over the crowd, with inside "FEDERICO YOU ARE GREAT" written in red. Someone else holds a simple "THANK YOU" sign. Authorities and celebrities swarm out of the church, between two wings of crowds throbbing with curiosity, and they go to meet the small TV crews ready to pick up their comments. After the throng thins out, moving against the current I finally manage to get inside the basilica. The immense hall, built out of the ancient Baths of Diocletian, is normally free from furnishings. But now cluttered as it is with pews, chairs, wreaths, and garlands, it looks unrecognizable. It is a magnificent grand hall, teeming with voices, imbued with incense. I am enveloped by the sweetish smell of dying flowers, which remains unchanged in my memory since I was a child, when I visited the graveyard on All Souls' Day. I walk through the imposing nave. I go almost all the way to the high altar, and I sit on a prie-dieu left unoccupied. The propitiatory rite for that last farewell to Federico apparently has not been exhausted. His many devotees still linger, tearing flowers from the plush leafy pillows and wreaths lined up all along the walls. Standing in single file, waiting to leave, they all pick up a blossom to keep as a memento. A white Barberton daisy stands out among the green leaves, catching my eye. Someone has yet to choose it. I cherish the hope that it might be there for me. In fact, the solitary flower survives, miraculously untouched.

I cross myself with holy water, and I head out. The scaled golden vault of the Byzantine temple melds with the sky outside. A nervous sirocco runs through the spring-like air. Sprawled in their lewd postures, the Naiads in the fountain delight themselves with the water spurts, exhibiting their lust-provoking naked bodies, beaded with shiny drops.

I see again Oscar with Angelica and his circle of girlfriends: Giannella, Stefania, Lorena, and Milenda. The Norwegian neurologist is also part of the group. They all stand under the Exedra portico, held together by a mysterious force that prevents them from taking leave.

Oscar, however, must hurry away. He's expected at the works on Via Tuscolana for a final check on the new print of a Fellini film, the last one left to be shipped to America. And so he invites his girlfriends to accompany him. They all accept his invitation, including Else. As he starts walking to his car, they follow him in his retinue. I'm curious to find out how he will manage to squeeze them all in, so I follow him too.

"If the police stop you and confiscate your driving license, we'll drive" they warble, getting all excited.

I don't see Federico's face among them, but he is there, I am sure of it. Oscar must have contaminated my mind with his insidious fluids. But I know I'm right.

A whole month goes by. At the end of November, I decide to pay a visit to Giulietta, who now stays at a private clinic on via Pineta Sacchetti.

I have been told that her room is on the second floor. I wander about haphazardly, until I finally see a nursing station and a group of nurses crammed together behind the glass. They tell me to wait. One of them reluctantly leaves the group, and in a few minutes Mariolina, the actress' sister shows up. In the brief span we spent exchanging the usual polite remarks, Giulietta had the time to wear the turban with which she hides her baldness. I hug and kiss her. Sobbing she clings to me, and her thin fingers get entangled in my jacket collar. She brings to mind the distressing image of a tiny bird with its wings broken. During the night, she fell from the bed, and tumbling to the floor she cracked a rib. She is dismayed at seeing that harrowing streak of bad luck. As soon as we disengage ourselves from our embrace, Giulietta removes her vexing headgear, thus revealing a tiny bald skull, which gives her the incorporeal look of a frightened extraterrestrial. I help her sit up. She leans against the pillows, then she lights up a cigarette and starts sucking on it as eagerly as an infant suckling at her mother's nipple. Her only contact with life seems to lie in the smoke that she inhales into her lungs. Other than that, her aghast eyes are drowned in agony.

When I leave, Mariolina escorts me down the corridor and then to the elevator. She did expend her energies to help her sister for months on end, and now she is worn-out beyond description. She's a nervous wreck, and she always looks like she is just about to burst into tears. Mariolina, too, is an inveterate smoker, and when she coughs she produces the same wheezing and hollow sound as her sister. She wishes to give vent to her grief. Giulietta is no longer self-sufficient. Even though her brain tumor has stopped growing, at least for now, the lesion has reached her cerebellum: she must be cared for all the time.

On my way out from the clinic I run into Rinaldi, who is just arriving. I have not seen him since the day of the funeral. He, too, is there to see Giulietta, whose days apparently are numbered.

He seems very upbeat. He is just back from Milan where he

met with his publisher to discuss the revision of his novel and set the delivery date. He is living this lucky turn of events with special intensity.

"When can we get together?" he asks hurriedly. "Are you free for dinner?"

There is still something vital that he wishes to tell me. By now I am his confidant, the only one who might not mistake him for a lunatic. I gladly accept. I am as eager to find out the latest developments as he is to narrate them.

Outside it is starting to rain: it is a freezing drizzle almost changing to sleet. Some streets already shine with Christmas lights and are decorated with vanes and festoons.

At the *trattoria* in Prati where we agreed to meet, the air is fragrant with good smells, and the atmosphere is warm and friendly thanks to the extremely kind waiters. Despite my distressing visit to Giulietta, I find it easy to regain my good mood, and Oscar definitely helps life reclaim its rightful place.

Oscar resumes his narration. "As you may remember, that day, November 2, when we met at Studio 5 and I confided to you about Federico and me, only Else Jacobsen was present. Angelica had yet to arrive. Her resolve was such that she decided to attend the funeral, even if it meant deserting the film set once again. The film producers threatened her with repercussions, but she did not care.

The rain poured down incessantly all night long. I left the theater when it was still dark outside. While I was driving on the Appia Antica, I came under such a heavy shower that the wipers could barely clear the rain off the windshield. It really looked like a cataract of tears, an inconsolable weeping.

Else came home with me. As soon as we arrived at my place, after she took a hot shower to take the chill off her bones, she curled up under the comforter and fell asleep immediately. When I joined her in bed, she pressed her body against mine, wanting my embrace despite her torpor. While half-asleep, she kept caressing me, until she had me completely.

Sleep swept over us while we still were breathless.

The phone rang at dawn, sounding like an explosion in my

brain: it was Angelica, calling from the airport.

"Should I come by your place, or should I go directly to the church?"

I did not know what to tell her. She absolutely wanted to arrive early enough to get in and find a place at a pew. She didn't want to be left outside, among the anonymous crowd. Then she sensed that I was not alone. She asked me to repeat the names of the basilica and the square several times.

"I'll get a cab. I'll see you there: do look for me!"

After the funeral, she joined the other girls to go the filmworks. Verzini, the pressman, was not there. He was suddenly taken sick with the flu. There was, however, his daughter Ambrina waiting for us. The "beautiful Ambrina," as Federico would call her, was sheathed in a shiny pair of silky pants. That small crowd invading the little projection room did not surprise her in the least. Actually, she banded together with us: she offered coffee and ordered to have it delivered. Swept along in the general euphoria, she even decided to sit with us, as if we were at the movies.

"I'll keep you company: I've never seen it anyway."

On the program was *Variety Lights,* the first film directed by Fellini, pairing with Alberto Lattuada.

The lights were turned off, and we plunged ourselves into that collective dream, guided by Federico. With "his" peerless faces, Peppino De Filippo, Carla del Poggio, Giulietta Masina, Carletto Romano, he drew us into a life-restoring fun, he enveloped us in its serene and contagious joy.

The black and white print was wonderful, impeccably restored, ready to join the others for the New York retrospective. The audiences across the ocean would have the good fortune to rediscover a giant of cinema!

I was happy with the reprints. I suddenly realized that the passion I poured into that work out of respect for Federico was actually meant for all the people who loved him, for that seemingly endless and silent crowd who for a whole day paid homage to his coffin. It was meant for his vast audience all over the world, who was going to have a unique, not-to-be-missed opportunity to celebrate his films in ideal conditions, on a big screen at a true movie theater.

When the projection ended and the group disbanded, not having any plans for the night, Angelica coasted to my place as if she were bound to a temporary mooring. We sank on the couch and started watching the tape of the funeral broadcast live on RAI earlier that morning.

Revisiting those images through the panoramic but sharp eye of the camera was deeply unsettling for her. Being the actress that she was, the full screen shots of her dazzling figure in the pews especially intrigued her. With her black sunglasses, her light make-up that dramatized her paleness, she looked incredibly sensual, a metareal incarnation on a level with Anita Ekberg in *La Dolce Vita.* Every time the camera returned to her provoking queenly figure, I stopped the tape and rewound it, watching it two, three, four times, so as to satisfy her vanity and rekindle it at the same time. In the row of kneelers behind her was Michelangelo Antonioni, with his lean face in which one could read a transparent, unstoppable emotion. Angelica absorbed every moment of the funeral rites, watching them with fearful concentration like a little schoolgirl. In the meanwhile, she was starting to lose the unjustified slight grudge that she held against me. She still had on the clothes that she was wearing at the funeral. A longuette skirt with long slit on the front, which teasingly revealed her long legs up to the groin when she was sitting; black semi-sheer stockings, which enhanced her tall and graceful figure; naughty Belle Époque shoes, ankle high, with cylinder type heels.

However, something troubled the beautiful Angelica: I could feel it. It was as if she was scrutinizing herself, searching her soul for what eluded her. While slumped on the couch, she welcomed my head on her shoulder, but she granted me no more than sporadic, idle kisses on my hair or forehead. All that relaxation made me fall asleep. I roused myself from my torpor towards the end of the recording, when Father Angelo Arpa, Fellini's Jesuit friend, wearing ecclesiastical paraments, approached the pew where the grieving relatives were to whisper consoling words. That image was immediately followed by Giulietta's heartbreaking gesture. When the coffin was being carried out, she lifted her arm with all her residual energies, her rosary loosely wrapped around her fingers, to say goodbye to her spouse.

Did it happen then or did it happen before?

The brush of Angelica's body against mine provoked in me an unexpected arousal. My excitement was so evident that when she noticed it, she looked at me with reproach and surprise. Nonetheless, she sluggishly came over to assay how impudent I was. My indecent reaction proved to be infectious. Going from feigned rebuke to sincere action, she bent at once over me. The sunburst of her flowing wavy hair spread on my lap, and she set herself to work with zealous skill. I could feel a ravenous lust, a maelstrom of passion and life; but I also savored uneasiness, a bitter taste from yielding to that degrading pleasure, to that barren enjoyment.

All this while those mournful images, so garish, sharp, and solemn were still filling the TV screen: the stern ceremonial gestures; the priest's chant; the cloudy faces and the tear-reddened eyes of the public in the pews; the utterly dismayed look of Federico's closest friends. And that coffin with him inside (but was he really there?) covered with flowers; and the two of us (but was it really "us?") scandalously "messing around" (Federico himself would have used that expression), maneuvered by Stromboli, the irreverent and skillful puppeteer.

Angelica was absorbed completely in her task, which she performed fervently; and yet, I must confess that I did not feel her to be my lover at all. Once again, I had the clear sensation that I was acting by proxy, that I was alienating my own nerves and blood.

Our intercourse ended there, exhausted in that act, with no need to rekindle our love-game. Out of the blue, she told me that she was indisposed and that she was bleeding copiously. Her enchanting pale face, her bluish circles under her eyes gave her a languishing, lunar look.

The dream that she had "seen" the night before Fellini's death came back to haunt her through a series of visible signs: my penis becoming smaller and smaller, and her blood flooding the whole arena.

Angelica and I spent the rest of the evening talking and dreaming. She would have liked staging a play in Greece, in which she interpreted the many female characters that were created by Fellini: Anitona, Cabiria, Gelsomina, and Gradisca. She burdened herself with expectations, fancying herself as Federico's Hellenic muse, his ambassador in the land of Myths. She left the next morning to return to Greece.

Fellini's funerals could now be considered really over. To the journalists he gave fifteen days worth of news. To the public the premiere of his film that he would never shoot. And to me the love of his women, so impalpable that it was all but vanished.

"Is the dream over?" I ask stubbornly, not satisfied yet.

"I don't know," he explains. "Unusual events are still happening to me, and I have trouble interpreting them myself. For those who believe in such things, they are fortuitous coincidences, carefully engineered. Personally, I believe in subterranean communication, in sacred signs from the beyond, in brain waves. And in free imagination. I have never felt so close to portents since he died.

A few days ago, I was driving home late at night, when I saw the Circo Massimo cloaked by fog. It was as if a light steam was rising from that immense bowl. For some mysterious magic, only a few ethereal slender trees emerged from the white cloud hovering under the clear and starry sky. It was a powerful theatrical effect. A fantastic vision, quite similar to the vapor hovering over the near and distant fields that I saw from the train, when I went to visit Federico at Ferrara's hospital. A gray merging of mist and sky, a world frayed into cotton wool, into blurred outlines that became more and more tenuous towards the milky horizon, which was instead still and dense like a film backdrop.

I stopped the car and stepped out on the grassy edge of that millenary stadium.

Sometimes, when I sleep alone, especially in the still of night I experience auditory hallucinations. I pick up fragments of voices floating in the ether. In that place, at that time, the illusion was corporeal: I felt as if someone was holding my arm. No one was near me, however. A sacred fear came on me.

"Don't leave: stay with me," I whispered on impulse, addressing that incorporeal presence that was asking for attention. If only it could hear me.

There are signs, ectoplasms, impalpable bequests concealed in the creases of a veil, to be discovered by those who know how to find them.

I don't know if that was his last gift.... Days ago I was in Milan. I had to work out a few details regarding the publication of my novel, which was about ready to hit the bookstores. During his stay at the hospital in Zurich, several times Federico talked about an attractive mulatto girl who worked there as a nurse. She was the one in charge of the phone: she would stand on the threshold while he was talking, making sure that he did not exceed his allotted time and did not get too tired.

If you remember, I once mentioned to you that her beauty awed Federico, so much so that he described her to me with his usual fiery enthusiasm and extolled her likeness with verbal fireworks. Since the girl dreamed to be an actress, he invited her to send him her pictures to his studio address in Rome, and he promised to summon her at the earliest opportunity.

Given what happened afterwards, all projects fell through. However, I came upon her pictures by chance. They had her name written on the back: Isis, like the Egyptian goddess. I studied them closely, trying to piece Federico's description together by looking at her features:

"To see her is to suddenly discover the elusive attributes of femininity," he said excitedly. "You're held there, enchanted and grateful. It's like an epiphany: the shapeliness of the lips, the harmony of the ears, the delicacy of the cheekbones, the brightness of the eyes. It's like plunging back to the origin of creation. You find yourself in front of the first woman, and she's there for you to admire. And you realize: That's what skin must look like! The fashion of her arms, her neck, her nape, her eyelashes are nothing short of astonishing! She's the exact archetype of female charm."

Since then, the girl had moved from Zurich to Milan to take a try at a career as a model. I gave her a call to return her pictures. I arranged a convenient time and place, so that I could see her in between my work engagement and my flight back to Rome. I went straight from the publishing house to her apartment, which was somewhere around Viale Lodi. Her place looked like a pied-à-terre turned into a photographer's studio. As she opened the door, a young enchanting queen appeared before my eyes. With brazen spontaneity, she pointed out that her breasts were now rounder than they appeared in the pictures, thanks to a surgical touch-up imposed by her agent. She seemed proud of it, and amused as well: she unbuttoned her shirt and watched my face for a sign of approval. To show my unconditional subjection, I bowed and kissed the birthmark standing out on that round forbidden fruit. I was guided by a blind impulse, by an irrepressible desire, but she seemed neither surprised nor indignant in the least: my homage was expected–inevitable, I should say–being part of a prearranged design.

She, too, was scheduled to leave for Rome, where she was expected the next day for a screen test. We were on the same evening flight. And so we could share a cab to the airport!

Isis showed up right on time at the residence lobby where I was waiting for her. She was wearing a suede leather coat with fur trim. She advanced majestically in her ankle-high boots, with the elegance of an African goddess. She had a pretty flat nose, and tiny ears, like a lioness.

Her body was that of a Creole: she had strong and slender thighs, like those of a gazelle; supple and luscious glutei; and incredibly protruding breasts. I looked admiringly at her slender hands, at her delicate nape that her short hair left uncovered, at her uniform complexion, as smooth as satin, that only dark races can boast. It was a vision, a fine arabesque that Fellini had described with astonishing precision: another illusion of his, no doubt.

And so we rode to Linate. By tacit understanding, we sat very closely on the taxi back seat, made intimate by the complicitous dusk. Once we were at the airport, past the metal detector, in search of some privacy we chose a secluded spot in the vast hall near the window. Isis took off her coat. Under it she wore a cashmere waistcoat left unbuttoned, beneath which was a white, semi-transparent sleeveless body suit, with a low neckline that emphasized her bursting breast. I placed one arm affectionately around her shoulders, and I slipped my fingers under the wide armhole, reaching for her turgid breast flesh and hardened nipple, and then I lingered there, unashamed. Seemingly indifferent to what I was doing, she did not react or shirk me. But I knew that she was moved: I could see it from her mouth, from her parting moist lips. So encouraged, I moved my lips to hers, barely grazing them.

"You make me shiver: you cannot touch me like that," she said in a serious tone, warding me off like a sensible little schoolgirl. Her words, however, clearly collided with her temptation to give in.

Trying to stem the surging tide of desire, we stood up: from bad to worse! Our temptation grew beyond measure! I drew her close with no more qualms. The little taste I had of her curvaceous body had whetted so much my appetite that I could not quench my craving! I even sneaked my hands under her skin-tight body-suit, going for her silky naked tits.

She obligingly reciprocated with her supple body, by gently swaying her underpants-clad pelvis. Alas! That public place was an insurmountable obstacle: our prelude to bliss would not have a follow-up! To allay the torment, we decided to go to the bar. At the precise moment we entered the food court area, there was a sudden break in the stream of music coming from the wire broadcast: it was a moment of suspension, of void. Within a few seconds, there sounded the unmistakable second movement of *La Dolce Vita,* with its hopping, oneiric melody. Out of an endless repertoire to draw from, somehow they decided to broadcast that unique and yet universal theme, right then and there, with perfect synchronicity. The tune had no relationship whatsoever with the previous or following one, it had no possible connection to other soundtrack melodies or other Nino Rota's compositions. The most famous music from the most famous Fellini film was conjured for us, out of nothing, by an arcane, magic coincidence.

Federico was with us. For a brief moment, I even thought that I could feel his material presence, his voice, his smile, even the familiar touch of his hand caressing my hair: a long shiver ran down my spine.

Isis and I gazed at each other. She gave me a strangely intense, questioning look, as if with new eyes. I am sure that she did not recognize that tune: she was too young to know it. And she could not possibly realize what it meant for me. In any case, she did not know that much about me to fully understand the portent, the innermost reason that made me startle. And yet, she was startled as well.

"What was that? A ghost?" she whispered.

Translating Federico F.

I too am untranslatable.
Walt Whitman, "Song of Myself"

Gianfranco Angelucci's *Federico F.* is a semi-fictional novel that chronicles the last nine months of Italian film director Federico Fellini's life, from January 1993, when he received his fifth Oscar– a lifetime achievement award–to October of the same year, when he died of a brain stroke.

Angelucci was Fellini's assistant and personal friend for over twenty years– twenty-eight, to be precise–during which time he worked alongside him in various capacities, foremost as his screenwriter. In 1987 the two co-authored the screenplay for *Intervista,* a film on Fellini's cinematic art. Angelucci is also the editor of various publications on Fellini's works, among them *Amarcord, Casanova, And the Ship Sails On, Ginger and Fred,* plus a photo-book on *La Dolce Vita* and another one on Fellini's entire opus titled *Un Regista a Cinecittà.* As a TV director and producer, Angelucci authored a two-episode homage to Fellini, each segment respectively titled *Fellini nel Cestino* and *I Protagonisti di Fellini.* In 1985 he filmed the ballet *La Strada* set to the music of Nino Rota, the author of the most memorable Fellini soundtracks. In 1993, he saw to the restoration of Fellini's entire film production. After the director's death, he took charge of the Fellini Foundation in Rimini. In short, by reading his biography alone, we get the sense that Angelucci's professional and personal life was strictly intertwined with that of the Maestro, as he deferentially refers to him in his novel. He slowly became Fellini's alter ego in real life, in the same way actor Marcello Mastroianni was his alter ego on the screen.

Angelucci does incorporate this notion of shared identity into his *Federico F.* at both the thematic and structural levels. The book is built on overlapping and confused narrative planes. The adjective "confused" is used here in the Latin etymological sense of the word–*confusus,* mixed together or fused together. The plot develops through a threefold diegetic frame, as a set of Chinese boxes. The outer frame is the story told by an anonymous narrator, an acquaintance of Fellini, in which we can clearly recognize Angelucci as the fictional writer. The middle frame is the story told to the narrator by a young apprentice named Oscar, another thin disguise for Angelucci as the scriptwriter/assistant director. In fact, the character's full name, Oscar Rinaldi, evokes a fusion of literature and cinema–Oscar epitomizing Hollywood and the film industry, Rinaldi being evocative of Rinaldo, a character from Tasso's *Gerusalemme liberata* related to Ariosto's Ruggiero. Finally, the novel's diegetic inner frame is made of the events from the life of Oscar, whose identity is partly fused with that of the Maestro, in that some of his actions are a projection of Fellini's will. The director's influence on him becomes more and more apparent, so much so that Oscar can be labeled Fellini's mental and physical extension.

The theme of shared identity is addressed early on in the novel, in a passage where the anonymous narrator describes the puzzling relationship that develops between Fellini and his ghostwriter Oscar. The passage is worth quoting here at length, given its centrality in the general economy of the novel and of the present discussion:

"I knew that Oscar Rinaldi had been at Fellini's side through his entire illness, until his very last hours. In fact, he had been at his side for decades, mostly as a friend, but also as an aide and scriptwriter. He helped Fellini draft a few screenplays, and he was always the first one with whom he would discuss a new idea for a movie, a subject, a film treatment. In time, Oscar became the ghost of Fellini, his ghostwriter, a sort of writing alter ego, a logographer, as he gleefully used to describe himself:

'I write what they ask me to write, in whatever form they prefer.' [. . .] The two of them played hide and seek through their writings, to the extent that it became quite a challenge to distinguish them apart. Federico was constantly overwhelmed with all kinds of requests: interviews, speeches, prefaces, and statements. If there had not been someone to help him, he would have spent all day just replying to the thousands of solicitations that came to him from all over the world. He got along well with Oscar. He treated him like a son, or maybe like a younger brother, a pupil, even though he never wanted to consider himself the master of anyone. Nonetheless, in a veiled way Oscar could evoke the figure of an apprentice wizard.

The film director had sincere affection for him; their relationship was based on congeniality and respect, but above all on close familiarity [. . .]. He and Oscar shared an intangible complicity, a peculiar affinity that was quite easy to discern. Leaving aside the great gap in age, differences between them were minimal. At any rate, if one of them could be considered an eternal adolescent, it was Federico. Oscar was not a kid anymore, either. In the end, even their human, personal experiences came to resemble each other. They say that when two people spend a lot of time together they grow more and more similar, or at least that is the general impression."

Within the main theme of identity exchange lies the sub-motif of creation and restoration. Like author Angelucci also the fictional character of Oscar sees to the reprint of all Fellini films for an imminent New York retrospective. In his appointed capacity of restorer, Angelucci/Oscar acts as the Maestro's proxy. As the novel suggests, Fellini is ambivalent about the restoration of his opus. While showing interest in the technical details of the restorative process, he wryly relinquishes the task to Oscar. Fellini's attitude stems from his real-life conviction that he must avoid lingering on his past work lest he should be encapsulated by it. Consonant with his belief, Fellini refused to see his films after their official release and was averse to discussing them from a critical standpoint. In those few instances when he conceded talking to interviewers about his work, his comments proved to be rather elusive and misleading. Even more disconcerting was his tendency to distort facts about his personal life, like his fictitious juvenile escape from home to join the circus, which became part of his hagiographic biography. Going against the grain, Angelucci questions the canonical view of Fellini "a born liar"–to paraphrase the title of Damian Pettigrew's recent documentary on the director. He instead suggests that Fellini loved to create very complex edifices of partial truths, of "secrets on top of more secrets."

Angelucci's novel reveals how creatively Fellini treated personal events, as if they were screenplay ideas to be developed. He reworked facts through the prism of memory, laying more importance on their emotion than their factuality. His creative slant is illustrated by the "croquette" episode, which sees Fellini and his newly found friend Rinaldino shivering in front of a deli shop, an unlikely occurrence since it takes place during the summer heat. As Oscar aptly points out, what counts is not the accuracy of the story but its artistic essence: "I found it quite peculiar that their teeth were chattering with cold in July. But I also found it unnecessary to question that story, because that is how Federico related it to me. He conjured from memory that Charlot-like scene, which unfolded exactly as he would have filmed it. . . ." From this and other episodes, it appears that Fellini recorded reality as if it were a semiotic flow. In other words, as Angelucci says through Oscar, it is not so much a case of Fellini creating a willful lie but rather of recreating reality according to his cinematic vision, of translating events into personalized memories, and memories into films.

Angelucci's novel features several reflections by Fellini on his work, all of them proving that the director considered his films as personal creations, coalitions of external facts and private memories harmonized through his imagination. The identification of an author with his/her work is clearly perceivable in literature, especially in poetry. In Yeats' words, a poem is "an infinite concentration of the personality." Robert Bly goes even further by stating that a poem is an incarnation of the poet's substance and therefore no different from his skin or his hands. Fellini claimed the same rights to his films, which were made of such a personal substance that he totally identified with them: "I am my films," is one of his most famous remarks. Yet, as Angelucci reveals through Oscar, that mirroring of the creator into his creation ended with the editing process. After the release of a film's final cut, Fellini severed his ties with the actual physical product and never confronted with it as an external viewer. An exchange between Fellini and Oscar is particularly enlightening in this regard. The night Oscar suggests that they go and see the restored version of *La Dolce Vita,* the director balks at the idea: "I wouldn't dream of it!" he says. "We could go in when the movie has already started, no one will see *you.* . . ." Oscar replies, thinking his refusal might be caused simply by his desire to shun publicity. "But *I* don't want to see myself," is Fellini's sharply remark. The rebuke indicates his loath to see himself in the theater and his own image on the screen. Obviously, we are not referring here to his filmed countenance but to the objective correlative of his emotions, those concept-images that we have come to recognize as unmistakably Felliniesque. A few of them are featured in this novel: the sudden storm followed by torrential rain; the columns of cars at a standstill in chaotic traffic; the raging fire at the side of the road; the oversized breast of voluptuous women, etc. These trademark images with which Angelucci intersperses his narrative are the same images that roll before Oscar's mesmerized eyes while he screens the restored prints. These images *are* Fellini, they mirror his identity, but it is an identity frozen in time, a simulacrum of his being. Thus, while appreciative of Oscar's restorative effort, Fellini abhors facing his old self, albeit showcased in a new luminous print.

The identity transfer of creator to creation performs another important metaphorical function in the novel, as can be inferred from the ensuing passage in which Oscar describes his work on the negatives while struggling to finish the project on deadline. "Time was getting short, and new problems kept popping up at every turn. The original negatives of some of his first films had crystallized and needed meticulous restorative work, which had to be done by hand, frame by frame. The negatives of more recent films like *Amarcord* were so worn out that they could not withstand any more printing or regenerating, and could only be saved through a delicate process that was extremely expensive and time-consuming." The decay of the celluloid prints is to be read as a trope for the director's physical ruin. The meticulous loving care that Oscar pours into salvaging Fellini's brittle opus parallels the efforts by the doctors to halt the decline of his waning body. The fusion of the physical and the artistic suggested in the passage quoted above mirrors Fellini's actual view of creation. To him, in fact, there existed no clear-cut separation between abstract thought and physical matter. The reference in the novel to the theories of American neuroscientist Wilder Penfield, who posited the existence in man of an imaginative brain capable of generating limbs, is not accidental. Similarly, to Fellini there was no clear-cut separation between eroticism and creation. As Angelucci says through Oscar, "women were his creative magma, his placenta, his food." The creative function of the feminine is substantiated by a number of colorful comments by the director, who often remarked how to him lovemaking and filmmaking were in essence one and the same. After the stroke that deprives him of the full use of his limbs, this balanced interaction is shattered. "This son of a bitch has let me down," Fellini blurts out, railing against his body. His mind left unscathed, Fellini tries evading physical limitations by living vicariously through Oscar, the "wholesome terminal of his desire." He thus directs him, in the dual sense of the word of controlling him and guiding him as in a performance. Fellini's direction extends to a surrounding cast of women, who, as we already know from earlier films like *La Dolce Vita* and *8 1/2*, are allegorical representations of his creative power. Initially engaged in the restoration of Fellini's creative past–his filmic universe–Oscar is soon drawn into restoring Fellini's erotic present–his feminine universe. In other words, he goes from being his ghostwriter to being his ghostlover–two facets of the same prism. His encounters with Fellini's women are in essence filmic, as evidenced by Angelica's dream, in which the Greek actress and Oscar perform their sexual act in an arena before a crowd of faceless spectators.

Therefore, given its multiple nature–documentary and fantastic, literary and cinematographic–*Federico F.* can be read not only as an intimate account of Fellini's last months, but also as his final screenplay relayed to us by his alter ego Oscar/Angelucci. The staging sets of this unrealized film are Rimini and Rome, eminent places of Fellini's real life, and Ferrara, described here as the ultimate locus of fiction. "In Ferrara," says Oscar, "life pulse seems to slow down, time stops ticking; the palaces, the walls, the streets, the old houses, the aristocratic architecture of the courts . . . all concur to create the illusion of a city with foundations at midair. A city built on metaphysical abstraction, on psychic creation. To know that Ariosto once lived there makes you think that Ferrara is a borough born out of his imagination, materialized through a powerful alchemy, like the enchanted castle where Merlin allured knights and ladies to make his beloved Ruggiero stay." Angelucci here intimates Fellini to be Merlin reborn. Like him, he would resort to the arcane in guiding people's behavior. After his debilitating stroke, Fellini designs a map for all characters to follow, as if all they have to do is "act out an existing script." He exerts his influx on his virtual cast not through the written or the spoken word but through their subconscious, like a wizard operating by magic spells, like an alchemist combining chemical elements inducing visions.

The use by Fellini of techniques from psychoanalysis and alchemy can be traced in a number of his movies. As Angelucci reveals here for the first time, Fellini became involved with psychoanalysis while shooting *La Strada,* therefore at a much earlier time than critics generally thought. That experience spearheaded his later interest in Jung's work and the subconscious, themes to which he gave open artistic expression in *8 1/2.* The most evident illustration of the subliminal in that film comes from the character of Maurice, a telepath. In reading the mind of film director Guido, played by Fellini's alter ego Marcello Mastroianni, Maurice intuits the wordplay ASANISIMASA–a code for *anima* (AsaNIsMAsa), the Jungian feminine principle. As well known, Jungian psychology stands at the crossroads of psychology and alchemy. In unearthing ancient alchemy texts, Jung discovered evidence of a link between unconscious and alchemical symbols, and between chemical and mental processes. He found that those two distant arts, psychology and alchemy, shared the common goal of harmonizing the opposites and producing unity from fractured parts. These aspects of Jungian psychology are important in deciphering the final episode in *Federico F.* Committed till the very end to play the role they have been assigned, Oscar and his circle of friends embark in the quest of healing the dying director who has suffered a second stroke. They consult the *I Ching,* an ancient Taoist text also linked to Jung, who derived from it the notion of synchronicity. This he based on the randomness by which the sticks or coins used for divination connect with the diviner's mind, producing one hexagram out of sixty-four possible hexagrams. In response to the characters' query, the *I Ching* yields the hexagram 8, "UNION," with a mutating line leading to the hexagram 1, "THE CREATIVE." The group interprets the oracle as a clear invitation to come together to save Fellini's life. Led by Oscar, they go under Fellini's hospital window. There, they join hands in a circle, hoping to regenerate him with their psychic strength and to "bring a spark of light where the darkness fell." Yet, as they do so, they also invoke him "for nourishment and protection." Through a circular flow of energy, consistent with the Taoist view of the universe, the donors expect to infuse new energy into the receptor without suffering a diminution of their elán. As a matter of fact, they are enriched by him.

This episode, the last one in the novel before Fellini's death, is reminiscent of the final scene in *8 1/2*, in which all of the film characters, led by Guido/Mastroianni, join hands and parade around a circus ring. As many critics have pointed out, in Fellini's films the circular space, usually a circus-tent, performs the same symbolic function as the mandala in Jungian psychology. The ring shape that the characters form at the end of *8 1/2*, therefore, could represent the newly found unity of the Self as well as a magic locus for ritual healing. The end of Angelucci's novel performs a similar symbolic function, albeit with opposite results. Whereas *8 1/2*'s joyous finale announces the director's healing and rebirth, *Federico F.*'s ending foretells his impending death. Like the celluloid copy of his beloved *Amarcord*, Fellini's body is so worn out that it cannot "withstand any more regenerating." However, a number of signs tell Oscar that Fellini's creative power may have survived him. In fact, some subconscious influence still directs Oscar to consummate a sexual act with Angelica while the images of Fellini's funeral scroll before his eyes. Other portentous events subsequent to Fellini's death suggest the same. Among them, Oscar cites his vision of the Circo Massimo shrouded in vapors, an esoteric set that evokes Fellini's presence. "For those who believe in such things, they are fortuitous coincidences . . .," says Oscar. "Personally, I believe in subterranean communication, in sacred signs from the beyond, in brain waves. And in free imagination. I have never felt so close to portents since he died." Again, Oscar's statement directs the reader toward the Jungian theory of "meaningful coincidence" or synchronicity. Equally suggestive of Jung is Oscar's mention of "free imagination," which calls to mind the notion of "active imagination." Jung conceived "active imagination" as a technique to bring to surface the subconscious through coded images and symbols. This conscious visualization of psychic phenomena had for Jung the thaumaturgic quality of unclogging the wells of one's creativity. The euphoric state experienced by Oscar, deriving from his flurry of publications and assorted successful endeavors, is witness to that. As Fellini connects with Oscar via the subconscious, he performs the same function as telepath Maurice, favoring Oscar's individuation of his own "ASANISIMASA," his own creative principle. As Oscar tries healing Fellini, Fellini heals *him* and paves the way to *his* rebirth.

The visualization of the Circo Massimo shrouded in transcendental vapors represents Oscar's newly found ability to translate the subconscious into a conscious image. In fact, the whole notion of "translation" can stand as an effective metaphor for the creative process, intended here as transference of material between realms. As Jung noted in his *Tavistock Lectures* on analytical psychology (1935), the word transference can be used in both literal and metaphoric ways. It can describe the physical conveyance of an object from a place to another as well as the shifting of one form to another. In this sense, transference and translation are synonyms. At face value, the episode that sees Oscar and his circle of friends try rejuvenating the moribund director by conveying their psychic energy to him is an illustration of physical transference. Yet, the same episode possesses metaphorical value. As we know from Oscar's statements, it is Fellini who directs his virtual cast through their subconscious. They are, therefore, at the same time senders and receivers of Fellini's own creative energy. As they invoke the other, the other evokes them. Their ambivalent status is somewhat similar to that of Pirandello's six characters, who are made of the same substance as the author's mind. They personify their author, but only in part. As Poggioli points out in his excellent essay "The Added Artificer" (1959), although identifiable with their creator, Pirandello's characters are not strictly speaking his impersonation, but rather his "transference, in the psychoanalytic meaning of the term." The same can be said for many of Angelucci's characters, who, whether fact-based or fictitious, are the embodiment of the director's thought, the visual translation of his *persona.*

Translation as metaphor can be especially useful in shedding light on Oscar's figure and role. The almost chemical bond that unites Fellini to Oscar is in fact eerily reminiscent of the intricate connection arising between a writer and his translator. As Alexander Tytler states in his famous *Essay on the Principles of Translation* (1791), the faithful interpreter "must adopt the very soul of his author, which must speak through his own organs": a fitting image to describe Oscar as the voice and spokesperson of Fellini. Similar to the bond between Fellini and Oscar, the relationship between author and translator is generally one of dependence. Regardless of how much creativity the translator infuses into his work he remains a writing alter ego; regardless of his personal talent he remains a ghostwriter, the reflected image of the original creator, the negative in the camera obscura of the author's mind. Like Oscar, he is a *logographer,* one who says, "I write what they ask me to write, in whatever form they prefer." He is one who willingly lets his creative mind be impressed by the "sorcerous light" of the other, and willingly so. Yet, as much as the translator tries to achieve identification with the original writer, the best he can hope for is a type of transposition. We are not talking here just of the impossibility of translation from a textual viewpoint, of the inability to find suitable equivalents in the target language. Angelucci himself deals with these themes in his enlightening commentary "The American Translation of *Federico F.,*" herewith published. He proves his point by mixing again the literary and the visual, borrowing metaphors from the arts. For instance, his concern that a text cannot be poured from one language to another without its spirit dying calls to mind Shelley's similar argument in "The Violet and the Crucible." What we are discussing here is rather the impossibility for the translator to reach a perfect union with his author. As much as he tries molding his style to that of the original writer, he can never attain creative sameness with him. The essence of any creator remains unique and ultimately untranslatable. Nonetheless, the translator must strive for that sameness and make room within for the other. To use a cinematic parallel, the translator must become a blank screen on which both his image and that of the original author coexist. This is very much like the condition of Oscar, and, one suspects, of Angelucci as well.

Giuseppe NATALE
Las Vegas, 2005.

The American Translation of *Federico F.*

Like all forms of artistic expression, a novel consists of how it says things rather than what it says. The "how" involves many facets: the structure of the work, its pace and internal features, and foremost its language, its lexicon, that unique blend of sounds and semantics forming its style. This is its true identity.

Italian authors like Calvino and Eco, endowed with great analytical keenness, have already provided enlightening observations about translation. Therefore, I shall not venture into theorizing. Rather, I will limit myself to talking about my substantive, emotional relationship with the English translation of my novel, *Federico F.*

I must say that in the beginning I was hesitant. I was doubtful, fearful of the translation process itself. After being subjected to such a "reconditioning," would my novel still retain its identity? Or would translation change its character, its appearance, its "physiognomy"? How can a language be poured into another one without dying away?

I know English just enough to communicate, but definitely not enough to express myself, if by "express" we mean controlling the artistic outcome in relation to the endless combinations that language offers. Yet, even in my limited knowledge of English, I could see how complex this operation actually was.

I realize that my Italian is quite elaborate, in an almost mannerist way. My luscious, sweeping literary style stems directly from the crowding of emotions. Often, I feel I have to extend these emotions into language, into a sensual savoring of words. Hence my rather turgid prose. Moreover, according to some critics, my style is mostly visual, perhaps as an effect of my other profession as a film director, i.e. as a narrator of images.

Translation is an act of molting. Therefore, I thought it to be nearly impossible for a text to shed its old skin while retaining the luminosity, the smoothness of its original complexion. Furthermore, in order to transfer, or rather to cast my phrases into another idiom, was it better to have an English native speaker as a translator? Or was the exact opposite true? By possessing a more profound knowledge of the original language, by having a natural understanding of the most impalpable aspects of the original, a native Italian translator would avoid misreading and distortions while finding a target language equivalent. If the translator is not gifted with "perfect ear"–a quality which apparently is required from orchestra directors–if he cannot recognize timbre subtlety, if he cannot identify the variations of each string and wind instrument, how can he truly assimilate the source text and transfuse it into a new sound? In other words, is it better for the conductor to be a fine score reader, able to interpret every enigma on the stave, or for him to be a skilled ensemble leader, capable of swaying the orchestra into playing my notes faithfully? For the best results, shouldn't the two become one?

Federico Fellini–since we are talking about him we may as well call upon his authority–symbolically likened language to an *otre dei venti,* the bag into which Aeolus bottled up the winds. He used to say that language is more than just a mythical repository of sounds. For each sound there exists a representation, an image that forms its subtext and is as important as the sound to its comprehension. We, the readers, without realizing it fill up that *terrain vague,* that void between registers. We do so by resorting to a network of millions of cultural synapses holding verbal communication together. The "word" has its deep roots in this millenary, ancestral soil. When we first learn how to recognize and reproduce those sounds we also make them visible, we clad them in a physical body. A physicality of which we are hardly aware, but which is clearly perceptible to the ones hearing those sounds.

This set of verbal/musical signs varies from region to region, from city to city, even from district to district, let alone from a nation or a continent to another. For this reason, despite his sincere fondness for America, Fellini never accepted the invitation to move to the United States to direct a film there. To the very end, to the very last shot he remained faithful to his beloved Studio 5 in Cinecittà. He remained faithful to his language, to his multifaceted idiom made of thousands of different inflections. I am not just talking about regional or vernacular variations, but also of subtly phenotypic expressions: changes in tone-color, music, falsettos, cadence, volume. He relied on an inexhaustible modulation of utterances, very much like the legendary tapestry of faces that composed his films.

Now, a book rests on the written page, but, as Homer's *Iliad*, the mother of all novels teaches us, the book has its roots in the oral tradition of story-telling. Those pages–sheets streaked with ink lines–possess an intimate, unique sound. This sound, like the graphic sign representing it, directs us to another sign, thus becoming richly metaphoric. In art everything is symbolic, but, in the art of writing, symbols as signifiers are susceptible to ambiguous interpretation. The artistic word, like the poetic word, is naturally polysemic and leads the reader to endless semiosis.

Here the subject would become too wide. It is not my intention to dwell on general problems that those of us working in words dolefully know only too well. I prefer to go back to the translation of my *Federico F.*, which the translator kindly sent to me in installments, for several months, a chapter at a time. Chapters that I rushed to read voraciously, fearful to see in them not my own creature–whose traits were clearly sketched out in my mind–but a deformed face; or, if not deformed, a face altered by an inappropriate *make up*. Instead, I must say, every time my fear was pleasantly belied: I could still recognize my "creature," its broad lines perfectly preserved.

Was the translation problem-free? Of course not. A few hitches were inevitable. Hitches gave spice to the whole enterprise. There were a few amusing cases that might be worth recalling, in that they exemplify how translation presents an inexhaustible–and stimulating–range of problems. I provide you with a sample of them, which illustrate issues of lexicon, word-usage, word-definition, and culture.

First of all there was the question of how to accurately describe the pathology of Fellini's illness. Federico suffers a stroke, which disables him by leaving him partly paralyzed; a few months later he suffers another stroke that kills him. In medical terms he suffers an *ictus*, or ischemic stroke, that is a local anemia in the brain vessels caused by mechanical obstruction of the blood supply. *Ictus* is a

Greek term that is used today in the medical jargon to describe this pathological condition. It is interesting to notice that for the ancient Greeks of the classical period–of the time of Pericles, not of Homer–the brain disease we call *ictus* was thought to be caused by the strike of Jove's thunderbolt. *Ictus* was a divine sign, the sign that somehow the divine had touched you. It is not by chance that the ictus changes the balance of forces in the human body, which is ruled by the brain, and the stricken person changes with it. Now, the word *ictus* is still widely used in the Italian language to describe the disease. Even though the common user may not know the word's ancient roots, its potential connotations are still there, ready to be evoked. But apparently that's not the case in English. While *ictus* does exist as a vocabulary word, it is rarely used. The corresponding expression "brain stroke" perhaps still carries the etymological idea of an impact with the brain, but all other associations are lost.

Then there was the issue of the word *maschiette*. What is a *maschietta*? We could generically describe her as a *she-boy* or manly girl. This is a girl who adopts a masculine attitude, mainly for fun, in order to look more enticing, more attractive. A *maschietta* wears her hair short (perhaps with a bob hairstyle a la Louise Brooks). Seemingly she is free-and-easy, cheeky. Her male mask is very thin, however. Its function is simply to enhance her feminine side while pretending to deny it. Her house of cards is so fragile that one enjoys all the more making it collapse at the right moment. The *maschietta* prototype is an invention of the twentieth century, as opposed to the torpid, voluptuous female model of the nineteenth century. Through her clothes, a *maschietta* tries looking androgynous without relinquishing her femininity. She flaunts a masculine posture, like smoking with a cigarette holder, but then she unveils her legs from under her fringed dress, or she wears a male-hat that makes her look even more fragile and helpless. Her figure exudes a sense of ambiguous camaraderie, which people find attractive and provoking. This feminine type has lived past her historical time and is still with us, in an updated form. A *maschietta* is not to be mistaken with a *maschiaccia*, the type of young girl that we would call *tomboy* in American English. On the contrary, she is a very seductive feminine creature, presumptuous in her defiance, secretly ready to surrender. In the end, by resorting to the image of the girls from the age of Charleston, *maschiette* was translated as *flappers.* This was based on an intellectual rather than an instinctive decision. I will never know if *flapper* evokes the same image as *maschietta.* I am satisfied with thinking it might bring the same whiff of lust, of titillating transgression to the American reader. The above discussion about the term *maschietta* illustrates the subtext that words have and produce.

Then I remember the question of the coat. In Italy, we have a popular type of coat that we call *montgomery,* after the WWII British field marshal who used to wear it. It is a short coat made of soft wool, with a hood and braided loops for buttons. After WWII, it became a popular garment among civilians. Nowadays it comes in different colors, but it still retains the original style. The literal English translation, *Montgomery coat,* may be meaningless to the American reader. Even if it did refer to the same type of garment, I'm afraid it could not generate the same kind of emotional impact. In Italy, the *montgomery* is associated with the war of liberation (a perfect example of a *montgomery coat* can be seen in Orson Welles' *The Third Man,* as worn by the British officer). Clad in a *montgomery,* perhaps we Italians fancy ourselves being somewhat heroic, being in a trench fighting the tyrants. Perhaps it makes us feel a little bit more English, who knows, more informal, non-conformist, artistic even. More free. With *duffel coat,* the closest equivalent to *montgomery,* the original image loses entirely its romantic patina, its implicit nobility, its fragrance of adventure. However, *duffel coat* unmistakably refers to that type of garment, especially for the new generations, who do not even know who Bernard Law Montgomery was.

Problems of conceptual nature arose with the adjective *rarefatto.* In the novel, I use this adjective in three separate instances, three different contexts, and it works perfectly well in each of them: *un evento rarefatto* [lit. "a rarefied event"], *un periodare rarefatto* [lit. "a rarefied style or turn-of phrase], and *la rarefatta estate cittadina* [lit. "the rarefied city summer"]. Like the Italian language, also the English language uses this adjective metaphorically, albeit in a different way. The attribute *rarefatto* points to a form of border reality, a shaded area between the material and the immaterial. With the expression *aria rarefatta* we commonly refer to the thin air, the air poor of oxygen, hard to breathe. It is a technical expression. We use the same adjective to describe a climatic condition, or a mode of expression. Could a literal translation, *rarefied air,* lend itself to a metaphoric meaning the same way it does in Italian? Or do we risk creating an unintelligible word pair? What I call *frasario rarefatto,* that is an elusive, vague way of talking, shouldn't it be translated as *foggy language,* or *unfathomable language,* or even *esoteric language* rather than *rarefied language?* And do these terms retain the same vagueness and poetic quality as *rarefatto?* Then there is the case of *rarefatto* used to describe an ambiance, a state of suspension. By *estate rarefatta* [lit. "rarefied summer"], I describe a kind of mirage, a *fata morgana,* like when the asphalt evaporates under the sun blaze, or a kind of sea refraction, that optical quivering described by Dante in the famous verse, *conobbi il tremolar della marina.* Can *rarefied* convey the physical image and at the same time conjure the idea of endless waiting, of still time, of being trapped into inconclusive acts? All these meanings perhaps could be conveyed by the adjective *ghostly,* and yet the allusion to ghosts may cause inappropriate shivers down the readers' spines; they may evoke the clang of chains in deserted castle halls. Perhaps it would be worth using *rarefied* throughout, whether it fits or not each context, thus forcing the American readers to use their imagination and to create their own meaning, elusive as it may be.

A case that seemed impossible to unravel was the idiomatic expression *speculazione edilizia.* Its literal translation into English, *building speculation* is entirely inadequate and probably incomprehensible to the American reader. The phenomenon I am referring to is typically–although not exclusively Italian. Right after WWII, in the rush of reconstruction and in the absence of town planning, there developed wild economic speculation based on the construction of dwelling houses. Italy needed houses, politicians needed money, and therefore, as a result, apartment buildings were often raised in farmland areas, with no concern for the necessary infrastructure or proper permits. At *fait accompli,* the transgressing builders obtained some sort of pardon from the local authorities, which de facto made their constructions legal. Perhaps in better-organized nations–the United States first and foremost–no one could have made such lucrative profit this impudently. The bulldozers would come to tear everything down at the first sign of illegal construction. In Italy, everyone profited from this kind of corruption–citizens, politicians, entrepreneurs–and if the environment had to suffer the consequences, *pazienza!* Too bad! Let's deal with one problem at the time. A whole class of builders grew incredibly rich very fast. Its representatives were, and still are called with slight disdain *palazzinari*. They represented such a powerful economic force that they became grand electors of the ruling parties. Political films were made to denounce this immoral behavior, like Francesco Rosi's *Mani sulla città* [The hands over the city], set in Naples. In Italy, the expression *speculazione edilizia* clearly needs no explanation. In the United States apparently it does. We consulted with architects and urbanists, we checked American magazines and newspapers (a reportage in the New York Times tried to illustrate this Italian phenomenon). All for naught. Perhaps the most sensible conclusion would be to leave the expression in Italian and to explain it in a footnote.

These are just a few of the enigmas of translation!

Gianfranco ANGELUCCI
Rome, 2004
Translated by Giuseppe Natale

About the Author

Gianfranco Angelucci lives and works in Rome as a film director, scriptwriter, advertising expert, and TV producer. The turning point in his professional career and personal life has been his encounter with Federico Fellini in the 1970s, followed by a twenty-year long association with the Italian film director.

In 1970 Angelucci graduated from the University of Bologna with a dissertation on Fellini's *Satyricon.* He then moved to Rome, where he started working as a writer for cinema and television. During all this time he worked alongside Fellini in various capacities, but mostly as a screenwriter. In 1987 he authored the screenplay for Fellini's *Intervista,* recipient of a special prize at the Cannes Film Festival and the First Prize at the Moscow Film Festival.

Angelucci is the author of several essays on cinema, and has edited various publications on Fellini's works, among them *Amarcord, Casanova, And the Ship Sails On,* and *Ginger and Fred.* He has also edited a photo-book on *La Dolce Vita,* and another one on all Fellini's films titled *Un Regista a Cinecittà.* As a director, he produced numerous TV reports and a two-episode homage to Fellini, respectively titled *Fellini nel Cestino* and *I Protagonisti di Fellini.* In 1985 he filmed the ballet *La Strada* set to Nino Rota's music, and broadcast by RAI on Christmas' Eve. In 1993, Angelucci saw to the restoration of Fellini's entire film production. After the Maestro's death in the same year, Angelucci took charge of the Fellini Foundation.

Angelucci is also the director of a feature film, *Miele di Donna* (1981), and the author of two novels, *L'amore in Corpo* (1994) and *Federico F.* (2000), the latter a semi-fictional story on Fellini's last months.

About the Translator

Giuseppe Natale was born and raised in Turin, Italy. He has translated into Italian several major American novels, such as Toni Morrison's *Beloved,* Alice Walker's *The Temple of My Familiar,* Thomas Pynchon's *V.* and *Gravity's Rainbow.* He is the founder and chief editor of the translation journal *TransScribe.* He currently holds an Associate Professor position at UNLV, where he teaches Italian culture and cinema, and translation studies.

Sections of Angelucci's *Federico F.* were used as a practicum in a graduate translation workshop that Natale taught at UNLV. He would like therefore to thank those students who contributed to some early drafts with insightful ideas: Cara Minardi, Barbara Pasqui, and Jenny Toups. He would also like to thank Chris Arigo and Dick Gerdes for kindly agreeing to revise the translated text. Finally, a great thanks to Giuseppe Leporace for his invaluable help throughout this project.

www.ingramcontent.com/pod-product-compliance
Lightning Source LLC
LaVergne TN
LVHW010057110826
845155LV00028B/386

* 9 7 8 1 8 8 4 4 1 9 9 5 9 *